Marriage Games

CD REISS

Distributed by EverAfter Romance
A Division of Diversion Publishing Corp.
443 Park Avenue South, Suite 1008
New York, New York 10016
www.EverAfterRomance.com

For more information, email info@everafterromance.com

First EverAfter Romance edition October 2016.
ISBN: 978-1-68230-466-2

Marriage
Games

This book is dedicated to my sister and
brother authors in the indie publishing world.

For your sharing, your kindness, your ethical behavior in an
industry that could be so much less ethical—even if we've never
spoken, this is a reminder that you've created something beautiful.

Adam

Chapter 1

PRESENT TENSE

The morning my life changed was no different than any other. I woke. I showered. The tie I chose wasn't much different than the other ties in the drawer, and the suit I put on wasn't much bluer than my other blue suit. It wasn't my favorite or my most hated. It fit the same as every suit I'd had made after I got married. Bigger in the shoulders. Smaller in the waist. Sleeves more generous at the bicep. She liked when I worked out, so I did.

The morning everything changed, I felt the same as I always felt, more or less. I had plenty to do, but not too much. She was probably already in a meeting with our other editorial director. I was heading for a sheer drop into death at a hundred miles an hour while I looked up at the clouds.

The morning my life changed, I started a grocery list for the housekeeper.

The loft was bathed in light, trapezoids of sun cast over the hardwood. Twenty floors beneath me, the capillary of Crosby Street coursed the blood of steel and noise on its way to the artery of Lafayette.

My life changed on a weekday, with the gurgling of the coffeepot behind me, my jacket slung over the barstool, and the milk souring on the counter.

I put it away, because she never did.

I had no sense of impending doom. No gut feeling that that day was different from any other. It's unreasonable to expect I would. In an age of science and reason, why should I sense disaster before it arrived?

Yet I didn't see it coming.

Her handwriting—flowery, curlicued, an expansive rendering of Catholic School standards—was at the bottom of a typewritten note. I poured my coffee, assuming it was a deal memo waiting for my signature to go next to hers.

I was wrong.

It was the first time I was wrong about her intentions, but not the last.

Dear Adam:
  I don't know how to say this.

Chapter 2

PAST PERFECT

First times.

The first time I saw her.

I had the power. I held all the cards. The publishing empire her parents had built was crumbling with the entire industry. They had one willing buyer. Me. She walked into the conference room behind her father, John Barnes, who left his oxygen tank and his ego at the door.

The space folded around her.

The first time I saw her, I had to hold my breath.

The first time she spoke, I exhaled.

"Mr. Steinbeck," she said, taking her place among the lawyers and executives. My name was uttered with more respect than I deserved. She was a child of literature. Saying Steinbeck with respect was a habit.

"No relation," I said. "I've never seen a farm."

"Obviously."

Her hair was straight, brown, to her shoulders, and her eyes were the color of broken safety glass.

We sat. Opened our folders. Numbers got flung around. Her father's breathing became more labored. Emphysema. Three-pack-a-day habit stopped too late. She kept looking at him, getting more and more agitated as the meeting went on.

What would she do for him? If I pretended I didn't see her father's distress, would she jump in to help him? Would she make a hasty decision to get him out of the room?

The first time I tested my future wife, she failed. Or passed, depending on how you look at it.

"What you're offering," I said, "is a forty-nine percent stake in a company that no one else in the business believes will make money over the next five years. You've tapped out your credit, and you want R+D to come in, bail you out, and let you keep the keys to the kingdom."

"No one at R+D knows the publishing business and we have some ideas—"

"No one at this table knows the publishing business. But only one of half this table knows *business*. And you're not sitting on it."

I slid her a folder. It contained McNeill-Barnes's profit projections for the following five years. It was ugly. Even the best-case scenario had them drowning.

"You're past a simple bankruptcy proceeding," I said. "You've already cut too much staff to argue for the jobs you'll save. And as far as the chilling effect on American literature, no one gives a shit."

John Barnes's breath caught and he wheezed. He wasn't looking at the folder; he was looking at me.

"What do you want?" he whispered.

"The whole thing. No less. My buyout number's on the bottom of the page."

The first time I shocked my future wife, she didn't show it. Not much. But her lower lip went slack, and she blinked out of cadence. She closed the folder. "You're after the building."

I leaned back. "It's a nice piece of property." My eyes fell to her breasts. I could detect the entire shape of them from the slight shadow at her collar. I wondered what they tasted like.

"It's a converted SoHo warehouse."

She was about to make a point, but her father wheezed again. She lost her train of thought. I felt sorry for her. She loved him. Her devotion moved me. More than the taste of her tits, I wanted a taste of that devotion.

She tapped her pen and picked up her point. "This building? It's a unicorn for developers. For this number, we could just sell it and keep the company."

"Not with the liens."

The first time I cornered my future wife, I thought I'd won a decisive battle in a war I assumed I understood. Five years later, with the syncopated blast of an ambulance twenty stories below our loft and a typewritten note on the kitchen counter, I realized I'd done neither.

Chapter 3

PRESENT TENSE

Dear Adam:
   I don't know how to say this. But I have to.
   I can't be married to you anymore.

The note was two pages long. I couldn't read it. My coffee chilled in my hand.

Every drop of blood in my body rushed to my face, leaving me with an empty hole in my chest and rigid, white fingers that tingled before going numb.

I crumpled the note until it was a dense, tight sphere of betrayal, and I stuffed it in my pocket. I had to piss. Of all things. I had to walk to the bathroom, open the door, and take out my dick. Do all the things I had to do with this fucking cliff I was driving toward without brakes.

I called her. No answer. Voice mailbox full. Called again. Same. I texted.

—Where are you?—

—We need to talk—

No reply. I couldn't stare at the phone any longer. She thought she was leaving me, and I still had to piss. I had no time to think, much less manage these absurd bodily functions.

As I stood over the bowl, my thoughts ran out of me, rapping like a playing card in bicycle spokes, downhill faster and faster.

It's another man.

I'll kill him.

Check everything.

Lock out the banks.

Tuesday after the Unicef Gala.

Fucked her Tuesday.

She came.

Did she come?

Definitely came.

What did I do wrong?

It's me.

What's his name? I'll kill——

Apologize for nothing.

Get access to her email.

Where is she?

Apologize for everything.

She didn't mean it.

Do something.

Do something.

Do.

Something.

I slammed the toilet seat down. Fuck pissing. Fuck locking the door. Fuck this fucking walk down the fucking block. It was winter. I cut through the cold like a dull knife. McNeill-Barnes was down the block and I didn't have the bandwidth to be cold. Fuck all the shit I had to do when I should be doing something.

Chapter 4

PAST PERFECT

Diana. Diana McNeill-Barnes. What would I do to possess her? Would I change my cellular structure? Turn my back on my identity? Walk away from it, never talk about it, burn it so thoroughly into a pile of dust that not telling her wouldn't be a lie?

Would I make a bad business deal for her happiness?

"I'm going to do it," I said.

Charlie and I were at the Loft House—a hip little private club with original art everywhere and a membership waiting list as long as my leg. The top-floor restaurant overlooked the city on four sides. We were on the southern tip, where we could see the point of Manhattan jut into the ocean.

"Break her?"

"I'm going to marry her."

He shook his head, tapping his aboriginal cane. He was a war veteran in his late forties. If you knew history and heard his accent, you might be curious enough to ask him what was the last war Australia fought. He'd tell you "the ones that are bought and paid for," then he'd ask if you wanted to see his war wounds.

Best to decline.

Charlie had been the first to hear about her eleven months before. The first to question my instincts.

"How is it possible she's vanilla?" he'd asked the day after I took her to bed the first time. We were taking a spin around Central Park's six-mile loop, the rattle and tick of our derailleurs punctuating heavy breaths. He was slow because of his leg. "You can't do vanilla. It's not natural."

"What's the big deal?"

"It's like cats and dogs sleeping together. She must be a sub. She might not know it, but she has to be."

"I found her ex-fiancé in some douche Wall Street bar. I got him drunk and asked him a few pointed questions."

"How do you do that?"

"'Oh, hey stranger at the bar I was just dumped boo hoo were you ever dumped, oh, really the bitch. My girl wanted yadda in bed etc etc did you ever tie her up whatever whatever?' He says, 'No, she didn't even let me pull her hair when I dogged her.' Done. Confirmed. Took seventy-four minutes."

"All that proves is she's attracted to a closet Dominant, even if the wanker didn't know what he was doing. Did you ask her? Directly? Instead of dancing around the subject?"

"She had a girlfriend in college. Couple of months of light bondage, but she wouldn't let the boyfriend do anything."

He pushed himself off his handlebars to sit straight, arms out. "And you gave up Serena for this?"

This? For Diana. Serena was a child, and our prescribed time had ended already. Once I'd broken her on the last day, I was done with her. Diana was a woman, and she was eternal. I loved her. I'd spent a single night with her and hours over a negotiating table battling her and I loved her.

Between the bike ride in Central Park and sitting with Charlie in the club, drinking whiskey and telling him I was going to marry her, almost a year had passed. Diana was the sky and all the stars in it.

"You're never going to be right with yourself, mate," Charlie said, leaning back into the point of Lower Manhattan.

"That's bullshit we tell ourselves," I said. "It's justification. I don't need justification, and I don't need the lifestyle to have a life."

"Keep paying dues at the Cellar," he said before sipping his drink.

"No need."

"I'll pay them for you. Day will come when you can't deal with power sharing another night."

"I can function just fine."

He smiled. The parentheses around his mouth got darker when he didn't shave for a few days. "Function? My friend, I never questioned your manhood."

"Good idea." I swirled my whiskey around the bottom of my glass. "I could break her, sure."

The thought of it swirled my insides with the drink. It was too good. The idea of her on her knees with her hands behind her back. My balls went into a knot.

I shut out the thought. I loved her. *Wanted* to love her. Needed to love her, and the second she kneeled, she'd be nothing to me.

I put the drink down. "It wouldn't feel right. She's not built for submission."

"You can't just decide to be vanilla the rest of your life. It's not a choice."

"It's all a choice. And I choose her."

He brought his drink to his lips. "She must be quite a piece of ass."

Chapter 5

PRESENT TENSE

I can't be married to you anymore. You're a good man. You're good to me and my family. I can never repay you for how you helped us. But I've started to feel obligated, and I think the obligation and gratitude has clouded my judgment.

We'd started repairing the damage to McNeill-Barnes Publishing by renting out pieces of the building on short leases and putting the staff to work in the smallest amount of space they could manage. Five years later, we'd reclaimed two floors.

I walked through the penthouse with a sucking pain in my gut and a heart wrapped in wire. We'd built this together. Her father had stepped out of the day-to-day and onto the board, while she and I reshaped the business.

"Mr. Steinbeck." Diana's admin, Kayti, ran behind me. A single mom with a nose ring and a sweet smile, she kept my wife organized. "I have a message from—"

"Where is she?"

"Who?" Kayti chased me.

"My wife." I didn't stop walking toward her office. I could

see the shadow of a figure between the frosted glass doors and the windows.

"She left a message…"

I opened the door.

"Steinbeck!"

The figure was Zack Abramson, the executive editor. Nonfiction. The stuff that had put us back on the map. He snapped a book closed and put it on the Mission-style coffee table.

Diana liked warm things. Warm colors. Warm lighting. Warm sex.

"She's not coming in," Kayti finished.

Zack was a smug little prick who should have stayed in the acting business. He was sly and untrustworthy. He had a way of looking at people as if he had secret knowledge about them, which he didn't. But he was a formidable editing talent, and despite all that and more, I kind of liked the asshole.

"Did she say why?" I asked Kayti.

"Uh, no but—"

"Shouldn't you know that?" Zack asked, smugly, I might add.

"Marriage doesn't make you psychic." I put my bag on my wife's desk chair because I could.

"That's a really nice suit, Steinbeck."

"What did you want again, Zack?"

"Um, can I finish?" Kayti said.

"No," Zack said.

"Yes," I said at the same time.

Kayti wasn't flustered for long. "Diana said no one knows. Those were her one-two-three words to tell you. No one knows. But she wouldn't say more. So I don't know what that was about. Should I call her and find out?"

"I'll call her," I said. "Thank you, Kayti."

She nodded and left, clicking the doors closed behind her.

"Was there something you wanted?" I asked.

Zack pulled an envelope from his jacket pocket. "I wanted to deliver this personally to one of you. Thank you for the opportunity to work for McNeill-Barnes. Being part of this restructure has been a great learning experience. I'm offering my resignation."

I didn't open it. I'd had one too many good-bye notes that morning. "I'm sorry to see you go, but I won't try to stop you."

"Thanks for that." He slapped my shoulder.

"Any reason? New job? Off to get a real life somewhere?"

"My grandmother back home. In Dayton. She's sick. Dementia."

"And you're taking care of her?" I looked at him from his Tronton boots to his just-slightly-too-long hair. He didn't look like much of a caretaker, but I'd stopped judging people on their looks a long time ago.

"My mother and I."

"Take notes. It'd be a great piece. Actor turned journalist turned editor turned nurse."

He smirked. "I'll bring it here first."

He started out, and I stopped him. "I'm sorry about your grandmother. But your path to the door should not detour to your office. Your laptop stays. Per your contract, you submit all your passwords. Don't make me get legal after you. It's a bore, and you don't want to get served court papers in front of your family."

"Don't worry, my friend. I'm an open book. Give my best to Diana."

Her name cut right through me.

Chapter 6

PAST PERFECT

A man puts on clothes for the place and occasion. A woman dresses to make a point. When I invited Diana to dinner to discuss the terms of the deal where I would buy McNeill-Barnes Publishing to sink it or save it, she dressed to tell me something.

It wasn't just business.

We'd been going back and forth for weeks. She'd fought hard. She was tenacious and loyal to her parents' vision. It looked as if she'd let the ship sink before turning it away from the iceberg.

Her dress was New York black, cut to make me wonder about the shape of her tits yet again. She was too young for her position and her confidence. At twenty-three, she carried herself as if every one of her curves fit into the puzzle of the world.

See? Nothing about her was submissive.

"Fifty-one percent of a dying company isn't worth much, Diana."

I wasn't harsh or cutting, just truthful. She deserved the flat truth without punch-pulling. She'd earned my respect. I wanted to help her more than buy her company for parts. We were coming to the part of the negotiation where the deal lived or died. Once I finally said no or she finally said yes, what then?

"A living company is worth more than a hunk of brick."

"And Cynthia Wilt's entire backlist? And Norton Edge? You can keep it on life support with the IP you own."

She sank a little in both surprise and disappointment. I'd mentioned the company assets numerous times, but never the backlist. I figured she assumed I didn't know the worth of the backlist and was only after physical assets. Now, with her posture deflated, I knew she'd been hoping to use that as a bargaining chip at the last minute. I'd just killed it.

"Let's make a deal," I said.

I'd had a plan back-burnered for days. I hadn't thought about it consciously or run it by any of my team. I'd just let it simmer to see how it cooked down. When she arrived in that black dress, the back burner boiled. Buying the company and kicking her out wasn't an option. I had to see her again. And again. And again.

"Deal? I like that word. It kind of rolls off the tongue." She tipped her wine glass and watched the tears form on the surface. "Let's make one."

"I'll buy fifty-one percent and promise interest-earning cash infusions when necessary. I'll give you five years to get in the black."

She smiled as if this was easily done. She wasn't stupid or naïve, but excited by the idea of a chance, no matter how slim. I didn't know at the time that getting the company in the black was secondary to just keeping it afloat.

"But… " I let it hang to see if her smile disappeared. It didn't. "I'm in the day-to-day operations."

"With fifty-one percent of the vote?" She leaned back, tapping the bottom of her wineglass.

"I'm not shelling out the kind of money you need without oversight."

I didn't admit to myself the real reason the deal included me. I couldn't force myself on her. She wouldn't take what I had to give. She would never crawl to me. Never submit completely. I had enough women who did. I could get Serena back any time. But Diana... Diana was an endless fascination. I just wanted to watch her exist.

She smiled to herself and hid her eyes.

"What?" I asked.

She moved her hand to her mouth and looked at me in a way she hadn't before. "I've had too much wine."

"Two glasses? Come on." I poured her more. "Have another glass and tell me what's on your mind."

"Stop!" She laughed the command.

"You're about to agree to my terms." I put the bottle down. "I think you deserve to get good and drunk."

We clinked. She sipped, put her glass down, drank more, took a deep breath.

"Since we're going to be working together every day, more or less, I want to tell you something that's been bothering me."

"This is going to be great. Please." I moved my bread dish out of the way and leaned forward. "Go on."

She moved her bread dish out of the way and leaned forward. "When you first came to us, I looked you up."

"I'd hope so."

"Marine Park, Brooklyn. Family of electricians. Both parents died in a car accident when you were five. I'm sorry."

"Thank you."

"First in your family to go to college. A real bootstraps story. I couldn't find money anywhere. And here you are." The way she shook her head, like a drill boring into me ever so slowly. She could drill all she wanted.

"Full disclosure—the bootstraps are tainted. My grandparents loaned me money for my first down payment."

"And you're single at thirty-one. Never seen in female company."

"I'm here with you."

"This is business."

"Is it?"

Her finger stroked her pearls, her nail *tick-tick-ticking* against them. The tablecloth shifted when her right knee rocked back and forth. Every woman had a tell for when they wanted to fuck. Diana had ten, and I'd learned all of them.

"You think I'm too old to be single?" I asked.

"No. You're too handsome to be single. Too charming. Too sophisticated."

"Don't stop there. Go for broke."

She smiled, looked into the whirlpool of wine, her cheeks burning with a touch of pink. She bit her upper lip and avoided my gaze.

She's just looking down. That doesn't make her a sub.

"I just can't believe you haven't been snapped up."

"You're asking if I'm gay?"

"That would be a horrible injustice for women everywhere."

"I'm nothing if not just. And straight."

"There is a God." She gave me a quick flash of her eyes before she brought the wine to her lips, as if hiding behind it.

"Are you trying to seduce me before the deal is closed, Miss McNeill-Barnes?"

"We just closed it." She put her glass down, tapping the bottom as if she had a cue to hit. "You get to fuck me on my desk every weekday."

She used the word fuck like a piece of dark, bitter chocolate swallowed before it could be savored.

"Just the desk?"

"If that's what you want."

What you want.

She wants to please you.

Shut the fuck up.

I put the top of my foot against her calf and pushed her knees apart. She put her hands flat on the table, opening her mouth in a gasp. She aroused easily. With that, I could take her the good old-fashioned way and like it. It didn't have to be a big deal. It didn't have to be a lifetime of vanilla sex, even though I already wanted that more than anything.

"It's Saturday," I said, running my thumb across her hand and up her arm.

She warmed and bent under me. "Let's pretend it's Monday," she said, eyes at half mast.

"I looked you up too. Immaculate Heart. Volleyball. You've only ever worked at McNeill-Barnes. Met your fiancé while you were failing out of Vassar. Then you dropped him. Why was that?"

"Couldn't bear the thought of fucking him every night."

"Too boring?"

"Too rough. Treated me like a rag doll. But enough about him."

I stroked her arm. I didn't feel any satisfaction or disappointment in being right about how she needed sex. I'd already decided she was perfect. Already knew I'd take whatever she'd consent to give.

"I'll take you home because I've wanted to since I met you. But we're business partners now. This is not me fucking you on the desk every day, no matter how tempting that is. It's this weekend, then it's business. Agreed?"

She rubbed the edge of her wineglass with her ring finger, making a show of thinking. Slipping her hand around the bulb of the glass, she lifted it. "Where do I sign?"

I called for the check.

Chapter 7

PRESENT TENSE

I think it's clouded my judgment.

I'm sorry. I have to interrupt myself. I know the first thing you're going to think.

There's no one else.

I'm not cheating on you, and I never have.

This isn't about another man. This is about us. Me. You. Us.

I'd crumpled the note so tightly the ink had cracked. I couldn't stomach the entire thing in one swoop. She was talking at me. I had no room to disagree or question. I only had room to stop, reread, dissect, panic in the front seat of the Jag, watching the Meatpacking District come alive with restaurant-goers and dog-walkers. Ten at night on Gansevoort was a fucking carnival on cobblestones. What did all these people want?

I called the one man she would tell everything. Her father.

"Lloyd?" I said when I heard the wheezing.

"Adam, how are you?" I knew from his tone that he had no idea. He greeted me like the best son-in-law in the world, as always.

"I'm fine. Have you seen Diana?"

"Not since yesterday. Is everything all right?"

If she didn't tell him, maybe she wasn't serious?

"Yeah. Everything's fine. She's not picking up her texts."

"She's probably at the gym."

"Right. Okay. Thanks."

We hung up.

Did I miss something? A clue? A behavior that should have made me suspicious? Had I been so blind to her misery? I went from angry at her to angry at myself. Then I didn't believe her. This was a cry for help. Then fuck her if this is how she asks me to pay better attention. And did I not pay attention? Did she want more flowers? Why didn't she ask? Why didn't she tell me sooner, before she had to resort to this shitty tactic? When did it start? What did I miss?

I sent my hundredth text.

—Was it the baby?—

Chapter 8

PAST PERFECT

She was at her father's place again. He lived in a three-bedroom on Park Avenue in an apartment with maids' quarters. Fifteenth floor, overlooking the Avenue. He'd struggled to keep the co-op when McNeill-Barnes nearly went under, but it was where he and his wife had made their life together, and he insisted on dying where they'd lived.

So romantic.

The doorman greeted me by name. I took the elevator up to fifteen. The apartment took up the entire floor, so there were two doors in the hall. One with a welcome mat, thick molding, a table with an ivy plant next to it, and a little brass mailbox.

The other was just a white door with a rubber mat. Servant's quarters. I knocked on the plain white door and waited. Rustling. Voices.

Gilbert answered in his usual suit and tie. "Mr. Steinbeck," he said, stepping aside. "They're in the kitchen."

The kitchen was through a short landing on the back stairs and through another door. A shorter walk than the front door. I knew she'd be there, and she was.

A tea set sat on the kitchen table, and Diana's bare feet were up on the chair as if she wanted to fold herself into a fetal origami. Her father sat across from her. He wasn't wearing his mask and tank. His health had bounced back with the business.

"Hey," I said.

Her eyes were swollen and red-rimmed. Still the clearest tempered-glass blue, which made the red stand out and the shine of her cheeks more apparent. She put down her red journal. In it, she asked questions. Just lists of questions.

Who decided the speed of light?

Why can't some people sing?

What's in glue?

Where do they get the vitamins to make vitamins?

I was sure it was getting filled with questions about why we'd had to terminate her pregnancy. Some days she read me her questions, but with her curled up in her father's kitchen chair, I didn't ask her to.

She held out her arms for me like a child. Moments like this, I felt the truest bliss of my marriage to her. When I could take care of her, gather her in my arms under her back and knees, and carry her to the couch with her head on my shoulder.

I laid her across me on the couch and held her.

"It's not your fault," I said, taking my handkerchief from my pocket. "It's no one's fault. It happens."

"I hate it," she snuffled. "I hate that it happens."

"I know. I do too."

"I keep wondering what she would have been when she grew up."

"Nothing. It wasn't meant to be."

She spent another few minutes sobbing, and I held her even though my arms ached and I was thirsty. I heard her father behind us as he went to bed, his footfall still slow even though he was feeling better.

"Adam?" she said.

"Yes?"

"Tell me. Honestly. Are you upset?"

"Of course."

"You don't seem upset."

I was unhappy that the baby's spine had grown outside its body. The sonogram had been devastating, and the decision we'd had to make had broken my wife's heart. But it was the right decision for us. We couldn't bring a person into the world to do nothing but experience a few weeks of excruciating pain before dying. Having the baby so we could feel it and touch it would have been selfish.

Once the decision had been made, I wasn't upset about it, because it was right. And because Diana's collapse gave me the opportunity to take care of her. I'd bathed her after the surgery. I'd stroked her hair and fed her. It was as close to dominating her as I would get, and it soothed me. The buzz of anxiety and dissonance that followed me around shut off like a faucet.

"I don't like seeing you like this," I said. "That's the worst for me."

She laid her head back on my chest as if she couldn't look at me. "Will you always take care of me?"

My God. Why didn't she just ask me if I'd allow the sun to rise and set?

"Always," I said. "As long as you let me, I'll take care of you."

Chapter 9

PRESENT TENSE

Part of me wants to just exonerate you, but that's dishonest. You never gave yourself to me. Or maybe you're just not deep. Either way, I can't live with that. I want more. I want to love fully, and there's so much missing. Can't you feel it? I mean, it can't be just me. You're in this marriage too. But then I think you're not and you never were.

—Was it the baby?—

I went on another roll after that, but it was shorter than the others. I only had half a block to walk to the Cellar.

—When are you going to talk to me?—

—You can't just keep ignoring me—

Rob saw me before I was even close to the velvet rope. "Holy fucking shit." He held out his meaty hand. He wore a dark suit under a black trench coat that was spotted with new raindrops.

"Didn't you get a real job yet?" I asked.

"And leave this? No way." He undid the rope. "Man, the girls missed you. I did too, gotta say. Everyone's always asking where you went."

"I've been around."

"Are you back now? Back for good?"

"Just seeing some old friends tonight."

I checked my texts in the elevator.

—When are you going to talk to me?—

—You can't just keep ignoring me—

And a hundred before it that were much the same. Jesus Christ. I sounded psychotic. That wasn't going to work.

—Diana. If you want to make this about lawyers and money, we can do that. We can do all the things people do when they get acrimonious. But I can't believe you want that. I know because I looked at your email inboxes and outboxes. All your correspondence. No lawyers. You haven't moved any money and you haven't changed any of your passwords. So either you're a very good sneak or you're still the same honest, forthright woman I know. Now is the time to stop playing games. Enough—

I thought about not hitting Send. I'd just admitted to spending half the afternoon spying on her. I decided that was just tough shit. I'd seen what I needed to see and left her life as it was. She could change her passwords if she didn't like it.

The elevator stopped. I hit *Send*, and the doors opened when DELIVERED appeared below the message.

That was it. I'd texted everything I was going to text today.

I looked through the elevator doors. Everything in front of me was painted as red as rage.

Chapter 10

PAST PERFECT

I lost my virginity on a park bench at the age of fifteen. Blaire was fourteen and in her last year at St. Mary of the Fields. I was in my first year at Our Lady of Precious Blood High School. We'd been at Fields together, and when I aged out, we felt the brokenhearted sense of urgency common in teens.

I impaled her on that bench. Right under her little plaid skirt and leg warmers, tucked into a corner of the park, just after the sun set. I controlled the motion of her hips. When she moved without my direction, I had a disconcerting feeling I could only describe as not-rightness.

We did it a few more times then broke up. My best friend's mother, Irene, seduced me a few months later, seeing something in me Blaire wasn't qualified to see. Irene had said, "Do what you want to me. We are animals. Treat me like one."

So I did. I never looked back. Not until Diana.

After the dinner where we made our first deal, I took her to my place in Murray Hill. In the back of the cab, she crossed her legs and put on lipstick. Her hands were shaking. Did she know what I was?

I'd tracked down her past; had she done the same to me? Had she heard I was a sadist? A Dominant? A punishing fuck?

I hoped she had and still decided to do it.

She snapped her bag closed, and I whispered in her ear, using my Dominant voice, "Open your legs and touch yourself."

She glanced not at me, but the rearview mirror at the center of the windshield.

"The cabbie's right there." She was not amused or coy. She simply didn't want to do what I told her.

I asked myself how badly I wanted her, and I decided badly enough to risk the deal. The risk was greater for her than it was for me.

My condo was on the top floor, with a rooftop garden. I'd bought it to renovate and flip, but the lease on my apartment on Lexington was up and I decided to keep it.

I closed the door and turned on the lights. The place was spotless, but I checked anyway, following her gaze around the windows, the furniture, the curved stairwell to the top floor.

"Very nice," she said.

"Thank you." I only had eyes for her, with her feet perpendicular to one another, legs long below the curve of her hips. "The view's pretty good from here too."

She put her bag on the side table.

Take your clothes off quietly, get on the coffee table, on your back, and spread your legs so I can see your cunt.

I bit that back. "Can I get you something?"

"Water, please."

I went to the kitchen and came back with two glasses. Her dress was laid over a chair. She stood in the middle of my living room wrapped in a blanket.

"There aren't any curtains," she said meekly in front of the bare windows.

Drop the blanket and show New York your body.

"The bedroom has blinds."

"Is it upstairs?"

Crawl up the stairs. Second door to the left. Wait for me on the bed with your ass up and spread. I'll be taking that first. You are permitted to prep it with your fingers if you need to. And trust me, you need to.

I gave her the water. Her hand poked out of the blanket and took it. She drank, clutching the wrap at her chest. She gave the glass back to me, and I put it on the table with my glass. Then quickly, before she could change her mind or I could think better of it, I picked her up, blanket and all, and carried her up the stairs.

She put her hands on my cheeks and put her nose to mine. Her perfume smelled of oranges and orchids. When we got to my bedroom, she wiggled to her feet, still with the blanket around her. I drew the blinds and turned on the bedside lamp.

"Thank you," she said.

When I stood in front of her, she put her chin up and shook the hair out of her face. I took the blanket off, revealing wine-colored lace and a body that made my cock push against my pants. She'd gone all out. Her bra had a little crystal heart between the tits and pushed them up and together. Matching panties shaped like the letter *T* with an identical crystal heart at the center.

She reached for my jacket to pull it off, and I took her by the wrists.

"Give me a second," I said.

"You don't like it?"

"I want to just look at you for now."

That was true, but I also needed to create a few scenarios before we started. I needed to feel as if whatever simple thing happened, I'd planned and controlled for it.

I undid my tie without taking my eyes off her. Jacket. Shirt. I was working on my belt when she reached for me again, and I reacted by grabbing her wrist again. She stiffened. She wasn't supposed to reach without asking, but then again, she was supposed to do whatever she wanted and I'd reacted too fiercely.

I kissed the inside of her arm, and she relaxed.

"I brought condoms," she said.

Get on your knees. Take out my cock. Put your hands behind your back and open your mouth so I can fuck your throat. You'll breathe when I want you to say my name.

"Okay," I said, working my lips to her shoulder, up her neck, her ear, and finally, I kissed her on the mouth for the first time.

She was soft and just yielding enough. I tasted her wine, her water, her ambition, and her loyalty in that kiss.

I was a goner.

Chapter 11

PRESENT TENSE

Whenever I thought of leaving you, I felt two things. I felt relieved. But then I felt worried about McNeill-Barnes, and I couldn't do it. That's not a reason to stay with someone. I know you can understand that. We can figure out the business, but I can't figure out you. I don't feel close to you. When we're in a room together, I'm as lonely as I've ever been.

I didn't love the club scene, even when I had been a part of it. I didn't like chaos and noise. I understood how much control the free-for-alls took, but I liked intimacy.

The Cellar was a necessary evil though. The club acted as an organization with rules surrounding what would be assault outside its walls.

Every combination on the spectrum was available, depending on which part of the club you were in. Downstairs, in the actual cellar, nothing was off-limits. The sixth floor, where the dominant men and submissive women played, had its share of showmanship and chaos, but it was a more controlled, sedate scene. A bar. A bank of leather couches. A few back rooms.

"Adam?" the bartender said in shock. Norton was an actor and a Dominant. I shook his hand over the bar. "What's happening?"

"Don't get me started."

He put a short glass and napkin on the bar. A young man with grey eyes and conservative haircut sat next to me, talking to an older man I recognized. At the older man's feet curled a woman with a collar. He held her leash taut.

"We missed you." Norton poured me a shot. "How's married life?"

I took the glass. Did I have to answer that? I did, and I had to lie. I didn't want him to know about the note that morning. I still had hope that it was all a big error in judgment, and I only realized it when I couldn't tell the bartender my wife had left me. "Fine."

The room looked over the backside of the district. The windows had been treated so we could see out, but no one could see in. Which was for the best, since a state senator was on her hands and knees, deep in subspace, where dopamine levels were high and pain and pleasure merged. She was in heaven. I envied her Dom. Getting a sub there was the ultimate drug.

"How's the lady?" I asked Norton.

"Naughty." He waggled his brows. He and his wife worked the bar together. She wore his collar and called him Master, scrubbing the floors and wiping the counter when he told her to.

"Where is she?"

"Got a job as a graphic designer. She makes more than I do now."

"Well done." I looked at the couches. Rows and rows of them, with tables. I didn't want to talk about Norton's perfectly kinky marriage where his submissive wife could have it all. It was too close to what I wanted. "Have you seen Charlie?"

"Yeah. He's in aftercare four."

"Thanks."

I took my drink and walked toward the aftercare rooms. On the way, I was greeted with hugs and jovial backslaps. Henry offered me a turn with his sub. I declined.

Aftercare four had a black leather cross on the door with a

brass 4 in the center. I knocked gently, expecting he wouldn't answer if it was intense.

"Come in."

I smiled when I heard the accent, and I opened the door.

"Crikey," he said.

A naked woman was draped over his lap, ass bruised and red, slick with soothing cream. Her eyes were closed and a smile stretched across her face.

"I haven't stepped foot in here in years and that's all you have to say?" I closed the door behind me.

"You look like someone wrung you out, mate. Carrie, look who's here."

Carrie opened her eyes, and I recognized her. We'd done a week-long years ago.

She held out her hand. "Sir. Nice to see you again." I took her hand, and we shook as well as she could under the circumstances. She rolled over onto her back. "Do you want a drink, Master?"

"Club soda. And bring Adam a whiskey. Then you need to rest." He dotted the tip of her nose.

Charlie was a Dom like no other. Without the ability to fuck, he had to be more cruel and more tender than any of us.

"What happened?" he asked when Carrie went out.

For the first time since that morning, I wanted to talk about it.

Chapter 12

PAST PERFECT

There came a point when the bloody, wrapped up bundles of paper and napkins stopped appearing in the bathroom garbage pail and Diana was walking around the office like a normal person. Once I even saw her laugh through the conference room glass. I watched her talk to Zack as I passed. She was standing, arms crossed, legs apart at the width of her shoulders. Her eyes sparkled as she listened to whatever he was saying, and the sun caught the flyaway hair and bounced off as if flirting with it. Her clothes were more fitted than the sacks she wore after we lost the baby. It was impossible to look away from her.

That was my Diana.

I opened the door. "Are you ready for Easton?"

"Yes!" She gathered a stack of papers.

"Go get 'em, killer," Zack said.

She hopped, literally bouncing out into the hall.

"You seem… what's the word?" I looked up, scratching my head as if second grade vocabulary words had left me.

"Gorgeous?"

We walked down the hall.

"Of course, but also…" I put my hand on the frosted glass door of conference four. "Maybe after the meeting."

I pushed the door open and let her in. We were meeting with an upstate labor relations board over the expansion of a paper mill. Four of them. The mayor of Easton. Two second-rate public relations people. One very litigious and sharp lawyer in a fitted jacket and low heels. The conversation went downhill after the first minute of small talk.

"Our concern," said the balding mayor in the brown suit, "and our bailiwick, if you will, is to render guarantees from you that any new jobs are filled by the residents of Easton."

"We can't give guarantees," I said. "Not for every position you want."

"Why not?" chirped the PR woman with thin lips and straight brown hair. "We have a twelve percent unemployment rate. If we're going to sell the prop to expand the mill, our town needs assurances McNeill-Barnes can deliver jobs and we can deliver tax incentives."

"You can't just come in and build with no benefit to the community," the politician chimed in.

Next to him, a younger woman with a ponytail stared at me as if she wanted to burn holes in me. As I listened to the brown suit talk about his constituency, I dug around for her name.

Becca. Assistant. New hire right out of college.

"Sell them the new income tax base," I said. "Sell them the fact that we're turning an abandoned dump into a functioning structure. We cannot promise all four hundred jobs will go to locals, and the executive positions need to be filled out of Manhattan."

Our plan was to bring in experienced people as temps and train the locals, but we needed that to look like a concession later in the negotiations. We didn't want to tip our hand so far in advance.

"We'll do what we can," Diana said, right on cue. She was the good cop, as always. "We can fill positions from qualified locals first."

"We need it in writing," the lawyer said. "Numbers. As part of the incentive."

"No." I closed my folder.

"Here." Diana handed her a page. "A list of community initiatives. We can build a park and have low cost day-care on site."

She didn't even look at it.

"There's more," Diana said, tapping the page. "Consider it. We have a lot to offer, and so do you."

"We. Have. People." The lawyer poked the paper with every point.

"What you have is an existing structure close to our current site." I sat back and crossed my ankle over my knee. I could do this all day. "What you don't have is talent. We need to hit the ground running. We need people who know the machinery and the software. We need logistics people who know how to transport this particular product. This isn't about putting bodies in chairs. It's about the right people. Believe me. I've done this before."

"You're a corporate raider," Becca sneered. "You don't create jobs. You're like a little boy who buys things just to blow them up."

Becca had obviously gotten caught up in the heat of the discussion. I didn't take her comment seriously, and I was ready to move on when Diana leaned forward as if she wanted to launch herself over the table. I hadn't seen energy pour off her like that since the baby was diagnosed.

"This corporate raider happens to be the best man I've ever had the honor of sharing an office with. He's fair, and he's honest. He looks past the obvious. He finds value where other people see red ink. He's thoughtful and kind, and you need to show him a little respect."

Becca's face went from white to burgundy.

My wife picked up her files and stood. "Anything you need from us is in the folders. I'd like to thank you all for coming. I'm sure we can work something out."

She left. The door clacked behind her.

"Don't worry about it," I said to Becca. "We can reconvene later."

I nodded to everyone, shook a few hands, and went to Diana's office. She was already there, moving things around her desk as if she were a general moving troops over the field. I closed the door.

No word in the English language could describe how happy I was to see my Diana back again.

"You don't have to defend me from petty insults," I said.

"I'm sorry, but fuck them. They——"

I took her face in my hands and kissed her. I hadn't touched her since the baby. Hadn't kissed her anywhere but her cheek. And now with the full scent of her perfume and the feel of her skin, my desire rushed back.

She backed up, panting, lips blush pink. "Jesus, Adam."

I lifted her knee and put it around her waist, pushing my erection against her cunt. She sucked in air and groaned. I knew and loved that groan.

"Shouldn't. Bad professionalism," she said as if she couldn't make a full sentence. I could cure her of that.

"I love it when you're mad." I pushed harder, running the shape of my cock along the line of her cleft.

Your pleasure is mine. You come when I permit you, and you hold it until I do.

"I can make you come in seventeen minutes. Open your legs." I'd used my Dominant voice. I hadn't meant to.

"Wait. No."

The word no does not mean no in scene. Use your safe word or answer the trigger question incorrectly. Then everything stops.

"What?" The impatience in my voice must have been thick, because her reaction was sharp.

"I just... I just had this horrible thing happen with my body. I still don't feel whole and I just don't feel... I don't feel intimate, and you have no right to be mad about it."

I let her leg go and took my arms away. "I'm not mad."

"Your voice..."

"I was surprised. That's all. It seemed like you wanted——"

"I'm sorry."

"Don't be sorry."

"I think next week. Let's do next week." She put her hand on my chest, ran her fingers along the edge of my tie and straightened it. "Thank you. I know I'm being difficult."

"You're fine. Now come on. You can be the bad cop."

To her credit, we did have sex the next week. On Wednesday night. She wore garter and lace, came twice, sucked my dick like a champ, and fell asleep in my arms. It was almost like normal for two more years.

Chapter 13

PRESENT TENSE

I'm miserable.
I need to end this before I start to hate you.

"And you didn't know, mate? Not an inkling? Come on. Nothing happened to make you think she was fucking another bloke?"

Charlie had left his sub to nap, and we'd found a small table by the window. His cane leaned against it. A winter rain had started when I opened my story, and the clubbers and night owls below had found shelter, leaving a cold, empty street below.

"She's not cheating."

"You can't believe that."

"I do."

He looked away, his right foot bouncing. "You know what happened when I got shot, right? With my girl? My sub? I collared her a full year before. Fifteen years we were together, and not once did she care if I fucked her or not. But once I couldn't? Once they shot it off? I couldn't spank her ass red enough. She asked to be shared. Begged. And even then, she was off with four others. *Four.* You cannot trust women when they ask for something. It's never what they want."

"You're dealing with a self-selecting group of women."

"Were you fucking her on a regular?"

"Tuesday. I fucked her Tuesday."

"Did she come?"

"Yes."

"Did you come?"

"What?"

"Not 'did you ejaculate'? Did you *come*? Were you enjoying it? Or were you fucking her missionary while thinking about gagging her with your fist?"

I leaned back in my chair and looked out the window. Manhattan is never truly dark, just shaded differently. What I'd been thinking about on Tuesday night was not what I was doing. Hadn't been for a long time.

Charlie leaned forward and lowered his volume. "Do you think, for once in your life, she might be submissive? And you're not satisfying her? Maybe?"

No. I love her.

"You're living in the world of the Cellar like there's nothing outside it."

"All right, look." Charlie put his glass down as if he was just getting serious. "You know I thought this was a mistake, but divorce won't kill you."

"She won't even answer my texts."

"We still have the Montauk place," Charlie continued as if I hadn't spoken. "Take a sub. There are at least a dozen who remember you and a dozen more who heard about you. Take your pick. Do a thirty-day run like you used to."

I let out a quiet laugh. "Shit. The thirty-day runs. They were trouble."

"Just enough time for them to fall madly in love with you, mate."

No. There was no "them." Only one had fallen in love. The last one. Serena. It had ended right before I met Diana, and it hadn't ended well. Serena had been too young, a virgin, and she wanted a perma-Dom. I wasn't interested in loving a sub. The world we inhabited wasn't designed for people to be in love. It was designed for intensity, pain, pleasure, courtesy, and ritual.

"That was never the plan. The plan was to have enough time to get to know how to play them, but not enough time for me to get bored. I was transparent about that."

He shook his head as if there were no words for how fucking thick I was. "The main house is empty. Just do an auction and go out there. It'll be therapeutic."

My phone buzzed on the table, shifting a few inches.

I flipped it.

It was my wife.

Chapter 14

PAST PERFECT

Serena was stunning. A long stem rose with the thorns stripped. Pink petals wound tight around a cunt no man had touched, long brown hair ending at the top of her hard nipples. Her hands hung at her sides, and her eyes, which I knew were brown from the dossier, were demurely glued to my shoes.

"Charlie told me why you're here," I said. "But I need to hear it from you, in your own words. What I can do to you, and for you, needs explicit consent."

"I signed the contract, sir. I was pre-law. I understand it."

I dropped the folder on the desk. The back doors were open behind me. I could hear the waves beat the fuck out of the shore. I'd left them open on purpose. In October, the Montauk sky was the flat grey of a tin roof and the ocean wind had the first bite of cold. Goose bumps opened up on the tops of her thighs, but she stayed still, not daring to even shiver. Her discomfort, her stillness as the sheer white shift moved over her, made her submission plain.

"In your own words," I said, stepping toward her. "You went to Charlie. Why?"

"I heard he..." She stopped, drifting off in shame. "I signed it. It's right on the papers."

"You have to say it."

She swallowed. "He trains submissives. That's what I heard. So I went to the Cellar on tryout night to see if I could find him."

"You skipped a step."

I was close enough to smell her shampoo and feel her nerves.

"I want the whole story." I put a finger under her chin and made her look at me. She was about five-ten to my six-one, so her head tilted all the way back. Her tongue flicked over her lower lip. "From the beginning. You don't have to be ashamed here."

The pressure of her chin increased on my finger. She'd relaxed. All she needed was permission to explain how she knew what she was. A first-class masochist. A lovely and educated young woman who liked to be broken with pain.

"I was with my boyfriend, Keith. He went to the boys' school down the road."

"Where was this?"

"Brooklyn. Bay Ridge."

"Go on."

"We were kissing one night in his room. It was a couple of years ago. His parents were out, so he thought he was going to get me in bed. I thought so too. But it wasn't doing it for me. He never did, so I'd never let him touch me. But that time? He put his hands up my skirt, and I figured I'd let him. He put his finger inside me, and I was dry. I was always dry. I thought it was just the way I was. Normal."

"You're safe here," I said, leaning on the desk. I wanted her to feel safe, but not comfortable. There was a difference.

"Keith, well, he didn't think it was normal. He said if I was going to have the sex drive of a child, he'd treat me like a child. He spanked me. Right there in his room while I was looking at his Yankees banners. He called me names. He said I was frigid. He pulled my panties down and kept on spanking me. It was... my pussy..." She tripped on the word but gathered herself quickly. "It felt really good. And I was wet."

"What did he do?"

"I ran out before he could touch me down there again." Pause. "On my pussy."

"Call it a cunt." She looked scandalized. That got my dick hard. "Pussies are weak. Cunts are powerful. What you have is powerful. Now finish."

"I thought I was crazy or sick. So I looked it up on the internet."

She ended there. The rest was history. She met people who knew people, and she sought out Charlie, who used the word pussy like an invective. He trained her but couldn't fuck her. She was still a virgin. It was my job and my pleasure to relieve her of that. I had thirty days to do it, and I thought I might take twenty-nine just because I could.

"You are crazy and sick, but you don't have to be miserable."

"Yes, sir."

"You have a safe word?"

"Montana."

"Any reason?"

"I hate it there."

"I've never been."

"It's a shithole."

I smiled. I liked a sub with a salty mouth. "When I ask you your age or name, answer honestly if you're all right, and lie if you need me to slow down."

The Dominant asked a simple question when it might be hard for the sub to answer or if it was possible they were too distracted to remember their safe word. It let the sub know the Dom was concerned. It was the equivalent of "hey how are you doing over there?" and the sub had the option of lying or not answering if they weren't doing well. It wasn't as hard a break as the safe word.

"How old are you?" I asked.

"Nineteen."

"Good. That's how it will go. I ask. You answer."

She nodded.

"You have three things you can refuse," I said. "Have you thought about them?"

"Yes, sir." Her fingers flicked at her sides. "Choking."

"No breath play. One."

"I don't like being called a slut or whore or any of that."

Easy. I wasn't much of a name-caller. She was going to be a cakewalk.

"That's two."

"I asked for you," she said. I tilted my head, and she looked up at me before putting her eyes back on the hardwood. "I saw you at Charlie's Black Sword party and I asked for you to be the one."

I remembered her. Sky blue polo. Black pleated miniskirt. Seven-inch heels.

"Nice of him to comply."

"The thirty days…" she said.

"Yes?"

"Is it a hard boundary?"

"You want that to be your third limit? A lack of time limits?"

"I have to go back to school next semester, but…" She swallowed hard. "I don't know what I'm asking."

"The limit protects you, not me."

She licked her lip. The ocean breeze stuck three strands of hair to her lower lip once it was wet, and she didn't move them away. Must have tickled like hell.

"Forget that one. Do another." She balled her hands into fists then laid them flat again. All her emotion was in her hands. "Cross off sharing. Don't share me."

"No sharing. Done." I flipped through the document outlining everyone's boundaries and limits. She'd initialed everything, but I had to check. "You're your mother's primary caretaker?"

"Yeah. She had a stroke in June."

"I'm sorry to hear that."

"Thanks. It's all right. I had to take a semester off until we find a permanent nurse for her. My aunt's around for the month. My brothers and sister are in school. I told them I had a camping trip."

"A month-long camping trip?"

She shrugged. I didn't press her. Logistics were her business.

"You've gone over the rest? My working hours? Your free time? Meals? Everything?"

"Yes."

"And you agree?"

"Yes."

"How do you feel?"

Her right big toe crossed over the next toe, then they all curled. "Really, really excited."

"Good." I tossed the papers on the table behind me. "Me too."

"Thank you." She smiled at the floor. Which was good. She was going to spend a lot of time on it.

"Get on your hands and knees, sweet girl, and crawl upstairs."

Chapter 15

PRESENT TENSE

I don't know how to say this.
I don't love you anymore.

Seeing her name on my phone screen, I should have been nervous or tense. The anxiety I felt all day should have twisted tighter, faster, more intensely. I was feeling at home in the Cellar. I could breathe among friends. Her name should have amped me back up to where I'd been that morning.

Instead, I was relieved. Whatever this part of the journey was, it was over. I was going to travel from not knowing into knowing.

"Excuse me," I said to Charlie without showing him the screen. He didn't need to know. "I'm going to check the balcony."

He leaned forward, looking out the window at the balcony, which was only big enough for a small table with an ashtray and two folding chairs. "It's raining." He crossed his ankle over his knee.

It wasn't just raining. It was cold and pouring fat chunks of icy sludge. But I couldn't talk to Diana in front of anyone. I slid the answer icon over the screen and held my breath as I opened the door to the outside. I was about to hear her voice. It had been years. Hours, even.

"Diana," I said, recalling my goddess name for her. The prayer I said in her honor. "Little huntress."

"Don't."

The first word she said to me after leaving. Don't. There wasn't a submissive on six who would have said that to me.

I sat on the chair. My wool coat protected me from the wet seat but not the slap of the sleet. I moved my back to the wall, into as much shelter as possible.

"Did you read the note?" Her voice was husky and cracked.

"Where are you?"

Silence.

"I won't come. I'll leave you alone. I need to know you're all right."

"I'm fine," she said.

"Where are you?"

"We need to talk."

"I'm not talking about anything until I know you're safe."

"I'm safe."

I didn't answer. I let my silence speak for me. Let the slushy rain splat the balcony rail with tiny wet crowns that rose and disappeared. I tried to listen to her background noise, but it was silent.

She broke first. "I have somewhere to stay."

Loaded. Her statement was loaded.

It was loaded with things she wouldn't say and the things she did. Arranging an apartment in New York wasn't an overnight affair. But she wouldn't say where, or how, or how long she'd planned to move. I knew the market, and it was longer than three days. Which meant she knew she was going to do this, and she still let me fuck her on Tuesday.

"Was that a good-bye fuck the other night?"

"Don't make this ugly."

"You keep telling me what not to do."

"I'm sorry. I…" She gulped air. "This is so hard."

"I have to tell you something. Is that allowed?"

"Yes."

I bent at the waist until I was jutting forward toward the black bars of the balcony railing. My head was getting rained on and I didn't care. I wasn't relaxed about this. "I don't know what's happening with you. I don't know if this is the baby, or work, or if there's someone else."

"There's no one else."

"But it's gone too far. You let it get too far without talking to me. That's on you. I'm sure I did plenty wrong, but what you've done? You didn't give me a chance. You didn't let me love you the way you wanted to be loved. And make no mistake, Diana, little huntress, I love you. I have loved you from day one. I loved you more each day, and I'm going to keep loving you whether you want me to or not."

"I can't…" She sniffed. "Did you read the note?"

"I read your fucking note."

She was crying. I didn't know what to make of that. It gave me no pleasure, and coming from a man who used to make subs' tears his reason for getting out of bed in the morning, that meant a lot. But I wasn't soothing her. I wasn't going to tell her it was all right. It wasn't all right. It sucked. My socks were getting cold and wet and everything sucked.

A minute ago, I'd been relieved. Before that, I'd been determined, and now everything sucked and I was angry.

I wanted to be one thing for fifteen minutes.

I leaned back into the shelter. I had to piss. That was consistency for you.

"Don't cry," I said. "Please."

She took a deep breath. "I don't love you," she said with determination. "That's the end of it."

"Yeah."

"You don't believe me?"

"Did you tell your father you moved?"

"No."

"There you go. No, I don't believe you."

"I don't want to upset him. He cares about you."

She was baffling. She'd moved to another apartment. She'd left me a two-page note. How long did she expect to keep this a secret from her father? They were close. They talked every day. What was she going to say to him?

"What's your plan, Diana? You couldn't have started this without a plan."

She shot out a nervous laugh. "You know me. I only need half a plan before I start."

That was true. She was a starter. I was a finisher. That was why it was so perfect.

"You'll land on your feet, Adam. You'll find someone else. You're a great guy."

"Shut the fuck up." Maybe it was being at the Cellar. Maybe it was losing control of my life. I used my Dominant voice, the one that wasn't angry but broached no arguments. "Don't talk to me like that. Ever. When you're ninety and I'm a distant memory, don't even think of me with that tone."

And with that, she snapped to attention as if she were sitting right next to me at the Cellar. I didn't know if she gulped down the tears or just stopped on a dime, but business Diana showed up, kicking the door open in her New York black stilettos. She slapped her briefcase on the table and laid it down.

My girl.

"I need to discuss a buyout of McNeill-Barnes," she said with a rigidity that gripped my chest. "In the meantime, you need to excuse yourself from operations. I need full autonomy to run the company."

"No."

"Yes, Adam. This is my family's company. It's mine."

"Still no." I didn't know if I could run the business side by side with her anymore. But I wasn't going to agree to any changes in the fucking rain.

"All outstanding debts to R+D are paid," she said. "We're in the black. It's been five years. I've earned my seat at the table."

"You haven't earned a seat at the head."

"Yes, I have."

I imagined her in the McNeill-Barnes conference room in her power suit and fuck-me-if-you-dare pumps. I knew what her face looked like when she was ripping a printer a new asshole. Business Diana was more manageable than Crying Diana. I could talk to Business Diana. I knew the rules. I hated them, but I knew them, and I had a way to get my disorientation under control.

Bend over the table. Pick up your skirt. You're getting twenty strokes with my belt. Count them.

"Go back and read the contract. I'll meet you at the R+D offices at nine to discuss what you missed."

"I might be late. I'm up in Riverside."

Riverside?

The air felt warm on my skin. The sleet was boiling. That was how cold my body became.

I almost said something. Almost asked a question.

But that would alert her that I knew where Zack Abramson lived.

I tapped the red circle to hang up. Her name went grey and I went grey with it, and when it flickered away, the emptiness between us broke into separate universes.

She was beautiful in every way, and I'd been too nice. I'd let her consider leaving me and I hadn't taken a second to wake up to the fact that there would be other men.

Today. Tomorrow. Ten years from now.

Every cell in my body screamed.

I'd been confused and broken. But after the call, I had something I had to do.

Chapter 16

PRESENT TENSE

I barely parked the Jag on Riverside. It landed a foot and a half from the curb, but I didn't have the patience for one more parallel parking maneuver. He could be touching her right now. He could have his fingers in her cunt and his mouth anywhere. And she could be breathing in that way. That sticky-throated way she breathed when she was aroused. As if her throat got wet when her cunt got wet.

He could be on top of her. Pushing his soon-to-be-removed dick inside her.

All that was mine.

Her cunt was mine. Her thick-sexed voice was mine. When she closed her eyes to come. Mine. Her pleasure. I owned it. All of it. For-fucking-ever. Till death, you fucking shit.

"Hey." I smiled at the doorman and lifted a manila envelope. I'd stuffed a galley I'd had lying around the trunk inside it.

"Good evening, sir," he replied. He was a big guy, stretching his shirt at the belly. His long navy tie covered the popping buttons. He sat behind a little podium with closed circuit monitors of the exits and entrances and clipboards with guest signatures.

"Is Zack Abramson in? He's in seven-fourteen."

"I know where he's at. Was at. He left this afternoon."

I hadn't expected that. I'd expected the guard to take it upstairs. Then I'd call Zack and tell him to come downstairs to talk.

"Talking" meant "break his face."

"Can you give this to him tomorrow?" I thought maybe he'd been running errands all day and hadn't gotten back to fuck my wife yet.

"Would if I could. He left town."

"Dayton?"

"I'm not allowed to say. But if you want to leave that here, I'm getting his mail together. Sending next week." He held out his hand.

"I'll send it. Thanks."

I went out to Riverside Drive, crossed the street, and stood behind my car, looking up at the building. The sleet had picked up, going from drops to sheets, but I didn't care. Didn't feel their cold or their cutting friction.

One-two-three-four-five-six-seven.

Seventh floor. Zack had said he had a view over Riverside Drive, so she was in one of those apartments. She wasn't fucking Zack. Not tonight. Maybe never, but definitely not tonight.

I saw her in the second window from the corner, slim and straight. Unmistakable to the man who loved her. She cradled a teacup and looked out at New Jersey through the same veil of sleet I watched her through.

How long was I going to do this? Watch her in the freezing cold? Chase her down? Lie to doormen? Want a woman who'd turned her back on me months ago?

I couldn't shake the jealous rage over any man who touched her. I couldn't let go of the longing or the loss.

But as I got into the car, shivering, I realized there was only one cause for my pain. I didn't have to be a man without anger or jealousy. They were symptoms of another disease. I needed to become a man unburdened by love.

I didn't have a plan yet. I didn't have a beginning, middle, and end. Just a concept without form. I didn't articulate it to myself, but somewhere on the back burners, something started stewing. Something difficult, bold, and utterly callous.

Chapter 17

PRESENT TENSE

First times.

The first time I tried to sleep in our bed knowing she didn't love me anymore, I didn't sleep. I barely moved. The noise from Crosby Street rumbled, honked, shouted, clacked, gradually less and less as the moon moved the light from one side of our bedroom to the other. By three in the morning, I could hear the rooftop pigeons across the street coo and flap, rattling their chicken wire coop in the freezing cold.

I stretched across my bed. Was it our bed still? Or was the property transferred when she no longer had a place next to me?

The first time I doubted my decision to marry her, I wasn't sure if I was sleeping or not. How had I missed the manipulation? The calculation? She'd needed me to save her family business. But I was going to save it before she offered herself to me. Way before I asked her to marry me.

It wasn't that.

I owned her. She was mine.

But no.

Vulnerable. Powerless. I couldn't hold what I possessed. The feeling was freefall. The earth coming into sharp focus as I hurtled toward it at the acceleration of gravity.

I don't need to punish you to paddle you. I don't need an excuse. You're mine, and I can paddle you when I please. Because I feel like it. Now bend over the table, arms out, palms down. Do you need something to bite?

The first night of the rest of my life, I imagined breaking her. I imagined her crying for mercy. For release. For me. The smell of her skin. The taste of her tears. The color of the parts of her that got my cruelest and kindest attention. How would she beg for my forgiveness? How would I take her then? Gently? Would I bend her body? Her mind?

My fantasies crossed into psychopathic. Anger and dominance had no place together. Revenge and sadism never played in the same scene. The idea was to cause pain, not damage, and rage clouded a Dominant's judgment.

Yet the scenes I imagined with such clarity were familiar. Years before, I'd managed them all with utter control and complete consent.

The first time my wires crossed, I scared myself, and the fear was cathartic.

Chapter 18

PRESENT TENSE

The R+D offices were in midtown, in the center of a glass column on the west side. In contrast to the McNeill-Barnes offices, they were sharp and cold, modern and noncommittal. We bought things and either built them back up or stripped them and sold them for parts. I'd started with the Williamsburg, Brooklyn, property my grandparents helped me buy at a fortunate time in the market. I lived in a studio south of Metropolitan and bought another property, then another, leaving little for myself to live on, until the next real estate boom left me with enough to leverage for greater and greater loans.

I made money and explored kink through my twenties. Sometimes I breathed.

The subway wasn't luxurious, but if I wanted to get anywhere at eight in the morning, it was the fastest way to go. No matter how expensive the car, it was still subject to the laws of physics, and the streets were jam-packed with things not even a Jaguar could drive through.

My phone rang in the lobby of my building. Lloyd Barnes. My father in-law. Soon to be known as a guy I wasn't related to by marriage.

"Hey—" I stopped myself before saying *dad*.

"What the hell is going on?" His breath was wheezy. Stress.

"With regard to?"

Lloyd came to me when he wanted it straight. His daughter protected him from anything that might upset him. Even the smallest production glitch was a secret. He only heard about the spina bifida because he called me and I told him without preamble.

"My daughter."

"Is she all right?" I was stalling. I knew what he was calling about.

"She says you're splitting up. What did you do?"

The phone would die in the elevator, so I hung back in a corner of the cold stone-and-glass lobby, away from the push and bustle of people getting to work.

"When I find out, I'll let you know."

"Is she protecting you?"

No. She wasn't protecting me. I had no idea what she was doing except leaving. Maybe it was that simple anyway. Maybe she was just sick of me and wanted to move on.

"She wants out. I have nothing else, Lloyd."

He wheezed. I heard a whoosh and waited as he got his oxygen tubes in his nose.

"I'm not happy," he said.

"Neither am I. But there's nothing I can do about it. Diana wants what she wants, and if she wants to end this marriage, she's going to do it."

"That's her mother, you know. I loved her, but when she wanted something, she wanted it."

"Self-determination's a great quality until it's directed against you."

"You'll stay with us, I hope?"

He meant McNeill-Barnes. Not the family.

"I haven't thought about it."

"Think about it then."

"I will."

I hung up and went to the elevator. What did I want? What was my self-determined desire?

Diana. How was I going to get her back? By her presence or my absence?

• • •

R+D ran itself, more or less. My business partner, Eva, took care of much of the day-to-day while we built up McNeill-Barnes. Walking back into the office for the first time since Diana's note felt surreal. I was already a different man; I just didn't know how different.

Eva was a tightly put-together lawyer who had moved into corporate management. She had a short black pixie cut and pant suit. She changed the seven earrings in her left ear to match her suit or her mood. Today she was red.

"Adam," she said, falling into step with me through the reception area.

"Eva."

We went through the swinging doors to the inner offices. We each had a corner, and the other windows were bordered by seven conference rooms.

"Your wife is here with Rhonda Sidewinder. The divorce lawyer."

"They're early."

"What's going on?" She rarely got personal with me, but the concern in her brown eyes was real.

"Everything. Can you grab my contract with McNeill? I'm sure Rhonda has a copy, but I want to glance at it beforehand. And please do it yourself. If you have Brittany pull it, the whole office is going to talk."

She handed me a folder. "I had a feeling you'd need it. Your McNeill-Barnes contract is in there too."

"Great. Thanks."

"They're in conference four." I started to go, but she touched my arm. "Who's representing you?"

"No one yet. Look, this happened yesterday. It was out of nowhere."

"What are you going to do?"

"Fight for her."

I turned away before I had to see the sympathy in her face.

Chapter 19

PRESENT TENSE

First times.

The first time I saw my wife's face after she left me, she looked different. I thought maybe she'd changed somehow, but I knew I was the one who had changed. Not enough to stop loving her, but enough to see her from far away.

The first time I saw ice in her eyes, I knew it was a thin veneer, put there to make it possible for her to finish the job.

The first time she looked like a stranger to me, I knew it was false. She wasn't a stranger. She was my Diana. My huntress. She was still mine.

And when I looked right at her and she cast her eyes down, I recognized the performance of the gesture as hers. Very much hers. But I'd changed, and I didn't see what I wanted to see. I saw what was always there.

Chapter 20

PRESENT TENSE

This is the bottom line. I don't love you. It's not there anymore. It's not anything you did or didn't do. I've tried to talk myself out of it. I've tried to rekindle it. But it's not there. I'm dead inside.

I'm sorry.

~Diana

She'd taken off her wedding ring. She tried to hide it by folding her right hand over her left, but as the meeting drew on and on, she had to take a drink of water. I caught sight of her left hand before she put it in her lap.

"We understand that the company bylaws fail to provide a clear procedure for valuation of shares in the event of a buyback," Sidewinder said, "but my client would like you to sell her your fifty-one percent of the company at cost."

Diana put the glass down and her right hand joined her left hand in her lap.

"Cost?"

"What you bought them for."

"When the business was underwater and I wanted to break it

apart and sell the pieces?" I turned to Diana. "We've been sitting here for an hour for *this*? You want me *out*?"

"My client wishes to appeal to your good will."

"What good will?" I kept my eyes on my wife. "How long did you know?"

Her eyes joined her hands. In her lap. I slapped the table and she jumped.

"How. Long."

"I don't see that it matters," she said.

"Mister Steinbeck, we can reconvene when you've acquired counsel, but this—"

"It matters. I need to know how long I was fucking a stranger."

"—is not acceptable."

"And me?" Diana cried, the fire back in her eyes. "Who was I fucking?"

"Maybe you should make me a list."

"Never, you freak." She leaned forward, left hand flat on the table. "I never. But what were you doing last night?"

The word freak stopped me, and in the pause, Rhonda Sidewinder filled the gap.

"Mr. Steinbeck. I was hoping this could proceed without—"

"What do you mean?" I asked Diana.

"—revealing certain measures we've taken. But last night you were seen walking into a known sex club."

I maintained a steady expression and didn't move. I made sure I breathed. But I felt as though I'd been hit in the gut. I didn't want Diana to know. I didn't want her lawyer to know. I'd kept my past from my wife for as long as I'd known her, and she was finding out how I'd lied to her and myself the entire time.

"How long, Adam?" Diana growled, bottom lip quivering. "How. Long."

"Jesus, Diana, it's almost like you care."

Rhonda Sidewinder was known as a shark who never let an emotional moment get in the way of advocating for her client. "This won't play well in front of a judge. Nor will standing outside and watching her in a window."

"You put someone on me," I said.

"In the interests of—" Rhonda started but Diana interrupted.

"It was Regina's idea, and I'm glad I did it."

"Your *therapist?* She suggested you put a tail on me? Is that ethical?"

"She thought you were cheating." Diana shook her head. "I did it to rule it out, because I thought she was wrong."

"How long have you been going to sex clubs, Mister Steinbeck?" Rhonda asked.

I wasn't answering. Not right away. Diana was upset, and I wanted her to just sit there and feel like I felt for a minute. As if she'd lived a lie for five years. Because fuck her and her ringless finger and her time in Zack's bed. Fuck her detective, her therapist, and her lawyer. Fuck her attempts to kick me out of the business. Fuck her.

I loved her but fuck her. If she'd had the detective on me for long, she would have known I hadn't been to the Cellar since we were married. She had one night's worth of evidence. The night she left me. And it was burning her up from the inside.

Good.

Fuck her.

"As I was saying," Sidewinder continued, "adultery is cause. We intended to make this convivial."

"So you had me followed." I didn't take my eyes off my wife, and hers were glued to me. I didn't know what we were saying to each other. We were just battering rams of hurt and betrayal.

"We can skip the separation and just serve you. But as an article of good faith, we'll go back to irretrievable breakdown status if you agree to sign over the title to the Jaguar."

I turned my attention away from my wife and on to Sidewinder. "What?"

"And the parking spot on Lafayette."

The parking spot in the underground lot was the first thing we had bought together. We laughed about it and fucked in the front seat, in the spot, because it was ours.

"I can't believe this has come down to a car."

"Taxis won't take Daddy's oxygen tanks," Diana said.

"Buy your own car."

"It *is* my car."

I stood. I'd had enough of this bullshit.

Chapter 21

PRESENT TENSE

She knows.

The car, the detective, the terms of the separation, all of those overwhelmed me, but as I walked out of conference four, the only thing on my mind was that Diana knew I was at the Cellar.

Eva saw me in the hall on the way to my office.

"Guess who I just saw in the bathroom," she whispered. "Upset."

"Christian Grey."

"What?"

"Random questions get random answers."

"I don't officially advocate you going into a women's restroom."

"You're a piece of work, Eva."

"I know." She walked past me and didn't look back.

Justine, our staff architect, came out of the ladies' room just as I walked down the hall. When she was gone, I went in and locked the door. The clack echoed like a gong.

Diana spun, hands clasping the edge of the counter behind her, the water still flowing. "What are you doing in here?"

"It's my office."

I stepped toward her. She didn't move.

I leaned behind her and shut off the faucet. "Your lawyer isn't interested in anything but her bill. You know that, right?" I snapped paper towels off the roll and handed the piece to her.

"I can't meet you alone." She wiped her fingers. "You're too… I don't know the word. I can't think when you're looking at me. I just—"

"I thought you were fucking Zack Abramson."

Her eyes flashed. Anger or recognition? Couldn't tell anything anymore.

"That's why I went to Riverside Drive," I said. "To kill him if he was."

"From the BDSM club?"

"Directly."

"How could you? You're worried about me with Zack, and you'd just paid some woman tie you up and spank you or whatever?"

I laughed so loud I thought the whole office would descend on the bathroom to see what the joke was.

"What's so funny?"

"Look, I have nothing against male subs, and the femdom rooms are packed, but—"

"How long have you been into this shit, Adam? From the beginning or after? Is this why you're distracted when we make love? You wish I was something else?"

I stepped back. What she'd said was insulting. She'd missed the entire point and hit the bullseye.

As if sensing the crack in my armor, she went in. "You say you love me. How can you? You had this whole other life and never shared it. What kind of marriage did we have? Tell me, how deep does this go?"

"I'm saying this once to you personally, and once in front of a lawyer if I have to. I shouldn't have to repeat the truth more than that."

I looked her in the eye as she scanned me back and forth, *flick flick flick*. Her eyes couldn't stay still. She could have known me but never loved me, or loved me without ever knowing me.

"I haven't been to the club since before we dated, and you're the only woman I've touched since then. Period."

"You went before? This is a thing for you?"

"Yes."

"Why didn't you tell me?"

Because I loved you.

Because I was afraid you'd like it.

"Do you want the car?" I said. "I'll sign it over. One hundred percent."

"What's the catch?"

"You give me five minutes. Right here. Right now."

"I'm not having sex with you."

I smirked. Somewhere in there was an opening. She was interested. Curious what I had in mind. I owned her attention. Her lawyer could have banged down the door and not moved Diana's dial a single notch. "I won't touch you."

She swallowed and tilted her head just a tiny bit. That was the curiosity. "What is this?"

"You'll have to pull your skirt up."

Her brows knotted. "I said I wasn't having sex with you."

"And I said I wasn't touching you. You want to know about me and what that part of me is like? I'm going to show you. It won't hurt. It might even be fun."

She just drilled, pushing her intention forward, trying to see through me.

"Pull your skirt up." I said it without acknowledging the possibility that she'd do anything but what I commanded.

It felt good to use those words and that tone. It felt good when her eyes went to the floor.

"Trust me." I said it so low she was just within range to hear it. "Five minutes. Then we don't have to fight over the car."

I stepped back and set my watch with a beep. It wasn't about the car for her. The Jag was the least of her worries, but it was a tangible justification.

For the downcast eyes. For the way her breathing changed. For what Charlie knew and I suspected but wouldn't acknowledge.

Maybe every bone in her body was vanilla. Maybe.

"Quit any time," I said. "Just say the word."

She laid her hands on her hips.

Curled her fingers.

Gripped fabric.

Pulled up her skirt.

The tops of her thighs came into view then met at the crotch. I was hard already and made no move to hide it. She noticed and stopped moving the skirt.

"Higher," I said as if telling her how to center a picture over the couch. Higher was where it had to be. It wasn't a request.

Up it went. Cotton underwear in a pink so pale they were almost white. Tiny falling raindrops of hair at the edges of the fabric. The surprise of the hair pressed against the base of my balls.

Diana kept herself completely smooth, all the time. It was a priority for her. If she let it grow, that meant one thing. She didn't think anyone was going to see it. Not me, but more tellingly, not Zack or anyone else. Those little hairs were a relief.

"Now what?" she asked.

"How do you feel?"

"Weird, Adam. Really weird."

"Why?"

"Because I'm standing here with my skirt around my waist? Because you told me to? For a car, no less, which is creepy."

She was so honest. I ached for her honesty.

"Not for the car. So you don't have to fight for the car."

"Whatever."

"It's an important distinction. You're not obeying me for an object. You're obeying me so I do something. Take an action or don't."

"You think that's not weird?"

"No, I don't. And we have four minutes." I stepped forward. Part of her discomfort was in the physical distance between us. I'd stepped away so she didn't feel threatened, but my gaze was keeping her from relaxing. I kept my eyes on hers. I could smell her perfume and feel the shortness of her breath. "Are you turned on?"

"Sex isn't going to get me back. I'm sorry—"

"Touch yourself."

I remembered that first night in the cab. She'd seemed so solidly vanilla she wouldn't even play. But alone, in the bathroom, her initial shock and offense lasted only a second before she pressed her lips together and reached down, shoulders angling, hand thrusting as if checking to make sure her cunt was still there.

We have hundreds of bones in our bodies, and sometimes we won't acknowledge the preferences of the ones that scare us.

"Are you wet?"

"A little."

I gripped the edge of the vanity and put my lips near her cheek, millimeters from touching her.

"You don't love me anymore," I whispered. "But I could always make you wet, and you always came for me. Like our Italy vacation. In Florence. Coming back from that club, in the little alley. Against the wall. I ripped through your underwear."

Her breathing got shallow and fast.

"I fucked you in the dark, and when you came, you screamed my name so loud all the lights in the apartments went on."

"That was good." She turned her face toward mine.

When her lips nearly touched me, I pulled away just enough. "I said I wouldn't touch you."

"I changed my mind."

I wasn't fooled. Her arousal was talking. "Are you wet?"

"Yes."

"How wet?"

"Very."

I owned her. She'd do whatever I told her. But I wanted something very simple. I wanted her pleasure. "Take the juice from your cunt and rub it on your clit. Make it wet."

"Adam."

"What?"

"What's come over you?"

"Do it." I felt her arm move against me. "Rub your clit back and forth. Be consistent. One-two-one-two."

When I felt that she had it, I stepped back. She stopped. Her knees were bent slightly and her fingers had taken her cunt from the side of the crotch, not the waistband. She never ceased to surprise me. Her shame was apparent. So was her arousal.

"One-two-one-two, huntress."

"Is this your way of getting back at me?"

"One-two-one-two. Let me see you come. You're so beautiful when you come. You've gone this far."

I didn't think she'd continue with me watching her, but her clit must have been throbbing and hard. Her body must have been able to override her mind, because she moved her finger again, closing her eyes. Her cheeks reddened and her knees bent more deeply.

"In Florence. An hour after we got to the hotel. I came so deep in you that night. I fucked you from behind with your leg up on the dresser. I wanted to thrust my whole body inside you. I loved you that much. And I gave up who I was. Last night, at the club, I remembered what I was. I was a man who was obeyed. I dominated women, and they submitted to me. The result was what you're about to feel. Complete pleasure."

She let out a long, low groan, leaning on the vanity, twisting. I could have fucked her right then. I could have bent her over the counter and pounded her. But that wasn't the point. No. Watching her hand move under her clothes because I commanded it. That was the point.

An *uh* escaped her throat. Years of marriage had taught me that meant she was about to come.

My watch beeped.

"Time's up," I said.

Her eyes went wide. Her hand stopped.

"Thank you," I said. "We're done. I'll send you the title to the car. You might want to pull your skirt down, since I can't lock the door from the outside."

It was hard to walk away from her panting, bent frame without tasting her cunt or even seeing more of her reaction, but I turned the corner, unlocked the door, and left the bathroom.

Chapter 22

PRESENT TENSE

It wasn't until I got to the corner that I realized I was shaking. Not from the cold, which was significant. Blood had been dumped from my heart and was coloring my entire body hot red. She'd done what I told her. I'd dominated her for five minutes. Owned her. Pleasure and shame, every submissive bone in her body had been mine for that little bit of time.

It all came back in a flood. I was high on dominance. I remembered how it had felt with other women, but it was a hundred times more powerful with her. After such a long time away, the surge of adrenaline and endorphins made me feel like a perfectly tuned instrument.

I stepped onto the street in my flat-bottomed shoes, the melting ice creating new treacheries, and I knew I wouldn't fall.

Walking across, my feet counting one-two-one-two-one with the rhythms of the street, the sounds of the city, the wind on my face, the towering obelisks above, I was threaded into the fabric of the world.

I heard the yellow cab before I saw it. The wheels didn't screech—the street was too coated in melting ice for that. They made a splashing crackle as the hulk of metal barreled toward me out of control, so close. No way to run. No way to jump or dodge.

Yet I was in complete control of myself. I was right in the world. I felt the substance of my existence and the calculations of my thoughts.

I took one step sideways.

The cab missed me by an inch, skidding to a splashy stop.

With that lurching yellow car and the collective exhale of everyone who saw the skid, the door behind me closed. My journey had to go forward, back to who I'd been.

Chapter 23

PAST PERFECT

McNeill-Barnes company archives.
Transcript of Lloyd Barnes's retirement speech.
The Claude Hotel Ballroom
June 21st, 2012.
Staff, authors, and their guests in attendance.
Full guest list in appendix.

My wife and I took this company over twenty-five years ago from another team forged in the bonds of marriage—my wife's parents, Richard and Bertha McNeill. Dick and Bert were pioneers. Together they published and nurtured some of the greatest American authors of the century. True literary giants. And mostly because of Bert's influence, they published some of the most esteemed female authors of the generation.

Martha and I tried to maintain that vision, but we had a slow leak in the business. Technology. Changing tastes. We kept her afloat, working day and night, but by the time Martha couldn't fight off the second round of cancer, we were struggling to see a future.

And I can't imagine a future without McNeill-Barnes. The only thing that's kept me alive this past year has been the slow, steady, incremental revival of this company, thanks to my daughter, Diana, and her future husband, Adam Steinbeck.

(raises glass)

(guests cheer)

What a joy to give the day-to-day operations over to my daughter and another husband-and-wife team. It was my dream to pass them a profitable and historically relevant publishing house. I've downgraded that a little.

(cries of denial)

I'm passing them a company rife with potential to create and release important work in this new century. Most importantly, I'm passing it to family. I'll die happy if this company stays alive and in family hands.

You two need to have kids, stat.

(laughter)

Chapter 24

PRESENT TENSE

Two days had passed since I dominated Diana in the bathroom at R+D. Since then, she'd worked from home, and I'd jumped between publishing and real estate development.

I carried around five tons of pain where she used to be. But those minutes of submission, as reluctant as they were, they were minutes of heaven I never thought I'd have.

I thought about her constantly.

My wife and I worked because I was a planner and she was the creative mind behind our life together. She had ideas and ran at the starting gun, but midway, she'd get distracted and move on to the next thing.

That worked. Because I liked finishing. She wanted a condo down the street from the McNeill-Barnes building and attacked the purchase single-mindedly. When we talked about reviving the publishing business, she had the idea to diminish the importance of fiction in their catalog and pump new life into long-form journalism based on the questions in her journals. She started both projects. I finished them.

What had there been besides work?

Us, together. In the office, in bed, in the kitchen in the morning, strategizing, coming up with ideas, these were my best memories of Diana.

"Let's sleep in," she'd asked once. Maybe a year into our marriage.

I'd stroked her arm, feeling her eyelashes flutter on my chest. Saturdays were the only day to get anything done, and we had to do it. The financial bloodletting was slowing, but we had to keep pushing.

"We can sleep in tomorrow."

She'd gotten up before I finished the last syllable and she was in the bathroom before I could tell her to stay still a second, another half an hour wasn't going to hurt.

I hadn't gone to her cousin's wedding in Minnesota. She'd only taken two days leave for her aunt's death in New Jersey because we had a pitch meeting in Los Angeles. We'd lost the baby, and beside screwing regularly, we hadn't made any effort to time sex with her cycle.

Every step was another way we failed each other.

I ached. My joints. My head. My heart. I ached with emptiness and helplessness. The pain was physical. I tried to jog it off on the salty streets. Piles of snow built up on the curb, leaving less room for joggers, and I veered right to avoid a stroller. My shoulder brushed against the green subway railing.

Without pausing or missing a beat, I ran down the stairs and got on the Uptown A.

Fucking train. I couldn't tell how fast it was going because it was so goddamn slow. I needed to say what needed saying. We had been too focused on work. That was the problem.

I got off on Riverside Drive and jogged west in the Saturday twilight. I had so many things to say. All obvious. All puzzle pieces clicking into place.

The lights in Zack's apartment were off. I looked at my phone for the time, but I didn't need to. It was dark enough for her to need the lights.

It was almost the end of the month. Did she move out? And to where?

I slid the bar to make a call. She had to answer.

But then I saw a little app that would tell me when a phone was stolen. Was she still on my account?

I sat on a cold bench by the Hudson River and tapped the icon.

In half a second, her phone showed up. Downtown.

At the Cellar.

Chapter 25

PAST PERFECT

Did you never dominate her? Did she never submit to you, even a little? Take a command? A strong request?

Open your legs.

I didn't shave yesterday.

I don't care.

Or the day before.

I open her legs. It's dark. It's late. We haven't had time to breathe all week. We haven't made love in eight days, and the sight of her in the office is driving me insane. Seeing her in the morning as we talk about leasing parts of the SoHo building through the shower doors gives me a boner I never consider relieving because I know the schedule. I know where we have to be and when. But I can smell the delicious tang of her cunt.

I kneel on the bed and open her legs at the knees.

I'm so tired, honey.

She is tired. It's not a ploy. I run my hands down her inner thighs, and when my fingers reach her cunt, it's wet. She groans.

I bend her knees up and apart. She is deliciously compliant.

I can't move. So tired. We have to be up in four hours.

She can barely make the words.

Don't move then.

Can't.

Just let me take you.

Okay.

I fuck her. When she moves, I tell her to stay still. When her eyebrows tense and her mouth opens, I shush her.

Don't move. Stay absolutely still.

Adam. Adam…

Shh. Not a word.

I love you.

I can tell she comes when I feel her muscles tense and release. And when I come inside her, I own the world.

Chapter 26

PRESENT TENSE

—Are you at the Cellar?—

—What, mate? It's tryout night. We're
at the Loft Club—

—Diana's there—

—Diana your vanilla wife?—

—I'm uptown. I need you to go over
there and make sure she's all right.
I'm coming ASAP—

—We're on our way—

—Thank you—

—You owe us, big time—

Chapter 27

PRESENT TENSE

I didn't ask who "us" was. I assumed it was Viktor or another lifer. Another body. Someone who lived by rules and codes. Someone willing to run off to the Cellar on my behalf on tryout night.

I had too much to do in the meantime.

Sweaty gym suits wouldn't get me far in the club, and I was at the northwestern tip of a very crowded island. I wanted to be at the southwestern edge.

—Diana, what are you doing?—

I had two hundreds in my wallet and I gave one to the cabbie. "Get me to TriBeCa in five minutes and you get the other hundred." He took off like a shot.

—Don't talk to anyone—

She didn't answer. The signal in the bottom floor—the actual cellar—was notoriously hard core. So was the view. Latex bodysuits and slapping leather. Nipple clamps and tit torture. Scat had a separate room, but some nights you could smell it down there.

That's what I imagined seeing through her eyes. She'd see chaos where I saw control. When I saw it through my eyes, it looked like contented people satisfying their needs. It looked like a place without judgment.

She wouldn't see it that way. She didn't know every stroke was part of negotiation, consent, and contracts. She didn't know there was a board of people who settled disputes with excommunication and fines.

I checked for her phone's location, and no new signal came through. Just the old location.

Tryout nights were tame by normal standards because anyone could show up, but for some in the community, the extra people was the appeal. The increased risk of exposure was a turn-on, and the acts downstairs could get incredibly outrageous just for the sake of it.

She was fine. No one would hurt her or touch her. She was protected by the rules, and she very well might have gone with a friend or two. Maybe she went with a date.

I had to put that out of my mind before I broke something.

The cabbie earned the extra hundred. I promised another hundred if he waited.

I scrubbed down in record time and got into a suit, barely looking at myself in the mirror before grabbing the jacket and running out.

There was a crowd outside the velvet ropes. Rob and Carol were checking people against a list and letting others in just because they looked as though they'd be scared. Fear was great entertainment. They opened the rope for me.

"It's tryout," Rob said.

"I know." I slapped him on the shoulder and walked in.

My phone dinged.

—I see her—

—On six—

I went to my phone locator. Found her. New signal. Same place. She was out of the dungeon.

I got into the elevator with a woman in latex pants and a collar and her Dom, who wore ripped jeans and a leather jacket. He held her leash loosely, and when the brass doors closed, I saw the three of us in the reflection. Scenes were not permitted in elevators or halls, so we all stood, facing front, on the way to male domination. The Dom to my right quietly yanked the leash, and the sub smiled subtly.

I fixed my tie in the reflection in the brass.

My ring was still on.

I was about to see her, in the club, on the sixth floor.

Relief-plus-elation-plus-dread.

My lungs weren't big enough for the size of the breath I had to take.

The doors slid open to the red hallway.

Chapter 28

PRESENT TENSE

My space. My room. My world.

Five steps to the door, ten to the bar, and that's how long it took to get my shit together. Diana was under my protection in my domain. Nothing and no one would touch her but me.

I saw Charlie first, and he pointed at the bar. Fucker was just watching.

She sat at the bar between two men. Viktor and Braden. I knew them, and I knew why they were talking to her. She was beautiful and inexperienced. Their intentions were crystal clear to me, and I fought the urge to take their faces off with my bare hands.

I had to hold my breath and mitigate my expectations against the reality.

I expected her to be meek and scared. Kittenish. Overwhelmed. Wide-eyed.

The reality was that she was the woman I'd married. I married a boss. I married a sharp, creative mind. Not that any of those traits kept her from glancing nervously at the nearly naked woman curled at Viktor's feet, but Diana was engaged in a conversation as if everything around her was completely normal.

And she was everything. I couldn't hear her when she spoke, but I knew she sounded clear and confident from the way she made eye contact. Nodded when Viktor answered. Put her drink to her lips.

Her blouse was buttoned all the way, but I could see the heave of her chest, knew the shape of her tits, how to make the nipples hard. The things I could do to her in that club, half a room away.

Open your cunt. Bend over. Count with me. Beg for my cock.

I couldn't put them all in order.

She touched her necklace, one of her tells for arousal, but the knowledge that she was wet was pushed away by the wedding ring on her finger. She'd put it back on. Probably to keep men away. That didn't work in the Cellar. If you were there, you were there to play or learn how to play.

Calmly. I walked toward her. She saw me a few steps away, and her chin went up a few millimeters. Brazen, like a teenager caught with a cigarette and not putting it out. Viktor, a Dominant who couldn't stand the thought of losing a woman's attention, reached for her face.

I took the last step and grabbed his wrist hard.

Viktor was a Russian oligarch who'd escaped the KGB in a cargo ship, but if he'd touched her, I would have broken that wrist.

"Let go, friend." He elongated friend as if it was a temporary condition.

"She's mine." I let go. "And I don't share this one. Friend."

Viktor picked up his drink. "Shame you feel that way. It's what they need."

He looked down at his sub, who rested her head peacefully on his leg. He stroked her cheek. Her smile widened.

My wife touched her necklace as if frozen. I couldn't gauge her emotions. Mine were muddled as fuck. I didn't want her to be there, but my dick thought it was a terrific idea.

You don't want her getting any good ideas.

"Vick!" Charlie's voice cut through the noise.

"You Aussie fuck!" Viktor replied jovially.

Charlie glanced at me and nodded as he shook hands with the man, letting me know he'd saved me and I owed him plenty.

"Diana," I said, "what are you doing?"

She looked at me, lips tight. "I have the right to be here."

"I didn't say you didn't. And you don't have to be defensive. Let's talk about this separate from everything else. Without all the baggage or the divorce. Just talk to me." I put my arm on the bar and motioned for Norton. "What are you drinking?"

"Ginger ale," she said.

"Good choice."

"I felt like I needed my wits about me."

"You do. Do you want to stay or go?"

I wanted her to stay because if she left, I might not see her again. This chance to show her the world I'd left for her wouldn't come again. I didn't know if I wanted to attract her to it or scare her away, but I wanted to know what was possible.

She didn't think about it long, but deep, checking my face, the room, her own breath before answering. "Stay."

I ordered two ginger ales.

She eyeballed Charlie. "Was he at our wedding? The Australian guy with the cane?"

"Yes. And a few other things. Events. Whatnot."

She'd had no idea who he was to me. She'd shaken his hand and made small talk knowing nothing. Of course she looked as if I'd betrayed her.

"You didn't tell me you were coming," I said.

"Neither did you. For five years."

"I stopped when you came along."

"I don't believe you."

"It's true."

"Oh, I believe you didn't set foot in this club. But you were here." She scanned the room, with its ambient music and soft lighting. Men in suits and women doing their bidding. Her gaze landed on Viktor the Russian chatting with Charlie, then moved down to his sub curled at his feet like a contented kitten.

"I knew it was something," she said. "All that time you were phoning it in."

"That's not true—"

"You think I couldn't tell?" She looked right through me, breaking my defenses to bits.

"I love you, Diana." I growled it, taking her arm. "You're not for this. Did you want me to drag you down here? For what? I'd hate myself for ruining you."

"I loved you too. Past. Tense." She yanked her arm away. "And I've been blaming myself for a year now. But it wasn't me. It was *you*."

She snapped her bag off the bar and walked away, twisting on her high heel and speeding off.

Fuck this.

This was my world, and I could do shit here I couldn't do anywhere else.

I took a single step, picked her up, and threw her over my shoulder.

The air went out of her. She beat my back and cried my name as I carried her to the back and around a corner to a bank of doors with leather numbers. One was ajar. I kicked it open with a *slap*. The black room was lit by a single red bulb.

I slammed the door closed with my foot, clicked the *occupied* sign, and dropped her. Her lips were parted and her mouth was twisted into a snarl. She punched my chest so hard the air went out of me. I grabbed her wrists with one hand and pushed her against the wall.

"Don't you fucking touch me!"

I kept my hands where they were and pushed into her.

Her eyelids fluttered. She'd be touching her pearls if her hands were free.

"What did you say?" I whispered. I smelled the arousal on her.

Breathy, without aggression or a struggle to get away, she said, "Don't you fucking touch me."

"You came here to see something? You came here to learn

about me? The guy you don't love anymore? Why? What's the fucking difference?"

In the silence that followed, a *thwack* could be heard through the walls. And a long female cry that was a cross between pain and orgasm. And another *thwack*.

"I need to know where I went wrong." Tears glistened on the edges of her red eyes. "And fuck you for lying. You let me think I wasn't good enough."

I let her wrists go and punched the red shade button behind her.

The wall opposite the door opened to a window, and yellow light flooded the room, washing her face in pale yellow. I didn't turn to the window but kept my attention on her as she did.

"You tell me where you went wrong," I said. "Were you not good enough? Or was this just not what I wanted for you?"

I gave her room to face the window. I hadn't known what would be there when I kicked the door in. Could have been any number of kinks, but as it turned out, it was mine.

Diana faced the window. I saw her in the dim reflection, her eyes wide, cheeks slack.

And through it, a sub was bent over a bench, bare feet dirty on the bottoms. Her wrists were tied to a vertical pole on each side of her, and her shoulder blades nearly kissed. Her straight blond hair was tied into a knot out of the way of the tears streaming down her face and dropping onto her parted lips.

Her Dom was in grey slacks, clean shoes, and a crisp white button-front shirt open at the neck and rolled up at the sleeves. I didn't know him, but he was in his late twenties and handled the wooden paddle as if it were an extension of his arm.

She was at an angle to the window so we could see her painfully raw ass and her face. He spoke to her, and she squeaked a response, nodding.

"He's asking her if she's all right, but he's not actually asking. If he said 'how are you,' he'd break the scene. It's a trigger question. He's asking what color the sky is, and if she says 'blue,' it means she's fine."

"Why can't he just ask?"

"He's playing the part of a man who might go to any length to hurt her, and it's her job to trust he won't."

The Dom pressed his sub's lower back down so her ass was high and tight, then he pulled all the way back and paddled her three times, fast on the already wounded skin.

Diana went rigid. I stood behind her.

"Breathe," I said.

She didn't. The sub's face was beet red and wet. He leaned and kissed it, speaking softly. She nodded, and I read her lips. *Please. Yes, please, sir.*

Unexpectedly, and with sadistic relish, the young Dom took one last swipe. The surprise made the sub scream, and I had to reach around and cover Diana's mouth before she did too.

"Hush," I said in her ear.

That perfume. The oranges. Her hair on my cheek. Her mouth on my palm, breaths hard. I put my other arm around her waist and pulled her to me, pushing my hard cock against her.

The Dom touched his sub's raw bottom. She squirmed as he worked his waistband.

"He's going to fuck her now. It's her reward for being a good girl."

I slid my hand down my wife's body, putting my hand between her legs. I'd lost my mind. Everything about this scene was not what I wanted for Diana, but my cock was raging and the heat through her pants was undeniable.

The Dom fucked the sub as the vertical poles shook.

"Every time he enters her, he pushes on her sore ass." I nipped her ear. "I hear it hurts like hell. But look at her. Look at her face. She loves it. She was built for it."

I moved my hand off her mouth and pulled her closer, my hand circling between her legs, mercilessly pushing the shape of my cock against her.

"You want to do that to me?" she asked.

I curved my fingers, getting the tips across her clit, hard and fast. "I love you."

She pushed against my dick, and we moved together. I groaned into the back of her neck, and she spun around, putting her back to the window. Her hair hung in front of her eyes and her shoulders jutted forward.

Behind Diana, the sub came with a cry we heard through the walls and her Dom slapped her ass gently to mix pain with her pleasure. He was good.

Diana put her hands behind her. "Are you this guy? You do what he does?"

"Why are you asking?"

"I want to know what you've been fantasizing about every time we made love."

I didn't want to do this. Every wall I'd built around this life was broken. If I told her what had been in my mind, the very foundation I'd built our sexual relationship on would shatter. "A lot of things."

"Like what?" She stuck her *t* as punctuation. Petulant little girl needed a spanking, and she wasn't taking "nothing" for an answer.

I could salvage this with something mild. Then I could try to get her back under the old rules. Promise the life we had with a little extra. Play the middle.

Or I could draw a line in the sand she'd never cross, effectively pushing her away.

Play the middle. Play the middle. Play the middle.

"Like this." I put my hands on the glass and whispered in her ear. "You are on your back. You are tied to the headboard by your elbows and your ankles. Your knees are around your ears, and I see your cunt is already wet. I slap your ass. The backs of your thighs. Sometimes with my hand. Sometimes I use my belt. When your skin is red, I hit harder, until it welts. I put my fingers in your hole, then your ass. You're screaming and squirming as I bring you so close to orgasm, but I don't let you finish. You're begging for an orgasm. Begging for my cock. Then I slap your cunt. Right on it. You scream, but it's not in pain. It feels good. I slap again and again, until your clit is swollen. So when I finally fuck you, my cock gives you pleasure and pain until you can't tell the difference. I own that. I gave you that. Everything you feel is mine and you give it to me. We're connected by your submission."

That wasn't the middle. That was me shredding the foundation of the last five years.

I had an erection that was so sensitive, I was going to explode at the slightest touch. Behind my wife, in the whipping room, the Dom sat on the couch with the sub over his lap as he rubbed lotion on her red bottom.

"You're sick," Diana whispered.

The sub on the other side of the room said something, and she and the Dom laughed together. He kissed her lower back. Her arm flopped over his knee. She looked wiped out and happy. I couldn't give my wife that connection. I loved her.

I pulled back from Diana's ear to look in her face. "I am. And I tried to protect you from that. But you had me followed, then you showed up here. And now that I've told you, your nipples are hard and you're flushed. You're swallowing every half a second."

"So? Just because I'm turned on, you think I'm going to love you again? It takes more than that."

"What will it take?"

"A miracle." She shoved me away. "I felt bad about leaving you. I really thought there was something wrong with me because I couldn't love you. But I don't feel bad anymore. I was in love with someone who didn't even exist."

She swung past me and headed for the door. I put my hand on it. Through the window, the sound of the Dom and sub laughing together. I knew the tension release of a good beating and the hours of laughter that followed. If I ever paddled a woman again, I'd bust my gut laughing. Fuck, I wanted that relief with my wife, but I didn't think I could bear everything leading up to it, or losing her after it.

"What?" Diana asked. More of a demand than a question.

I moved my hand. "Let me walk you out."

"I can find my way."

"Not without being a target for every Dominant on the floor."

"Fine."

She swung the door open. The shades on the window behind us slapped shut, and the hallway light stung my eyes. A few people were exiting rooms, and the hall was moderately crowded. I put my hand on Diana's back and walked her past a security guy who remembered me and out through another wide hallway with a red carpet decorated with white flowers that, if you looked closely, were actually abstractions of bodies twisting around each other in hundreds of sex positions.

That particular hallway was closed to tryouts. I was trying to avoid the bar, but I probably should have walked through it. The hallway was full of people chatting, yanking leashes, draped over each other.

"Adam?" A female voice cut through the conversation, all white noise and ambient music.

"Sir!" The voice came again when I tried to ignore it.

A hand on my shoulder. I turned.

"Serena," I said. I hadn't seen her in five years. She'd been nineteen in the Montauk house. There in the back hall of the Cellar, she was twenty-four.

The bud had blossomed.

She was five-ten with straight brown hair and bangs. Skin like silk. Lips that looked like fresh-risen dough, and a smile sweet and innocent as a child's.

She bowed her head. Bit her bottom lip. This alone told me she was still subbing.

"You can look up," I said.

She wore a collar on her long, slim neck.

"How have you been?" I asked. "Speak freely. As friends."

"Great! I just got back from Paris. I did a shoot with Ingrid Gravenstein for the *Breakout*."

"I have no idea what that is," I said, smiling. It was nice to see her.

"It's a short list of hot designers and their muses," Diana said from behind me.

"Oh, hey. Serena, this is…"

My wife? My future ex? My friend?

"Diana," I said.

The pause was barely discernible, but knowing the woman I loved, she noticed.

Serena bowed her head and bent slightly at the waist.

"Nice to meet you," Diana said.

"I was walking her out," I told Serena.

"Will you come back?"

"Yeah. Give me a minute."

"Thank you."

Still trained like a champ. I nodded and walked Diana to the elevators.

"Well," she said, "who's that?"

"I was with her just before we met."

The elevator doors opened and a crowd piled out. It was getting to be prime time on a tryout night. Worst night to be there.

Diana and I got in with a few other people. She didn't speak to me or look at me. Not even when the doors opened and we flooded into the lobby with the rest. Not at the coat check, except to insist on paying, which I wouldn't allow. Not as we exited into the street.

Only when I started to step into the street to hail a cab did she speak.

"You gave her up to be with me?"

I got back onto the sidewalk. "Yes."

"Do you regret it?"

"Not for a minute."

Her breath made a plume of steam as she exhaled. "Are you going back upstairs?"

"Do you want me to?"

"I have no right to you anymore."

"No. You don't. But…" Fuck it. I was just going to be as honest with her as I was being with myself. "I don't know if I'll go. What just happened with us, just now, it's clouding my judgment. I'm half drunk on it, and I can't tell if that's good or bad. For better or worse, I let you in. I showed you who I am. I'm happy in a way. Really happy. And I'm scared to death."

"You're scared of what?"

"That I pushed you away, and that I brought you closer. Both. Neither. Everything's changed. We aren't us anymore."

"I don't know you," she said. "We were never us."

I put my fingers to the bridge of my nose and pressed the ducts. The cold soothed them. "This was my fault. You leaving. I brought it on myself."

"There's plenty of blame to go around." She sighed another white plume. "I shouldn't have come here just because I was curious. It was completely unnecessary, and it's not going to change anything. We need to just cut the cords and feel hurt over it and move on."

"Let me get you a cab."

"I got it."

She took a step into the street, and a cab pulled up. I opened the back door for her. She slid in and leaned down. She was forlorn in the dark backseat, bag in her lap, nose red from the January cold.

"I'm going to need to come by the condo and get a few things," she said.

"You need to show up at the office," I said. "I won't bite you."

"Not unless you tie me up first." She smirked.

"Ask nicely and I might."

I slapped the door closed before she could joke about asking. A joke like that would get me in the backseat, and she'd either refuse my touch or accept it. Neither option was good.

The cab took off and blended into the river of brake lights.

Chapter 29

PAST PERFECT

Remember the time it was late? In the office? The time Diana leaned on her desk, crossed her arms, and looked out the window. She watched the last shoppers in the Prada store. She said that if she could change anything about her life—

"I wouldn't change a thing."

That was when we'd gotten Q2 financials back and they were minus .8 YOY, even with the downsize. That was at the bottom. Shit was bleak.

"I'd change these numbers," I said.

She didn't answer for a long time. "I wouldn't."

"Really?"

"We're free." Her form was a silhouette against the lit windows across the narrow street. "We're still privately held. We can do whatever we want. No one would question it, and if they did, fuck them."

I pushed away from my desk and planted myself in front of her. "Tell me, what's on your mind?"

She moved her attention from the checkerboard of light across the street to my face. "Fiction's dead. At least for us it is. We don't have the leverage to break new literary talent, and the genre writers are doing it themselves."

"Right."

"The newspapers can't monetize the internet. They're hemorrhaging. Websites can't pay journalists to research solid, deep pieces."

"All true."

"I think we should kill the literary fiction division. Get out of our contracts."

I crossed my arms. "That feels like suicide."

"No. We circle the wagons around long journalism. Book length. Poach established writers and editors from the newspapers. They'll abandon a sinking ship if we pay them."

"Okay, look, I get it. This shit sells. But stories that work in this genre are unicorns."

Even as I said it, I knew the answer, and the beauty of us was that she knew it too. Her eyes lit up, and together, we laughed.

Her journals with their thousands of questions.

"This is it," I said. "We find the best in the business to answer your questions."

"We put a call out."

"Lists. We list the best ones."

"Long-form answers. Experiential and research-based."

"We throw everything behind it."

We talked over each other for the next ten minutes, an entire plan falling into place.

And that was how we saved her family business.

Chapter 30

PRESENT TENSE

As Diana's cab disappeared, I thought I'd just go back to our place on Crosby and look at all her things. Maybe digest what the fuck just happened. Take a healthy mental break.

"Hey, mate," Charlie said from behind me. He leaned on his cane. Serena stood a step behind him, averting her eyes to the ground when I looked at her. "We're off to the Loft House. You coming?"

"Sure."

Fuck it. I was pumped full of unanswered questions and undefined emotions. Perfect time to have a couple of drinks.

The Loft House wasn't a sex club, unless you consider money orgasmic, but with an impossibly long waiting list that required recommendations from three members, the sexiness could have sprung from exclusivity.

That night it was sparsely populated, but there was still enough ambient conversation over the experimental classical music to keep our conversation safe. Charlie, Serena, and I were tucked into a corner. Since we were in a vanilla location where I didn't need such a clear head, I moved on to whiskey. Charlie never stopped drinking, and tonight it was rum. Serena drank only water with lemon.

"Who you keeping dry for?" I asked. If she had a new Master, he probably didn't let her drink, or she was only allowed to drink with him.

"I feel better when I have water," she said.

"You look wonderful," I said. "It's great to see you."

I wasn't thinking of her as a potential fuck, but she blushed and looked down, pressing her knees together. She wore a polo shirt, same as always. Sexless and plain. Sometimes she buttoned them all the way.

"She was the most sought-after sub in New York," Charlie said smugly. "Got her pick of the best. And I trained her, thank you very much."

"Never went to law school?" I asked.

"No. I didn't like arguing all the time, and modeling is more fun. More money too."

I knew the truth, and it was sadder. Her mother had died from complications of her stroke. Her father was useless for much besides haranguing her for her failures.

"She socks it away like a squirrel." Charlie was beaming like a proud parent. "Gotta love her."

She smiled. You never forget your first Dominant, they say, and Charlie's praise would always mean something to her. I wondered if I'd made an impression at all.

She excused herself. I must have wondered while watching her walk away, because Charlie cleared his throat as if he had a ream of crumpled paper wads in it.

"The wife," he said. "You back on? You and her?"

"Why?"

"Because I saw her. Same as you. She has potential."

I didn't even want to talk about it. "You said Serena *was* the most blah blah—past tense."

"Why do you care?"

"Making conversation."

"This thing you have?" He put his drink down in pause. "You never loved a submissive."

"I can't."

"Have you tried?"

"Once I break them, it just dies. It's not something I can control. Do you have a point?"

"Serena blames herself. Takes it out on herself."

"It didn't start with her."

"She's been with Stefan going on three years now. That's his collar. The arrangement satisfies her need for punishment and his need to touch everything you've touched."

Stefan was a charming fuck. He was one of the few rich painters in the world. He was educated, talented, and back-breakingly sadistic. Along with Charlie and me, he was one of the three owners of the Montauk house, and he denied hating me.

"Three years isn't spite," I said. "He must care about her."

"I'm sure he does. But they've been having problems."

"Do they both know there are problems?" My voice was laced with bitterness.

"Been tense as the last hour of a cricket match for months."

"And you want me to charm her away?" I asked.

"I like you better than that Scandie."

"I'm married."

"Good thing one of you sees it that way."

"Low blow, Charles. Low blow."

He nodded and waved an apology my way, acknowledging I was right without saying the words. It was enough for me.

"Alayne Kerry was asking about you," he said. "Not a repeat. Take her out to Montauk for a month. The main house is empty. You'll be Master Adam in the first twenty-four hours."

"What's in this for you?"

"Seeing you happy." He leaned back and crossed his legs. "Go. You'll be over your little vanilla wife before the first week. By the end of the month, you won't remember her name until you sign the divorce papers."

Serena came back across the room, head high, legs up to her neck, black polo shirt open to show her fashionable leather collar. I wouldn't try to seduce her away from Stefan. I was soon to be single, and I needed the Cellar. Stealing another Dom's collared sub could get me thrown out.

I was formulating another plan.

Chapter 31

PRESENT TENSE

Diana and I had spent the day at the office acting like adults. We had meetings and made decisions. We didn't talk about anything but work. The activity was a relief, in a way. In another way, I felt as if I were trapped in a bag and thrown in the Hudson.

We were too polite. I'd never felt more awkward in my life.

"I was thinking of coming by tonight to get some things," she said as she slung her bag over her shoulder. The winter sky was charcoal through the window behind her, and the rectangles of yellow light from the building across the street made an orderly grid.

"How long are you living on Riverside?" I moved papers around my desk.

"End of the month."

"Where to then?"

"I don't know. Dad says I can have my old room back."

"Sounds tempting."

"He never took down the One Direction posters."

"You can move back into the loft with me."

She froze with her hand on the doorknob. "I can't. It's too complicated."

"I understand. Come by after eight so I can be gone."

She nodded, rueful. "Thank you."

• • •

I had no intention of being gone.

I was back in the condo by seven forty-five. When she came in, she had a suitcase and a duffel. Thank God she was alone. I had a plan if she brought someone, but it wasn't as good.

"Oh, hi," she said when she saw me, keys still dangling from her finger.

"Yeah, hi. I decided to be here."

She dropped the suitcase. It clapped. Hollow. "Why? Did you think I was going to swipe your cufflinks?"

I laughed. "If you want the cufflinks, you can have them."

"I don't want your cufflinks."

"Can we sit? Because I want to talk about what you want."

She tilted her head up, eyes closed in pure annoyance. "I want a divorce. That's all I want."

"No, it isn't. You want that and more. Come on. Sit."

I indicated her own couch, with its cold modern lines and warm colors. I'd kept the light ambient and put a pitcher of water on the coffee table.

"Do I need my lawyer?" she asked.

"I hope not." I sat in a chair and indicated her spot on the couch again.

She kicked her shoes off and sat the way she always did, with her socked feet tucked under her. I remembered the sub in the viewing room, how she went on her toes when her Dom paddled her and how I could see the dirty bottoms of her feet.

I knew where I'd planned to start, but now that she was sitting there, looking at me with eyes the color of broken glass, I couldn't launch into the offer.

"When you got home from the club the other night, what did you do?" I asked.

"I really don't want to talk about the club."

Defenses up already. I was going to have to lower mine to draw her out.

"I need to," I said. "You don't have to do a damn thing for my sake. But I need to."

"Then let's talk about the club. You want to hit my pussy. I don't know what that says about you."

"The fact that I never did says a lot about how I feel about you."

She continued as if she didn't even hear me. "I mean, I know it's not in anger. But it's violence and it's weird. I don't understand how you can want to do that to someone you love."

"I can't do that to someone I love. That's the point."

She wasn't listening, she was looking deep inside herself. "I can't get my head around it."

"I'm concerned you think it's just violence and the sub gets nothing out of it."

"What does she get out of it?" She was leaning forward, drilling again. She wanted all the information. All the words.

I didn't know if it was just Curious Diana or if Aroused Diana was showing up.

"When you got home last night, what did you do?"

"Went to bed."

"Did you sleep?"

"Who could sleep after that? I was all turned around." Her face and posture told a thousand tales.

"You touched yourself."

"Shut up."

"I need to know."

"How is that your business?"

"How is it not?" I asked.

"Did you jerk off?"

"No. I went out."

"Where?"

Shit. I was derailed. How did she do that?

Just by being Diana, that was how she did it.

"I met up with Serena and Charlie, the guy with the cane. From the bar." I sat back, leaning into the new angle the conversation took. "He trained Serena years ago, then sent her to me."

"Right before we met."

"About five weeks before."

"Sent her to you? What does that mean?"

"Did you touch yourself after you got home? Under the sheets? Standing over the toilet? On your hands and knees?"

Long pause. She absently ran her finger along the pressed edge of her cuff. "What if I didn't at all?"

"I'd be shocked."

She spit out a short laugh, looked down. Lordamighty. It's amazing what a man won't see what he doesn't want to see it. Was she full-blown submissive? Or did she just have tendencies? How did I not know it?

Charlie's voice answered.

You knew it, you whacka. You knew it from the beginning.

"I didn't even get my jacket off." Her eyes were still cast down. "I dropped my keys on the floor and got on my knees. I did it right in the foyer. Then…" She smiled again, looking away as if laughing at herself. "Then I took a shower and made myself come again."

"Just twice?"

When she looked back up, her softness was gone. "What does it mean that he sent her to you? And why did it end? Was it because of me? You told me when we met you weren't with anyone."

"I wasn't with her. Not in the way I meant when I answered. Okay, look, I'll run it down for you." I had to just forget who I was talking to and spit it out. "Charlie trains subs. He finds their limits, tells them what to say and how to act."

"Do they pay him?"

"No, no, there's no money exchanged. It's not that. It's what he loves to do and it's totally with consent. Joyful consent. He's the best, but he can't fuck them. It's a war injury, don't ask. Serena was a virgin. He could teach her to deep throat and take anal using a dildo, but he didn't want to take her virginity with a piece of plastic."

"He's a prince."

"Do you want me to finish?"

"Yes. Sorry."

"She wanted me to take her virginity. So I did. I spent thirty days with her in a house in Montauk I'm part owner of."

"You own a house in Montauk?" she asked.

"Do not even think of suing me for it."

"I won't. Go on."

"Thirty days was the limit, and we agreed ahead of time. We did all the things she was trained to do. She came a lot. I came a lot. On the twenty-eighth day, I took her virginity and continued to fuck her until she was too sore to walk. On the thirtieth day, it was over and we drove home. The following Monday, I met you in a meeting with McNeill-Barnes regarding a buyout."

I didn't know what she'd think or ask. I knew what I told her had a dozen holes she'd fill with questions, and I knew as painful as it would be, I'd answer them honestly.

"You waited twenty-eight days?" she asked.

"I needed her to be sure. Also, it was torture for her, which we both liked."

"She's beautiful."

"She is. It took a lot of willpower, but it was worth it to see her beg for it."

"Wow."

"Wow?"

"This is… I mean, this is a whole thing. Jesus, I just wanted to get my stuff. I wanted my mom's wedding dress, and I bought underwear last week I never got to wear. And I was going to take the blue stock pot? The Le Creuset one? I had a note all ready in my mind I was going to write on the yellow pad. I was going to offer to get you a new one even though you never cook and now I'm just…" She shot up, standing in her sock feet.

"I'm going to do all that. I'm collecting my things right now. I don't know what your plan is, Adam, but it's not going to work. Getting me all turned on last night and trying to get me jealous today? I get it. But being horny and jealous isn't love. It's being a teenager." She stomped toward the bedroom.

"You're jealous?"

"No! Tie her up and fuck her all night long. I don't even care."

She pivoted on her sock and disappeared around the corner. The bedroom door slammed.

Diana was never jealous. She just wasn't. Not of Eva. Not of the women who flirted with me. She never worried when we were apart. She was incapable of it.

Without rushing, I walked to the kitchen, took the blue Le Creuset stockpot from the cabinet, and went to the bedroom. I opened the door. Her suitcase was spread on the bed and she had a mound of underpants in her hands.

"Adam, can you just leave me alone? You weren't even supposed to be here." She dropped the underpants in her suitcase and opened another drawer.

"I brought you your pot. And you don't even have to write me a note."

She grabbed it without looking at me. "Thank you."

I stood in the doorway, arms crossed, leaning on the jamb. She wasn't particularly graceful when she moved. She stooped and swung, throwing herself into her task as if the only point was to complete it without looking at me.

"How was work for you today?" I asked.

"Fine."

"Really?"

"Yes."

"Do you want to know how it was for me?"

"No." She slapped the suitcase shut. It was so full it bounced open again.

I got out of the doorway and went to the bed. "It was awkward." I closed the case and held it down.

She zipped it shut, poking pieces of fabric into the opening as she went. Still not looking at me.

I continued. "You know we're in for a long fight over the company."

She paused, stuffed in another sliver of cotton, zipped two inches, stopped, zipped... "It's a family business. Why do you even want it?"

"Because I own fifty-one percent of it and put five years of my life into it. And I'm not family. I'm thinking of liquidating. Best for everyone. That building is—"

"I'll buy you out."

"With what? Half a condo and a Jaguar?"

In one motion, she picked up the blue stock pot and threw it at my head. The cover slid off. I ducked before the bottom smashed my head open. It flew past and made a hole in the plaster wall, landing on the floor with a hard clunk.

"You're a motherfucker," she seethed, pointing at me. This wasn't how I'd intended the conversation to go. Not at all. "You have no business fighting over that company. It has my name on it. My father and mother's name. You don't even exist."

"You'd love that. You'd love for me to just disappear. I'm sorry, Diana. It's not my job to make your life easy."

"I know." She yanked the suitcase off the bed and it landed heavily against her calf. "It's your job to withhold for twenty-eight days."

"You *are* jealous."

"Grow up." She started out, right toward me, both hands on the suitcase, using her leg to distribute some of the weight.

I took the handle.

"I have it," she growled.

"Let me help you."

"Get off me." She looked ready to out rip my throat.

"You still have to pack the duffel."

"I just want to go. Can I go, please?"

"Yes. You can go." But I didn't move. I'd just confirmed she wasn't trapped. I put my hand over hers and took most of the weight of the suitcase. "Now let go of the handle."

She dropped it completely and gravity straightened my arm.

"You have the heaviest underwear in the city."

She smiled to herself. "Go to hell."

"I'm sure I will."

She crossed her arms. "You're not moving out of the way."

"I have something to say."

"If you say it, can I go? Not theoretically, but really?"

I switched arms. I wanted my right hand to cup her face from a foot away, to gesture the shape of my words. "You're not the jealous type. I get that. But this needs saying once and once only. For clarity. I don't want Serena. I don't want anyone but you. I've never loved another woman. I know you think I'm a different person than you thought you knew. Maybe you think there's the husband me and the stranger me. But neither guy ever loved her. I love you. Every version of me loves you. Today. Now. Always."

She fell back and sat on the bed, hands dangling between her knees. "I don't know what to say."

"Say you loved me once."

"I did. Adam, I went into this marriage with my whole heart. It's just… what do you want?"

To not want you.

"Besides you?"

"Yes. What do you want?" She asked it less defensively, giving me the perfect opportunity to tell her exactly what I'd been thinking.

Nudged to the edge of a tall building with a net I couldn't see past the clouds below, I asked one more time. "What I want? Now? With you on the way out the door?"

"Yes."

"Thirty days," I said, jumping off the side of the tallest building in the city. No turning back now. I leaned into it. "I want thirty days. You and me. Far away. Not a vacation, just thirty days where I show you who I was before I started lying."

The fall was endless. The cloudline below pulled away and closer at the same time, like the horror-movie door at the end of a long hallway.

Chapter 32

PRESENT TENSE

Where is love?

In my wife's Unicorn Journals, the query had been embedded deep in questions of how and why. The *where* was most interesting. Nicolla Masta started it as a dissemination on the parts of the body that experienced love. The heart—the historical center, and the genitalia—the evolutionary center.

Zack Abramson killed it. The piece went nowhere. It was DOA. And we weren't sending her all over the world to find where love was. Waste of money and time. It was everywhere and nowhere. We moved on to the underworld lives of garbage men in Naples. Not a bestseller, but not bad.

Of course, I'd been wrong. Love wasn't everywhere and nowhere. It just shifted around. Expanded, contracted, and moved like a nomad.

The morning after my wife refused to go to Montauk, love moved out of our loft, to the offices of McNeill-Barnes. Love was still as awkward as a thirteen-year-old boy with his first public erection. Love didn't fit in the space. Love was uncomfortable. Love wanted out but couldn't find the fucking door.

I could have worked at the R+D office, but I couldn't let her off the hook, and I couldn't make the case for keeping my piece of the company if I stopped showing up.

And I knew she'd say yes to going to Montauk if I played my cards right. It was a question of when.

When is love?

Should have attacked that question.

"Do you still need the Montauk place?" Charlie asked at lunch soon after.

"Probably not." I tapped the white tablecloth.

"How's it going with her?"

I shook my head. It was bad. We spoke at work, about work. She'd had divorce papers served and hadn't looked at me for the rest of the day, out of shame and guilt. But she was being strong. I respected that.

I'd gotten myself a lawyer and made it abundantly clear, through him, that I was not going to sign over the company even if she could come up with the value for a buyout. I moved back to my Murray Hill apartment but didn't tell her. Love wasn't in our loft anymore, and its absence made the space seem too big.

"Her father called me. You know what he said? He said, 'Don't give up.' And the more I think about it, it's because he wants me running that business. That whole family runs on that publishing house. Their identity's strung up on it."

"You ever going to let it go?" He speared a piece of meat with his knife and ate off the blade. "Start living? Come by the Cellar for more than a drink?"

When I stopped loving her, I'd let it go.

Or vice versa.

I felt an answer in the intersection of the business and my lies, not in the switch between them, but in the fulcrum where all things pivoted. Our love was there. She loved that publishing house, and I loved her.

Chapter 33

PRESENT TENSE

"What's this?"

Diana stood over my desk with a document typed onto my lawyer's letterhead. I glanced at it, then back at the inventory reports.

"A notice."

"You can't do this."

"Yeah, I can."

"We walk out with what we came in with. I came in with this company. We can fight over shares, but it's mine."

I put my pen down and pushed away from the desk. "I came in with a majority interest, which is tantamount to ownership in the great state of New York. See, definitions get muddled. Let's just let the lawyers figure it out." I stood and swung my jacket over my shoulders. "I have a meeting uptown. Do you have the October release meeting under control?"

"Yes."

"Great. Thanks."

I was almost out of the room, hand on the doorknob.

"Adam!"

"What?"

"Why?"

"Because I can."

It wasn't an answer she would understand. Her ambition was always tied to the strings of her heart. She didn't understand the hunger to just *have*.

I did. My attempt to force her into a buyout wasn't about mindless acquisition, but I understood the psychology of it. It had been my mindset until she came along.

"What do you want? Is it money?"

"I told you." I opened the door. "You. Thirty days doing what I tell you."

"That won't change anything."

"Yes, it will. I'll sign it all over to you for nothing. You'll win."

I didn't wait for her to ask for a definition of winning. She wasn't in this to win. She was divorcing me to get out in one piece.

That was my goal too.

Get out in one piece.

Chapter 34

PAST TENSE

"Please."

Serena was the first in her family to go to college. She was synthesized in mediocre education and middle-class values, but she overcame both. When she'd submitted to me, she was released from her responsibility to her education and her family. I was her vacation.

She was intelligent and learned the rules of sophistication quickly. Outside scene, she had a sharp wit that wasn't cruel or cutting. She could choose her future, though in the middle of our stay in the Montauk house, she only had the next hour or so on her mind.

"I have to get back to the city, pet. I'll see you tonight."

She wore only her white gauze gown and her collar. I'd left a polo shirt out for her, but she'd refused it. She was draped over my leg.

"Please." Her brown eyes were as big as saucers, and her light brown lashes curved up at the ends. Her lips parted. When she opened her mouth so I could come in it, I made sure to get some on her bee-stung lower lip.

I didn't love her. I'd never been in love, so I didn't know what it felt like. I didn't feel anything for Serena I didn't feel for any other sub.

But two things were different with Serena.

One, I didn't take her virginity after the first week, or the second.

Two, it became quickly apparent that I'd somehow let her develop feelings for me. She didn't say as much, but I knew women, and I'd inadvertently gotten to her.

"I'll take you when it suits me. Not you." I stroked her cheek.

She turned her head and dragged her lips along my palm. She mouthed *please please please* against my hand. I could see my watch near her lips. We did have time.

"If you ask again," I said, and relief poured over her face before I even finished the sentence, "I'm going to violate you in ways you may not like."

I said it knowing she'd like it. The idea that I could and would do things outside her limits was exciting.

"Please take me."

I sighed as if annoyed and pushed her off me. "Go outside. Get a stick at least a foot long and thinner than your thumb. Crawl back here with it in your teeth. Put it at my feet, then put your head down and your ass up."

She ran out, naked at the end of September. The front yard was covered in sticks that would do, but if I'd asked her walk for it, she'd happily die of exposure.

I didn't love her. Couldn't. I'd break her a dozen times before I even took her virginity, and every time I did, I'd feel satisfaction, peace, compassion, and power. But I'd never love her.

I'd never made a choice not to love. I tried, but I felt nothing. I was frustrated with myself, but I was coming to the conclusion that it wasn't the women. It was me.

She came in, closed the door, and got on her knees with the stick in her teeth. She did exactly as she was told and it pleased me. And her.

But I didn't love her. The perfect sub isn't always the perfect match. It was possible no sub was a match.

Chapter 35

PRESENT TENSE

The hardest thing I ever did was stop.

I stopped telling Diana what was on my mind. I stopped trying to get in her way. I stopped chasing her around. Once the lawyer's letter came to her, describing my intention to fight her for the company, I behaved like a calm professional and so did she.

That lasted two whole days. She texted me close to midnight.

—We need to talk about this
ownership thing—

A dozen jokes about possession crossed my mind. I tossed them. I couldn't pretend I didn't know what she was talking about.

—That's fine. My lawyer will relay the
message or we can set up a meeting—

—I don't want to talk to lawyers—

—I want to talk to YOU—

I didn't answer. I wanted to talk to her too. I wanted to touch her and whisper to her, but I couldn't.

She found me at the gym the next morning. I was on the treadmill, and she looked as if she'd walked a few thousand miles herself.

I didn't stop the belt. I hit the button to make it faster.

"Are you all right?" I asked, jogging six miles an hour straight into nowhere.

"You're not playing fair."

"How's that?"

"You're being emotionally manipulative and spiteful and it's not okay."

My legs burned, but I didn't stop.

"Did you hear me?" she shouted.

"I heard you."

"You can't demand a price for your shares and offer me less for mine."

She was loud. People were looking. Fuck them.

"Mine are worth more," I said.

"Can you stop that thing?"

"Why?"

She reached onto my panel and hit the emergency stop button. I nearly fell over.

"Because I want to talk," she sniped. "We were talking before, then this started." She waved a piece of paper.

My lowball offer for her shares had been meant to insult her. I'd obviously succeeded.

"It's for the best." I snapped my towel off the machine. "The only thing talking was doing was getting you to feel good about leaving."

"Can you explain this?" She snapped the paper in front of me, jogging to keep up. "How are your shares worth more?"

"They come with me attached. I made that business work."

"*We* made it work."

I put my hand on the door to the locker room. "Is irony completely lost on you?"

She gritted her teeth. Man, she was so mad, she could have

peeled the paint off the walls. I went into the locker room and wasn't surprised when she followed.

"We were equals. Which means equal share value."

I slapped open my locker. "I'll lower the price."

"Really?"

I peeled off my shirt. Two guys in towels glanced at the woman in the room, but she was Diana and she didn't care.

"Sure."

"Don't say thirty days."

"Thirty days."

"God damn you."

"A halt to new business development for thirty days while we sort this out." I kicked my shoes off and hooked my thumbs in my waistband. "Access to an operating account. Maintenance of the status quo, current production schedule maintained, and limited power of attorney to a third party."

"We can't even do that."

"Maybe." I stepped out of my sweat pants and stood naked in front of her. "My lawyer says between the common assets and the company assets, it'll take at least two years to litigate, so the thirty days might have to be extended." I wrapped a towel around my waist and grabbed my soap. "I'm a long distance runner."

The showers were down a short hall and through a room of bathroom stalls and urinals. She followed me the entire length.

"Is this spite? This is spite. I know it is."

"Call it what you want."

A guy standing at a urinal saw Diana and turned so she couldn't see him piss. "Hey! She don't belong in here."

"She doesn't." I stopped at the entrance to the showers. "Diana, honey, you should go."

"I'm saying this straight," she growled. "My father isn't going to be around much longer. McNeill-Barnes is a family business. It's *his* family business. If you take it from us, it'll kill him."

"Talk about emotionally manipulative."

"No joke," said the guy at the urinal.

The showers were separate rooms all in a row, marked with green or red flags to indicate whether or not they were occupied. I found a green flag and opened the door.

Diana stopped behind me. "He can't die without this company in his daughter's hands."

"Is that what this is about? Your father?"

"Yes."

"Wrong. This is about business. This is not about family. This is not about your mother's death wish. This is about you and me and business."

I tried to close the door, but she stopped it.

"The thirty days you want? That's business? Because it sounds personal."

"You caught me in a contradiction. Oops, okay? Close the door."

"When did you become such a monster?"

There comes a point when you win, and you can either soothe the loser into thinking there was something in it for them or you can kick them while they're down to make sure they know what just happened.

I pulled my towel off and hung it, exposing my cock again. "Wake up, little huntress. I was the one who kicked out leaseholders on a loophole when your 'family business' needed more room. I was the one who called writers to break contracts. I was the one who did the company dirty work for years. Now you're the dirty work. Deal with it."

I closed the door and turned the lock quickly. I was shaking so hard I could barely work the shower knob. I turned it on high and hot.

She pounded the door once, then nothing.

I couldn't gulp air quickly enough. I let the water scald me, letting the pain on the surface match the pain inside me. I never wanted to hurt her, but I had. I never wanted her to feel small or powerless. I loved her. I loved her with everything I had. I'd done the dirty work to protect her from anger and cruelty, and now I had become the very thing I'd protected her from.

I was well past the point of no return.

Chapter 36

PRESENT TENSE

Diana didn't show up to the office the next day. I checked her phone's location, but she'd shut off the locator service. It didn't matter. The end of the month was approaching.

Do or die.

Sometimes *do* meant wait, and I considered that. But I had a sliver of time between her leaving Riverside Drive and her taking down her One Direction posters.

She'd been right. I was being manipulative. I'd learned how to toy with people as a Dominant, but I used my skills during play and not outside it. I knew better. There was no excuse for me to slap and tickle my wife's emotions, except my hunger to make her feel something. I knew I was wrong, but I did it anyway.

—The loft—

—What about it?—

—I moved. You should live in it—

I slid my phone onto the desk. It was just about dinnertime. I had my coat and scarf on before she answered.

—Will you be out by Thursday?—

—Already out—

—Do you want it? I'll sign
my half over to you—

Another long pause. I was halfway down the block before my phone buzzed again.

—For what?—

I smiled at the screen. She was a learning machine and a worthy adversary. Moments like that, I didn't think about not loving her. I couldn't imagine it.

—One hour doing what I tell you—

The phone rang as I got to the front of our building. It was her.

"I'm not a hooker," she said.

"It's a two-million-dollar loft in SoHo. No hooker is that expensive."

"No sex. And don't even try."

"Define sex." I was curious. How did she define it? What exactly were her lines?

"It's not obvious?"

"No."

"We've been married four years."

That was the problem, wasn't it? We'd shared a bed and our bodies for that long and I didn't know what she meant by "no sex."

"I'm not trying to turn you on. I'm trying to talk to you," I said, pacing from the front of the building to the edge of the curb, confusing the hell out of the doorman. "Define what you mean by sex. Is it talking about sex? Describing how much I want you? Is that sex? Is it me touching you? You touching you? Is it kissing? If I can smell your cunt's arousal, is that sex? If I taste you? Or if I can sense you spreading your legs a little wider under the table? What's that? And if it makes me hard, is that sex? Define it. Draw your lines around it and I won't cross."

A puddle of melted snow had formed at the curb. It reached the height of the sidewalk and no higher. The temperature had fallen with the sun, and the puddle had frozen at the top. I poked it with my foot while I waited for her to answer. My toe made a divot in the crust of ice but didn't break through.

"I don't know," she said.

"Then how am I supposed to know?"

"I feel like if I say no to something, I'm saying yes to everything else. And I just…" She took a deep breath. "I just want to move back into my own place."

I was such an asshole. Constructing ways to eroticize our meeting so I could trade bites of submission for an asset I didn't really want. I was treating her like a whore. She deserved better. She deserved a man who would split everything down the middle and disappear. I wasn't that man. I was much worse. I was a monster. I demanded sacrifice. Recompense. I demanded to be made whole for all the love I'd spent on her. I actually felt compassion for the woman who had shattered my heart.

"Let me define it then," I said.

"Okay."

"I won't touch you unless you ask."

"I won't ask."

"And if I say anything that crosses a line, you can tell me. Just say the word."

"What word? I can't get into spiraling discussions about what's appropriate."

"You pick the word. Make it something that would never come up in conversation."

Her breath changed. I heard a rustle. She was either changing clothes or putting clothes on. Naturally, I got hard.

"I don't know," she said, the phone leaving her ear and coming back. Must be her putting a shirt on.

Or getting one off.

"Just pick a word."

I wondered if she was wearing a bra. Her nipples were thick

and hard when she was cold or turned on, and I hadn't given them a good bite in too long. I hadn't thought about them over the phone in months. Years maybe. My sexuality must have been more closeted than I thought. All I could imagine was her naked on the other side of the line.

"Pinochle," she said.

"What?" I'd lost my train of thought.

"If you cross a line, I'll say 'pinochle.'"

"Come over. I'll have dinner ready."

"God, this is so crazy."

"It is," I said before we hung up.

And it was. She'd chosen a safe word.

Chapter 37

PRESENT TENSE

I rolled my sleeves up, took off my tie, and got to work. I whipped up chicken and a wine sauce with the stuff in the freezer. I wasn't much of a cook, but I managed some green beans and warmed bread. My grandmother had always told me enough butter and salt made stones taste good.

She came in while I was setting my side of the table. Tiny snowflakes stuck to her hair. She'd done nothing to prepare. Her hair was a mess. She wore no makeup. Old jeans. Her favorite button-down shirt. A few bracelets she never took off anyway.

Just the way I liked her. Effortless.

"If I knew what you wanted out of me, this would be easier." She unraveled her scarf. It was blue with embroidered birds.

"I told you already."

"Thirty days for the company and an hour for the condo?"

"Something like that. Look, I'm not going to try to fuck you."

"So what are you going to try to do?" She stuffed the bird scarf in a pocket and pushed her coat buttons through the holes. I got behind her to take it. "Besides be a jerk, which you were totally being at the gym."

"Show you that you might enjoy a month learning about the guy you married. The one I lied about." I hung her coat. "I want to undo all that."

"I'm not going to fall in love with you again."

Would that ever stop hurting?

"I know. But you're curious."

"I am. I read The Book That Shall Not Be Named, of course. And after we were in the Cellar, I did an internet search," she said.

"How was that?"

"Hot sometimes. Scary sometimes."

"You can satisfy your curiosity with me. For an hour."

I pulled out her chair. She didn't go toward it.

I waited.

"I have this choice," she said, looking at the chair. "You have things I want, and you'll give them to me if I do what you want. If I don't, you'll make my life a living hell trying to get those things." She took her eyes off the chair and laid them on me. "When I put it that way, do you understand why it's hard for me to say yes to any of it?"

"I do. But you have more to gain than lose. And I can admit something I couldn't admit before. There's a part of you that might have enjoyed this part of me if I'd been a man and let you in. If I thought for a minute there wasn't a good chance you'd like it, we wouldn't be having this conversation."

"I'm not leaving you over sex."

No, it wouldn't stop hurting. Even when she used different words entirely to say she didn't love me, she still ran me through and twisted the blade. And I realized that it was getting easier for her to say it. She'd become immune to the venom of her detachment, and I kept on asking for the sting.

"The reason you're breaking up this marriage is irrelevant," I lied. "I'm not after 'why,' I'm after 'how.' And the 'how' I'm after is 'not that easily.' You don't have to like it. I don't believe in heaven. I don't believe there's a reward for leaving nicely or being the bigger person. I'm not ready to let you leave with everything. Not easily. Not without payment."

I indicated the seat again, but she didn't sit.

"Would you just sign everything over if you didn't think I was curious?"

The question was one of two things. Either she wanted to gauge whether or not pretending to not enjoy it would make the path easier, or whether or not her curiosity had gotten her and McNeill-Barnes into this situation.

"No. That's not how I do business." I pivoted the conversation back to the matter at hand. "You need to obey me, but I won't ask for anything I don't think you're ready for."

"How do I know you know what I'm ready for?"

"You have to trust me."

She ran her finger over the sharp edge of her front pants pocket. "An hour."

"An hour. And you say pinochle whenever you want."

She nodded. Blinked.

"Is that a yes?" I asked.

Her eyes went to me. Through me. She could hurt me again and again if I let her, because she went a few degrees warmer, seeping tiny droplets of tenderness through the seams in her disdain.

"Yes," she said.

She sat, and I pushed in her chair.

The clock started ticking.

"What did you make?" she asked when I took the cover off the dish.

"Chicken. I think."

"Was it in the container with the blue cover?"

"Yes."

"It's duck." She put her hands on the table. "I need a plate."

She started to get up, but I put my hand on her shoulder and gently pushed her back to sitting. "No, you don't. Just relax."

I sat down and put my napkin in my lap and duck on my plate. I cut it.

"You got an eyeful the other night at the Cellar," I said.

"Yeah."

I speared a piece of meat. "But what you didn't see is what a Dominant really does." I held the fork out to her. She reached for it. "Sit on your hands."

Her hand froze midway. "Literally?"

"When I talk to you like this, you can assume it's literal."

She lowered her hand, shifted her body, and slid her hands under her. I could see her wheels turning. My wife didn't take orders.

"Open your mouth."

She was so scared of herself and me. When she parted her lips, the rest of her face registered nothing but trepidation.

"When you do what I ask you to do, it gratifies me. I have the sense that everything is in its right place. I breathe easier. I think more clearly."

I held out another piece of meat. She opened her mouth.

"Don't open until I tell you."

"Okay. Sorry."

She wasn't supposed to speak, but I couldn't shush her. Too many rules too soon would turn her off. This hour wasn't about my enjoyment. I had to remember that and not get ahead of myself.

"It's all right. Open."

She did, and I fed her.

"Do I have to ask to chew?"

This was why Charlie trained them and I wore them in.

"You're not there yet. You can chew when you like," I said.

"Are you going to eat?"

"I might eat before you, after you, with you."

She took another bite.

"It depends on the guy?" she asked while chewing, and my mood darkened.

Other men. If she discovered she liked this, would she seek it out with other men?

Shake it off.

I took a bite of duck. It wasn't half bad. "I'm going to feed you. You're going to eat, and you're going to listen."

She nodded. She was still on her hands. They were going to fall asleep.

"Put your hands on the table."

She did it, palms down. The ring was gone again. I fed her a forkful of vegetables.

"Since we only have an hour and I don't want you to give me something you're not ready to give, I'm going to tell you what I'm not going to do to you and what I'm not going to ask you to do."

Before she could speak, I fed her a forkful of duck.

"I'm not going to ask you to stand in front of the window and get undressed. Slowly and purposefully, down to the skin. Your nipples would be hard, and your cheeks flushed, but I won't ask you to stand still in front of me, feeling how naked and vulnerable you are while I sit here in my clothes, just staring at how gorgeous you are. I won't ask you to turn around, bend at the waist, and hold your ass and thighs open for me. I'd probably have to tell you to spread your feet apart. This is so I can inspect you. I'd run my fingers over your cunt to make sure you're wet, but I won't tonight. And I won't get my fingers wet so I can slide them in your ass."

She let out a short, hard exhale. I wiped the corners of her mouth with the cloth napkin and tipped the water glass to her lips. She drank.

"The downside is you won't come. Because if you did what I just told you to do, my fingers would graze your clit over and over." I took the glass away. "You can spread your knees if you want."

The tablecloth moved enough to let me know she did.

I stood and got behind her. "I'd tell you to get on your knees and open your mouth. And then, my wife, I'd teach you how to let me fuck your face. Not give me a blow job, but to let me take one from you. With your hands behind your back, you press the back of your tongue down and I fuck your throat. But not tonight. Tonight all I want is your obedience. I want you to let me take care of you the way I'm supposed to."

She was practically panting. I had her.

I took a handful of her hair and pulled her head back hard enough to hurt. Her lips and eyes were open, and I kissed her. I probed her mouth with my tongue, let her groan fill my mouth. She tasted exactly as she always had. Like my wife. My partner. My very heart.

I reached around with my other hand and pulled her shirt open, popping buttons, yanking her bra up over her tits. She let out an *ah* into my mouth, and when I squeezed her nipple harder than I ever had, it turned into a long *aaaahhhh…*

I spoke so close our lips touched. "Define sex."

"Inside me. You inside me."

"I'm not going to fuck you," I said, letting her nipple go and lightly brushing the newly sensitive skin with my fingertips.

"This won't make me love you." The barb came through her teeth.

"I don't want you to love me." I squeezed her other nipple when I lied. I'd never been so cruel to them.

"Oh. God."

"Hush." I broke saying it, because her awakening at this touch was life itself. "Stand up."

I helped her to her feet. Her shirt was askew and her bra squeezed her tits down.

"You all right?"

"Yes." She started to right her shirt, but I held her arms still.

"No. Just like this. Take your pants down halfway to your knees."

She swallowed hard. I'd hit an uncomfortable spot. I could let it go right now. Forget the trade. Tell her I'd give her the condo even if she walked out.

"Go on," I said. "Or say pinochle. Then we can battle it out in court."

I licked one of my thumbs and put the other one in her mouth. She sucked it without being asked. My God. All these years. A long string of a thousand missed opportunities.

"Your nipples are so hard." I ran my wet thumbs over them and pinched. Her eyelids fluttered closed. "I've never seen you like this. You want to finish." It was risky to give up, but I was sure she wanted to come as much as I wanted to make her come. "Trust me with this."

Trust that I'm not holding your financial situation over your head in exchange for sex.

Hey, we all use what we got.

"No sex," I said. "My cock won't enter you. You're going to come. After you come, I sign the deed over."

She unbuttoned her fly.

Diana Barnes was meeting me halfway. She was taking everything I'd hid from her and opening herself to it. She pushed her pants down.

I twisted the chair around and sat on it. She couldn't walk well with her pants around her thighs, which was the point, so I guided her to my side. Her expression was open and docile. Waiting to be told what to do next.

"Bend at the waist and relax, darling."

I guided her over my knee, spreading my legs so her head had somewhere to rest. Her bottom was pale and round, soft and ready. I tucked both of her arms at her lower back and ringed the wrists with my fingers so she couldn't move. I slid my other hand along her wet cleft. I put two fingers in her, finding the bundle of nerves inside her wall.

She groaned.

My cock raged against her belly. I wanted to come on her. Mark her back and her pink ass.

I pulled out my fingers, circled her clit, then slapped each ass cheek with a *crack crack*. She squeaked. Groaned. The backs of her thighs went taut.

I put my fingers back in her. She was rigid and tight and—

"Adam!"

Mid-slap when she said my name, my hand landed with a *thwack*.

"Stop!"

I froze.

"Pinochle! Let me go."

I released her wrists. She stood, but her pants restricted her, and when I tried to help her, she pulled away quickly, lost her balance, and fell. She tried to catch herself on a chair, but that only sent it down with her.

Up on the heels of her hands, socked feet, bra half up and off, she was comedic as hell. But I didn't laugh. Sex was funny, and BDSM required an appropriate sense of humor. This, however, was not funny to her. So I swallowed a laugh and scrambled to help her up.

"No!" She pushed me away.

"You can't be surprised at a spanking."

She arched her back and got her pants up. Damn. Fuck, shit, and damn.

"I'm not. But…" Still on the floor, she put her bra back down.

"But?"

Frustration crept into my voice. I'd been snapped backward from the most pleasant free fall. I had to remind myself I was the Dominant here. I was supposed to care for her emotions as well as her body.

She stood and fastened her fly. Her shirt buttons were busted. She crossed the front panels of her shirt across her beautiful body.

I sighed into a deep well of disappointment.

"I'm going." She stepped backward, reaching behind her for her coat. "Don't follow me."

"Diana, I'm sorry."

"Don't be sorry. Just… I'll call you. About this. I'm going to call you about this. Soon."

She threw her coat over her arm and opened the door exactly as much as she needed to get out, then she closed it behind her hard enough to rattle the doorbell. Her blue scarf with the embroidered birds drooped out of the coat pocket and got caught in the door. I walked toward it.

By the time I got there, I heard a click of the key in the lock. I opened the door, bent down for the scarf. Diana stood at the door, waiting. I folded the scarf in two, put it around her neck, and looped it.

"Thank you," she said.

"I like taking care of you."

She walked down the hall without another word.

Chapter 38

PAST PERFECT

Night.

    Crickets.

    Her face in darkness.

    Pillowcase cool on my cheek.

    The blinds clicking in the breeze.

    A glint on her eye from the moon.

    Our legs twisted together.

    What should we name her?

    You're not even pregnant yet.

    But I will be.

    You're getting ahead of yourself.

    Lenore.

    No.

    It's my grandmother's name.

    Did your great-grandmother read a lot of Poe?

    Probably.

    You want a bunch of ravens circling the building?

    A pinch on my arm.

    On top of her.

Her mouth yields in the dark.
The crickets hear her groan.
I suggest a name.
I like Olive.
It's a color.
And a boy can be Oliver.
Kisses wet. Skin sore but ready.
My body trapping hers.
She whispers.
More please.

Chapter 39

PRESENT TENSE

I pressed my ear to the door. The elevator came. I imagined Diana going down it with her only-slightly-spanked ass and her damaged pride.

That was over. Nice try.

I packed what I could so I could complete my move to Murray Hill. The rest of my clothes. The toiletries I didn't use every day. Our wedding album. I flipped through it. We hadn't had a wedding reception. We'd had a party months after. Fuck that party. Fuck the Lafayette Hotel. Fuck the first dance and the last. Fuck her mother's white dress. Fuck the overcooked fish and her cousins from Minnesota who didn't like me.

Fuck all of them. Fuck me. Fuck my stupid decision to try to show her who I was. Fuck the throb in my balls and her safe word. Fuck my plan to fall out of love with her. It couldn't work without her. I was just going to love her forever. She'd always be the woman with her wedding gown dragging along Fifth Avenue.

I was doomed.

The condo was hers. She'd tried. I'd tried. I failed. I'd sign the deed over in the morning and be done.

I left the duck and plates for the housekeeper. I started a note about the change in residents. I wrote down the groceries Diana liked to have, the way she liked more pillows on the bed, a note to leave the drapes closed and blinds open when she left.

My phone buzzed. I thought it was the west coast printer, but it was Diana.

—I'm not going to call you—

—I can't say it—

—Just please swear you won't show this to anyone. Even if you marry some nice submissive girl one day and want a laugh about your ex-wife, please don't show this text—

—You don't have to tell me anything. I get it—

—No you don't—

—And I'm not getting remarried—

—Yes you are. You deserve someone who loves you—

—Is that what you wanted to tell me?—

—No—

—Don't answer until I say I'm finished—

—Ok—

—That's answering—

(...)

(...)

The phone rang as I watched the streaming dots indicate she was typing. Her name sprang onto the screen.

"What's going on?" I asked, then I heard street sounds on the other side. "You're not driving, are you?"

"I'm still parked. I just can't type it either. And I can't look at you."

"I decided something," I said, pushing the housekeeper note away. "I'm not sorry. I treated you pretty gently. I checked on you. I'm still your husband—it's not like I'm some stranger. I don't feel a bit of guilt, so if you're about to lay it on, forget it."

"Yeah."

That was all. Then it was street sounds and the car stereo. A podcast. She loved podcasts. Fuck podcasts.

"You can move in tomorrow," I said. "*Nuestra casa* is now *su casa*."

After a deep breath, she said, "Everything about this is bad. You and I are crossing lines. It took a lot of willpower to leave you, and here we are, having sex. Don't correct me. It's sex. And I'm all opened up. I'm allowing things… I run a multimillion dollar company. I brought it back from the brink of a hostile liquidation."

"By marrying the liquidator." That was a lie and this was bullshit. I grabbed my coat and keys and went out.

"Let me finish. I don't need to be spanked like a child. I don't need to take orders from you or anyone. I am your equal. I know all these things are true, and I believed you did too."

She took a long silence. The radio went dead. She must have shut it off. I nodded to the doorman and went into the cold crowded street.

"Can I answer that?"

I had no idea where she was parked, but she wouldn't get a signal from our underground space. There were so few legal spaces I'd probably find her in two minutes. I had the Jaguar's spare key. I clicked the unlock button. The lights would flash when I was in range. She wasn't on the block. I walked east.

"No, you cannot. Because this isn't about you or what you believe or think. I have to put that out of my mind. I had to remind myself that I know all that stuff is true. And so saying that, I have to ask myself what the fuck happened up there. I was all up in my head. I was thinking about how stupid this was and how you're just crazy and I needed to get back and put my stuff in the car and call the west coast printers before they leave for the day." She cleared her throat.

I clicked the car key. No car.

"Then you kissed me. You stupid ass, you always knew how to kiss. And I don't know what happened. I let it all go. I let you own me. No one owns me, Adam. No one."

I rubbed my eyes. For the first time, I thought this was all too complicated. I was dealing with the love of my life leaving me with a note on the counter, but I wasn't. Getting her to submit to me was a distraction from what I should have been doing. Getting the fuck over her.

"I don't know what you want."

"I want my family's company. All the copyrights. All the shares. Complete control. I want you and R+D out without a fight."

"On a strictly business level, that would never be on the table."

"And all debts and loans forgiven. All holdings and assets go back to me. Including the building on Broome."

"You know what you're asking? I put R+D into debt to cover McNeill-Barnes."

"Thirty days. That's the price."

I knew it would be. I knew she'd shoot for the stars. What if I gave it all to her and walked away? It would bankrupt me. I'd survive, but it was bad business. I didn't work that way. I played to win.

If I was going to put the last five years in the negative column and build my holdings back up, I wasn't doing it with a broken heart.

"Thirty days," she repeated, "and then it's over. No sex ever again."

I was about to interject that I'd be happy to never touch her again, but she didn't stop or slow down. The sound of her voice changed. She became more present. More real.

"It's over. No arguing. No more deals. No nickel-and-diming. I'm probably never going to want to see you again."

I spun when I heard her. She was right behind me, coming north on Crosby.

We hung up our phones. The wind bit her cheeks and her breath came in a pouf of steam. Her chin was up a notch and she stood like anything but a submissive.

"This has to be a choice," I said, aware of my contradictions even as I used them to get what I wanted. "I'll give you the contract. It's not legally binding, but it lays out our roles very clearly, and what's expected of you. It's a hard document to read. So buckle in. You can redline three things. They can be broad, but if they're too broad, I'll reject them."

Her eyebrow arched. "We're going to have a contract negotiation over sex?"

"It's not about sex. I might not touch you the entire time. It's about power and trust. These are the rules. No arguing. You come in as a sub. A good Dom respects limits. If you trust me, you'll do exactly what I tell you from day one to day thirty. You'll walk out with every asset we own together and a little more self-awareness than before."

Because you're submissive, little huntress.

Behind her, a cab skirted traffic, wheel in the curb, breaking ice and splashing the sidewalk with cold, filthy sludge.

I took her elbow and pulled her out of the way. The flying slush missed her, though I got wet below the knees. Even with all that movement, she and I kept our eyes on each other, testing, asking, feeling for questions we didn't dare ask.

"Send the contract," she said.

"I need you to agree in principle."

"I agree in principle. I'm terrified, but I agree in principle."

"I'll leave it on the kitchen table."

She nodded.

"Let me walk you to the car."

She started walking south. I stayed on her right side so I'd get splashed if another cab attacked. I didn't even think about why I was on that side, it was just what I did. We didn't talk. I remembered wondering how we were going to get a stroller down the street on garbage nights, when even the Michelin two-star restaurant on Crosby put bags of trash on the street for pickup. I'd seen couples wrestle with wheels caught in plastic. Some laughed. Some practically had to dump the kid to get the stroller out. We decided on the little pouches that let the baby rest on her mother's chest. A baby with a spine to hold her up. Not like our baby.

The Jag *blooped* across the cobblestone street.

"Thank you," she said. "For walking me."

I started across the street. "Not done. I'm a finisher. Come on."

She followed, and I opened the driver's side door.

She put her foot on the ledge and stopped before lowering herself in. "I spent the walk asking myself if I trust you."

"Did you answer?"

"I did. I have a lot of mixed feelings about you and about this deal. I think it's weird, but you must need it, and getting out of this marriage without years of litigation is valuable."

"Good."

She got into the car and I closed the door. As I stepped away, she lowered the window.

"I'll make a list of what I expect at the end of the thirty days," she said. "We can make it a rider to your contract."

"A rider to an unenforceable contract isn't enforceable."

"I may not love you, but I trust you."

I got out of the street before I got hit by a car. I was doing it again. Starting over. Reclaiming what I'd been. A pillar of elation built on a foundation of fear. Or the other way around. I couldn't tell them apart anymore because the fear wasn't about something happening, but a fear of who I was.

Chapter 40

PAST TENSE

We—Charlie, Stefan, and I—had decided the main house in Montauk wouldn't have any tools or accouterments on the first floor. We each had a room upstairs we kept the way we wanted and an adjoining room for our subs. Six bedrooms, five baths. Downstairs we had a library, sitting room, an indoor gym, and a room we called the ocean room because it led to the back deck and the short, rocky beach. Kitchen, dining room, office. Everything we needed. Some movable tools in cabinets and hidden hooks, but to the naked eye, the first floor looked as vanilla as anything a real estate broker would show.

We could divide the first floor in a number of configurations by opening or closing pocket doors. In the deep heat of summer, in the years when we all got along, the main house was a hub of kinky parties.

In the off-season, from September to early March, I could work half days in the office and get back to Montauk in under two hours, stay up until two with a sub who begged for a beating, and get to work while she slept it off.

I'd kept that schedule with Serena for two weeks. But on our second Sunday, it changed. We were in the back house, where hooks hung from the ceiling and shackles were bolted to the walls. It was an eight-hundred-square-foot studio space accessed by a stone path behind the main house. The larger room was fit with hooks, crosses, cabinets, whipping benches.

Sometimes I went the entire thirty days without picking up a crop or a lock. Sometimes, if the sub was right and I was on my game, all I needed was time and well-intoned words.

But if I wanted to shackle Serena's wrists to the wall so she was bent over, legs wide, ass up, I had to use the studio.

"She's stunning," Stefan said from behind the one-way mirror.

I was making her wait. She hated waiting, but the anticipation kept her on the knife's edge. "She is."

I picked a soft paddle from the wall. I didn't want to welt her. Then I'd have to wait until she healed to touch her, and taking Serena too far wasn't as much fun as keeping her close to the line. She was too eager to rush over her own boundaries.

"You sharing?" he asked, sitting on a chair facing the mirror/ window, legs stretched out and rubbing his chin. He was six-four. Nordic. Dark blue eyes, large nose he played to his advantage, and a bright smile that belied a devilish and unrelenting sadism.

I was glad she didn't want to be shared. I didn't want him to touch her. I didn't have a reason. I just wanted her to myself for thirty days.

"She redlined it."

He waved his hand. He'd come out for a few days to meet an architect about changing the studio into a separate stand-alone with a kitchen so he could live there and paint in the off months. "You have to push the limits, Adam. They're here to be pushed. You can't let them run the show."

"Thanks for the advice." I ended up with a riding crop. A blunt tool compared to my hands, but a little variety was good for everyone.

"She still a popper?"

"As intact as the day she was born." I went for the door.

"You know what I would have done?"

"You?"

"That first day—"

"You would have stripped her in front of a few of your friends, put a dildo on the floor, and made her sit on it so they could all watch her bleed onto it. Then each of them would have fucked her cunt. You'd take her ass that night during aftercare."

He looked back at me with that big Swedish smile. "Something like that."

"That's not how I do it."

"She would have loved it." He turned back to the mirror. "She'd remember it forever. But she wanted you. Two weeks and still a virgin. Too bad."

I pulled a lever on the side of the window, flipping the shades closed. "Jerk off on your own dime."

I shut the door behind me and went around back. Five steps through fallen leaves to the studio door. Five steps in the cold September air. The sound of the ocean behind me, a broken record of rising and falling breaks and whooshes.

Stefan, Charlie, and I had bought this house together, and we used it cooperatively. We joked and got along. Stefan and I had had some differences we worked out. Mostly. He'd found the property and I got roped in, but I didn't trust him.

If he took a sub's virginity the way he described, or enacted any scene in his repertoire for any reason, he talked with the sub first. If he pushed limits outside the sub's comfort zone, he told her he was pushing limits during the scene. He obeyed the rules.

But still, he'd pissed me off.

"Good evening," I said when I walked into the studio.

"Good evening, Master," Serena replied, hair covering her face.

"How are you doing?" I could see the wet sheen between her legs.

"Fine, Master."

"Do you like waiting?"

"No, Master."

"Wrong." I thwacked her with the crop. "You like whatever pleases me."

"Yes, Master."

There was something rote about her answer. Something a little too rehearsed. That wouldn't do. Maybe Stefan was right. Maybe I'd let her have her virginity for too long. I'd let myself become infatuated with her looks and her purity. It wasn't about her anymore; it had become about me. It was never supposed to be about me.

I tossed the crop aside. I didn't want to be Stefan, which in a way, was also about me. I brutalized her that night while I made plans to shock her the following day.

Chapter 41

PRESENT TENSE

Diana's redlines came back while I waited for Charlie. He owned a small store that took up half a floor of an old garment factory on 38th Street. It had no name. Just a thick wooden door, a male receptionist, and rooms of every kinky accouterment a deviant could imagine. Every piece was hand chosen. Everything was expensive as fuck. And if you had the money, it was all worth it.

Her redlines came in an email.

1) You only hit me with your hands.
2) I will not crawl or call you sir. I will not be humiliated.
3) No gagging with anything. I always need to speak.

Too broad. A clear case of submissive overreach.

One. It wasn't the sub's place to redline such an enormous number of tools. She could say "no paddling" or even "no wood," but asking me to use only my hands was unacceptable.

Two. Humiliation was too subjective, as well as unpredictable. Sticking my fingers in her mouth was part of the deal, but if she was humiliated by it, that was now on me. Crawling and using respectful names for the Dominant were two totally different things, but they both illustrated the truth of submission. Crossing that much off kept me from achieving the dominance I needed to make this worthwhile.

Three. No gagging was acceptable. But making sure she could always speak? What if my dick was down her throat?

I'd negotiated contracts with her before. This list shouldn't have surprised me. Then I realized what was missing.

Anal. Sharing. Videotaping. Fisting. The dozens of pain-delivery systems that were on the list but I didn't use because they bored me. What about actual sex? I wouldn't have been surprised if she'd crossed that off entirely, but she hadn't.

"Hey, mate." Charlie came into the waiting room with two short glasses of scotch.

He sat on the sage-green brocade chair that matched the couch I was on. A long, low slate-topped table stretched the length of the sofa. The two windowless walls were covered with black-and-white art photos of men and women in the throes of bondage and ecstasy.

He handed me one of the glasses of scotch, and we clicked them together. "What brings you?"

I let the searing heat burn my throat as the scotch went down. "I have nothing at the Montauk house, and I'm taking it for a month. I gave Silver the list."

"Good for you. Main house, right? Stefan's in the studio."

He'd succeeded in converting the small house into his personal painting studio and punishment ward with a kitchen and its own power. I was out of the life and Charlie was fine in the main house, so we allowed it.

"Main house is fine. He alone?"

Charlie laughed to himself and moved to the chair next to me, propping his cane against the arm. "He needs them more than they need him."

"Someone should tell him that."

"What would be the point?"

I took a swig of whiskey. "So it's Serena or another one?"

"I think they're trying to rekindle the old fire."

The Silver Domme came in carrying a wooden box. She balanced perfectly on platform heels in her tight black pants.

"Adam!" she said when she saw me. "I didn't even believe it when I saw your name on the list." She put the box on the table, hugged me, and kissed each cheek. We sat, and Silver put her hands on the box. "I wasn't sure if it was you, but I got your favorite things."

Her smile was lascivious yet not flirtatious. She and I played the same field position. It was a smile of understanding.

Charlie leaned back and sipped his drink. "Mind if I stay for this stroll down memory lane?"

"Stay," I said.

Silver opened the box. "Now, we have another few things I gathered in the back room, but I wanted to bring these out first."

She laid out a birch paddle with three holes in it. A braided brown riding crop. A set of adjustable nipple clamps I couldn't imagine using on Diana, yet—

"The paddle comes narrower, and we have one with no holes and SLUT carved backward—"

"No."

"I remembered." She smiled again, taking out a black stick. "Not your thing. We also have rubber crops. This one's single mold so to prevent breakage, and the handle side also leaves a nice mark."

I leaned forward, tapping my fingertips together as she brought out rattan canes and more paddles in different sizes and colors. I said nothing. Silver was unfazed.

But would Diana be fazed? I had to look at these through her eyes. She'd done internet searches and seen plenty, but if I brought these out to use on her, I was sure she'd be frightened. More than anything, I didn't want to scare her.

"Should I bring out the bindings?" Silver asked.

"Please."

She left the tools on the table and went through the door to the back. I knew how to use everything she'd presented. I knew how to welt skin without opening it. I struck hard, with accuracy, safely. I made them beg for more, because I made sure that the more pain they experienced, the more pleasure it was paired with. In the end, it was about pleasure and freedom. But everything on the table was redlined. Was I going to accept her line in the sand? Or was I going to rub it out and draw my own?

"Who are you bringing?" Charlie asked. "If I know her, I can pick for you."

"Diana." I said it so softly I barely heard myself.

When Charlie didn't answer, I looked at him. His eyes were slightly wider and his mouth was just open enough for shock.

"Diana," I said with my full throat. "My wife."

"You've got to be fucking with me. The same woman who left you a note on the counter?"

"She's agreed. Saw the contract."

"Wait, wait, wait. *The* contract. The boilerplate? The one with gangbangs and electroshock?"

"Yes."

He fingered his cane, twisting it half clockwise, then counterclockwise, as if he were drilling a hole in the floor. "Do you have any idea what you're doing?"

"I've done it before, Charlie."

"Oh. Done it before, have you? And how did you get her to agree to do this with a husband she wants to divorce?"

I put my glass on the table. "Can we fill that up?"

He looked at me suspiciously. Tapped his phone. A second later, a man swooped my glass away and replaced it with a new drink. Before he'd even closed the door behind him, I downed it and clicked the glass back on the table.

Silver wasn't coming back. Charlie ran the entire operation from that phone. He could have a dozen dancing girls strut in by tapping it.

I picked up the three-holed paddle. The empty circles cut down air resistance so the paddle moved faster, hit harder, pushed the sub's capacity for pain and her ability to submit to the limit. The first time you paddled them, it hurt. If you gave them emotional comfort and a fifteen-minute orgasm, they brought it to you in their teeth the second time and bent willingly for its hard kiss.

I leaned back, feeling its balance in my palm. This tool of domination. Built to help me release the winding knot of a world I couldn't control. Those slices of time in safe spaces where a woman gave herself to me, and I gave myself to her. I missed the emotional connection. It wasn't love. It wasn't ever love, but it was deep and thick, nearly psychic the way a Dom and a sub could click together.

"I own most of her company," I said. "I rescued it. If she wants it back—"

"No," Charlie interrupted. "Absolutely not."

He snapped me away from the memory of that feeling of control. Brought me back to the world where I had to answer to society for my actions.

"*Absolutely not*, what?"

"She's not in a position to consent, mate."

"Believe me, she's capable of reading and understanding a contract."

He put his elbows on his knees, leaning more right than left. I knew it hurt when he bent like that.

"She doesn't know you. You're going to trap her on the tip of Long Island in storm season, with you and a few dozen paddles while you get back in practice? What are you trying to do? Get revenge?"

"It's not revenge."

"You can really hurt her." Charlie stamped his cane. "It's too much. If she's not trained slowly and fully consenting, you can break her mind. Is that what you want?"

"I'm not going to do anything she can't handle."

"Have you ever spent more than a few hours with a sub who wasn't trained and willing?"

"She's willing."

"She. Is. Not. She can't consent cleanly."

"She has the contract."

"You're holding her life's work hostage."

"Hostage? She's holding *me* hostage. She has my guts in her hands. I don't care about the company, I care about her. She's my life, do you understand? Have you ever loved a woman? Have you ever held her at night so tight because you couldn't sleep thinking something might happen to her? Have you ever built a future around a woman? Ever thought of every tomorrow, every year, every decade with her? Dreamed of your old age holding her hand? I can only function with her in my life. I can only breathe if I know she's there. I gave her my fucking soul and she threw it away. Months ago, maybe years ago. She made a decision to throw me away. She's prepared for this divorce, and I'm swinging in the wind. Raw. With nothing. No defenses. Now what am I supposed to do?" I stood and threw my coat over my shoulders. "This is not about money. It's not about some publishing company. Not for me. If I don't do this, I have no chance of recovery. I'm as good as dead."

He didn't stand, but looked up at me from below, still twisting his cane. "No, you're not. Don't do this. You'll get over it. You will."

"Yes, I will. I'll be in Montauk starting Saturday." I went for the door and was almost out before Charlie spoke up.

"You might want to hold off until Serena's gone," Charlie said. "Avoid unnecessary emotional complications."

"I don't have any complications about Serena."

"But Diana might. Seeing your last sub on the property? She's going to be vulnerable as it is."

He was right, but his solution was shit. Everything would change in a week, or days. I had to take Diana now. This moment.

"Thank Silver for me. I'll send a list of what I want delivered."

Before he could answer, I left, striding past the receptionist, into the hall where, thank God, an elevator waited.

What I was doing was wrong. I was treating the love of my life like a device. I was using her against her. I was holding her hostage until she freed my heart.

I knew it. Charlie knew it. Maybe Diana knew it.

The hope that she'd accept my offer and the planning that went into it kept me from breaking down. I feared that breakdown more than I feared a life alone. The inner chaos, the loss of any sense of self outside pain, I wouldn't stand it. I couldn't see through it. Becoming fully saturated in the pain that roiled inside me had to be avoided at all costs. The abyss was too deep. I needed to jump over it.

It was raining ice when I got to the street. I put my back against the building and tapped the cold glass of my phone.

—I accept your redlines—

She came back right away.

—I want one more—

Of course she did.

—You only get three—

—No scat or whatever you call it.
I don't want any poop or pee—

I smiled. God, I loved her. But she was a pain in the ass.

—Not my thing—

—You have no idea what
a relief that is—

—Let's meet with Lloyd. We can put
McN-B in his hands for a month while
it's in a holding pattern. If we have
to, we work mornings from out there—

I fell into the comfort of everyday thoughts, everyday talk, business as usual. To have that again. For it to be a month ago…

It took her too long to answer.

—Diana?—

—We run it as equals. If we're working
you're not the boss of me—

What was obvious to me wasn't to her. I didn't know if she'd be able to separate work time from play time, and if I was being honest with myself, I didn't know if I'd be able to either.

—I wouldn't have it any other way—

That was the most honest thing I'd ever said to a woman or myself. I wanted her at my side as a partner. That was the abyss I couldn't see past.

I hailed a cab up to R+D before I had to look so far into that vacuum that I fell in.

Chapter 42

PAST PERFECT

The real estate agent had excused herself so Diana and I could talk. We stood in the space a few feet from each other. The wood floors shone with new gloss, the white walls reflected the blasting summer sun through the huge windows. Crosby Street passed by, twenty stories below with tires rattling against the cobblestone street. A voice from the sidewalk. Another returning the greeting. An undulating rustle of white noise from blocks away.

"What do you think?" she said, voice echoing off the emptiness.

"It's pretty big."

"Do you think we can fill it?"

With our stuff. With our life. With our memories. With our children.

"Yes."

She smiled and looked at the high ceiling. "I'm so happy."

"Why's that?" I took her by the waist and pulled her close.

Her eyes were pale and clear in the bright room. Her mouth held all her warmth and expressiveness. She was incapable of lying through it.

"You want the long version or the short version? Pick the long version."

I held her even tighter. "Why go short when long's available?"

"You make me happy," she said. "I can't believe I ever thought I was going to marry anyone else."

"That guy?"

"That guy. He wasn't you, and I must have known it. It was you. Always you. You make me feel loved all the way through. Even the dumb stuff I do. Even when I have a really bad idea, you pay it full attention and you sort through it with me. It's like you know there's a germ of something good there and you want to find it. And can I tell you something else? Sometimes I look at you and I can't believe you picked me. You're so wise. And thoughtful. And handsome. Like, super handsome. I'm sorry but I love you." She closed her eyes again and shouted to the ceiling, "I love you Adam Steinbeck!"

I laughed. She delighted me, filled me, lifted me.

She put her hands on my cheeks and made me look deeply into her eyes. "Promise you'll never leave me."

"I promise. But if you really want me to promise…"

"What?" she asked suspiciously.

"We should probably get married."

Her mouth and eyes went wide.

"Let's!" She said it as if I'd suggested a cruise.

"I have to get a ring."

"Let's do it now!"

"Now?"

"Now! Grab a couple of friends who can witness. Go to city hall. Right now!"

"Wait, wait. Don't you want to do all the things?" I circled my hand in the air as if trying to pull "all the things" out of it. "You know. A bouquet? A party? Walk down an aisle in a white dress?"

"I have my mother's in the closet. I can run home and get it. We can get flowers on the corner. Oh, Adam, let's just do it right now, when it feels so right. Let's not wait for all the stuff. Let's not get distracted by caterers and photographers. I hate seating arrangements. I get stressed out just thinking about it. Let's just get in a cab and go get married."

Her enthusiasm infected me. She was light, life, energy. Everything.

What wouldn't I do for her, when she gave me so much?

I would have married her in an instant. So I did.

Chapter 43

PRESENT TENSE

The Montauk house had a full-time staff of two that included Thierry, who drove a long black limousine, and his wife, Willa who took care of the cleaning and cooking when someone was in the big house. They lived in a third structure on the east end of the property, took care of repairs, maintenance, and were unfazed by what they saw.

Thierry pulled the limo up at five o'clock Saturday morning. It was dark, and the air had the thrum of the day's potential. When he opened the back door for me, we shook hands and he told me how good it was to have me back. That was the extent of it. He drove from Murray Hill to SoHo, to Crosby Street, where Diana and the doorman waited with—I counted—four suitcases, one trunk, and a toiletry case.

"Take them back up," I told the doorman. I gave him a ten for the chore.

"Why?" Diana asked as he went into action. "I need—"

"Nothing. You need nothing. I provide you with what you need, and what I don't provide, you don't need. Think of it as a vacation from adulthood."

"That's the exact opposite of the way I want to think of it."

I held out my hand. "Regardless. I'll need your phone."

She didn't move. I pointed at her right-hand coat pocket then put my palm up for it.

"What if work calls?" she asked.

"They'll call me, and if it's important, you and I—together—will put the fire out."

She still hesitated.

"Okay, listen," I said. "When you're there, you're mine. Your time, your boredom, your isolation, these are my tools. If you're texting your friends or reading the news, you're not with me. I need you *with me*."

"What if there's work?"

"I brought your laptop from the office."

She took out her phone, weighing its importance in her hand. "This scares me."

"I'm not trying to scare you. But you said you trusted me. If you do, there's no reason to be scared."

She stretched her arm just a little, as if she really wanted to pull it back. I took the phone and put it in my pocket.

"Good." I almost said *good girl* but caught myself. We were still in the world, where that was condescending.

"I want to take my journal."

I thought about it for only a moment. I could cut her off from the world, but I couldn't cut her off from her own thoughts.

"Yes. All right."

"It's in the top bag."

I unzipped it, and the red leather popped through as if it were dying to get out. I handed it to her. She hugged it to her chest.

I held my hand toward the open back door of the car. "Shall we?"

Her hair blew back from her face as she watched her bags being taken back up, and onto her reddened cheeks when she looked at the back of the limo.

"Once I get in there," she said, "everything changes, doesn't it?"

"You wanted change."

"I guess I did."

I left it there, letting her look at the open mouth of the limo, wondering if she'd let herself get swallowed.

She did. My Diana bent her knees and took my hand, letting me help her into the car. I got in after her and let Thierry close the door. The outside world was snuffed out.

The car pushed forward. Diana sat across from me, knees pressed together, hands on them, looking into the space between us. Her wedding ring was where it belonged. I wanted to believe she'd put it on because she kept changing her mind about leaving me, but then I hoped not. If this was over, it was over. I was taking my full thirty days and walking away. I had no intention of looking back.

But that was tomorrow and this was now.

"Diana."

"Yeah?"

"You look beautiful."

"Thank you."

"How do you feel?"

"Scared."

"Thank you for telling me. You should always answer honestly even if you think I won't like it."

Instructing my wife how to speak to me. Was irony or justice being served?

"Do you have any questions?" I asked. I was falling into the natural use of my Dominant voice. I still had to remind myself first, but it took less time to process.

"I can't think right now."

"We'll go very slow."

"Yeah," she croaked.

"Your safe word is 'pinochle?' Is that right?"

"Yes."

"And for the trigger question, I'll ask you your name. You'll say 'Diana.' Your age, your address. If you take too long to answer or say anything but the truth, I'm going to change whatever I'm doing or slow it down."

"I read that in the contract."

She was walking on a wire. Tension surrounded her like a suit of armor. I usually enjoyed a sub's discomfort, but this was something more than that. This was a call for me to help her relax.

"Take your shoes off," I said.

She flashed red for a second, looked away, then slowly shifted her feet until they were out of her pumps. She curled her toes in her black tights as if they embarrassed her. We got on the highway, the seams in the asphalt making a *thup thup* against the tires. No traffic. We'd be there in a few hours, traffic gods willing.

I slapped my knee. "Right foot."

She lifted her foot and I took it by the Achilles, bringing it up to my knee. The sun was rising, washing the black sky blue.

I ran my thumb along the bottom of her foot, the matte nylon of the stockings dry on my skin. Pulling at the toe, I pushed my fingers against the fabric, stretching it into a cone, then I used my left hand to spread the knit apart until it ripped.

She gasped as I shredded her tights up to the knee. She was going to cry. She thought I was going to get very rough before we even got into Long Island.

"Hush," I said, running both thumbs along the bottom of her foot. "This is a foot rub. You have nothing to be concerned about."

She snorted a little laugh that would have gotten another sub welted. But she did it while leaning back and relaxing her shoulders.

"What are you worried most about?" I worked from the tender part of the arch outward with increasing pressure.

She cringed a little when I pressed hard, but she didn't pull away. My wife loved a deep-tissue massage. She went to an old Korean guy with hands the size of dinner plates and forearms as wide as Portuguese loaves.

"Everything," she said.

"Pain?"

"Yes."

"Discomfort."

"Yes."

"Having sex with me again? Which—" I was about to remind her there might not be any sex, but she cut in before I could.

"Not really that. More…" She grimaced then relaxed when I went deep into the ball of her foot. "Ickiness."

"Ickiness?"

"Seeing things I don't want to see. Being something that doesn't feel right." Her face changed as she watched my hand on her foot. "I'm afraid I'll be afraid of you."

I squeezed and pulled each of her toes. This little piggy was mine. This little piggy was also mine. This little piggy got a spanking. This little piggy got the paddle. This little piggy went *yes yes yes* all the way home.

She wasn't afraid of me. Not yet. She might be. If everything worked out, I wouldn't care if she was.

But in the limo to Montauk, I didn't want her to be afraid. I had a box of things in the trunk that had been chosen for their innocuous looks.

I put her foot on the floor and gently lifted the other, putting it on the same knee. I tore open the stockings, and because she wasn't shocked the second time, she wrested her foot through the hole. The foot part came off, and I tossed it aside.

I rubbed that foot the same way, maybe harder. She relaxed.

"The last time I rubbed your feet was in the hospital."

"Yeah." Her voice was no louder than a breath, and her eyes stayed on the hands folded in her lap as if she instinctively knew what to do and just needed to give herself permission to do it.

"Before we lost Olive." I pressed her foot between my palms, curved then squeezed.

"Lenore. And we didn't *lose* her," Diana continued. "We got rid of her."

"She wasn't going to make it. She was going to live a week in extreme pain."

My wife knew this. We'd discussed it. She'd cried for a week then stopped abruptly, as if she'd run out of tears. She focused on getting better as if it was a project she had to complete.

She was terrible at finishing things.

"Taking care of you during that time was one of the most satisfying things I've ever done," I said. "You let me bathe you, advocate for you, tend you. I wasn't happy about losing the baby. But being there for you made me very, very happy."

"I never—" she blurted, then stopped herself, softening her tone. "All that time... I never felt so lonely."

And there, New York City... there you have it.

The time I felt closest to her was the time she felt most alone.

I took her foot off my lap. "Did you read the contract carefully? Anything besides the list? I want to make sure you know what's expected of you."

"I did."

"When I walk into a room? What do you do?"

She stuttered. Swallowed. Seemed to shrink inside herself. "Present myself to you?"

"It's not a question."

She nodded slightly. Her hands were folded so tightly the knuckles were white.

"You present me with something to fuck."

"Adam..."

"You don't have to call me sir because you redlined it. But you no longer address me by my name. That's a privilege that's earned. You start from zero. I got into this car after you and you presented me with nothing. You should have been on your knees with your mouth open, at the very least."

Her face was beet red with contained rage. I was going for purple.

"I said I might not fuck you, but that doesn't mean no contact and it doesn't mean you make yourself unavailable. It's not up to you. It's completely up to me." I leaned forward. She looked as if she wanted to become part of the leather seat. "And let me assure you, if I remain unsatisfied in any way, there are going to be years and years of filings before you hold my shares."

"What happened to you?" she whispered.

"Get on your knees."

She didn't move.

I pointed at the floor. "What did you think this was, Diana? Did you think I'd fuck you sweetly once and let it go? Even seeing that contract?"

Her mouth opened but nothing came out.

I reached forward.

Cupped her jaw.

Drew my hand behind her neck.

Up the back of her head.

Made a fistful of hair.

She squeaked.

Her hands gripped my forearms as I pulled her forward.

And down.

Until she was on the floor. She got her knees under her, but I didn't let go, bending her head back so I could see the pores of her cringing face.

"This is what you signed up for. Feel free to change your mind any time."

Her eyes closed. She swallowed so hard I heard it.

"You are my submissive. You will kneel at my feet."

I let her go and sat back.

I thought I was going to have to turn the car around. When she kneeled upright in her ripped stockings, looking at the blurred motion of the trees, I thought she was going to pinochle out. I almost wanted her to.

But she fell forward, put her hands in front of her and her forehead on the carpet. Her ass wasn't up, but she was kneeling, naked toes pointed against the floor mat.

I wasn't going to last the whole month. Submission made her honest, and obviously I wasn't ready for her honesty. Maybe after thirty days I'd be able to hear about how lonely she'd been with me.

Maybe I'd grow a thick skin when it came to her, or we'd form an emotional bond I respected and she didn't.

She'd sue me. I'd lose because I'd taken her to a remote house in Montauk to dominate her. The contract and her consent would be inadmissible in court. Everything would go south. My life would be a disaster.

But I'd be over her. I couldn't imagine the day I wouldn't love her, especially not with her submission at my feet. The bare satisfaction of it, the peace, the rightness of my sexual dominance over this woman in a controlled setting was better than any drug.

Worth it. All worth it.

Chapter 44

PRESENT TENSE - DAY ONE

After fifteen minutes at my feet, she laid her cheek on my shoe. I leaned down and stroked her hair. We were in that position when the car turned onto the private road at the other end of Long Island and stopped at the gate to the house.

Diana looked up.

"You can sit," I said before she could decide to do it herself.

Thierry pressed the number sequence on the keypad while Diana stared at me from the opposite seat. I couldn't tell if she was mad or curious.

"How was that?" I asked.

"I slept a little."

The gates opened and the car pulled forward.

"Were you scared?"

A slight knot at the brow. A tightening of the lips. She didn't know what to make of the change, and I wasn't going to explain it.

"When I looked all this up, I didn't believe you could be that way. When I went to the Cellar, I didn't believe it. Not you. Not my husband."

The car pulled around the circular drive and stopped at

the front steps. The two-story house had been built in the late nineteenth century. It had thick wood beams, leaded glass, and porches everywhere.

"And now?"

"I believe it." She put her shoes on her bare feet.

As she spoke, I could see out the window behind her. Two people came from the side of the drive from the studio. I knew who they were.

"You don't have to get out of the car."

Stefan and Serena stopped at the bottom of the front steps. They were both fully dressed in coats and boots. Serena wore a collar attached to a leash.

Stefan yanked the leash, and Serena fell to her knees. Diana turned when the links clicked on the pavement, shock registering on her face when she saw them.

Thierry opened the door. We were blasted with cold. Serena's prone figure on the cold ground. Face hidden. Hair splayed out.

"Thierry can drive you home right now," I said, putting my foot out the door. I thought she was going to stay in the backseat and go back to the city. I could hear the ocean crashing behind the house.

"Adam," Stefan said, holding out his hand.

I got out of the car and shook it. He yanked the chain, and Serena looked up.

I didn't know if seeing Serena's face would inspire Diana to get out of the car, or if seeing that there would be other people around gave her comfort. But slowly, with eyes going from Serena to Stefan to me, she stepped through the car door.

"What do we have here?" Stefan asked.

"This is my wife," I said.

Her stockings were torn and her coat was open.

"Well, well, I assume we redlined sharing?" He said it to her. I didn't want him speaking to her. At all. But his eyes were all over what was mine.

I could hear Thierry behind me, unloading my box of equipment. I wished he'd hurry.

"Mind your own redlines," I said.

"That's a no." One side of his mouth went up at an evil angle. "Us either."

"You're in the studio?" I asked.

"Yes."

"Good. Stay there."

He jerked Serena's leash and made eye contact with my beautiful wife. "Come visit any time."

"Good-bye, Stefan," I said. "And Serena."

A perfect submissive, she glued her eyes to the ground and kept her hands at her sides.

Stefan waved once and turned down the side path, pulling his pet behind him.

"Follow me." I spun and went up the steps. I usually put my hand on Diana's back and let her walk before me, but things had changed. Now it was her job to be at my heels.

Did it make sense that both felt right? That in Montauk, I could let her walk behind me in a subservient position, but in the city, I walked behind her?

It didn't make any sense, and it did.

Once she was inside, I closed the door, shutting out the cold and the wind. Only the sound of the grandfather clock interrupted the silence.

I faced her. She looked all over, taking in everything. The walls of glass, the open rooms, the wood floor, the oversized nature photographs. Willa had left flowers on the hall table.

"We are the only ones in this house except for the following. Thierry and Willa live in the cottage just east." I pointed generally east. "Thierry won't come in without asking, and Willa comes to do some cooking and cleaning. Nothing they see will surprise them, but we are going to work around their times. The studio house on the west is currently occupied by Stefan and Serena, whom you just met. They have no reason to be in the main house unless invited, and the studio is absolutely, positively off-limits to you. Understand?"

"Yes."

I took off her coat, untied her scarf, put it in her pocket, and hung it in the front closet. The stairs to the second floor were by the front foyer, and the office door was on the other side. She faced the back of the house, which overlooked the ocean through high, wood-framed windows. She crossed her arms, looking past the horizon, where her worst fears were.

"Questions?" I asked.

"Will you invite them? Serena and Stefan?"

"Maybe."

"For dinner?"

"For whatever I want." I stood in front of her, blocking the view. "Your room is upstairs. It has a red door and it's connected to mine. Everything you need is there."

"Wait. We're not sleeping in the same bed?"

"No. Not even in the same room. It's your space. There are clothes for you. Unless I have something laid out for you, you can wear what you want. The white nightgown is what you wear to bed unless I say otherwise. You must leave your room for meals and when I need you, but if you're not servicing me, you can go wherever you like except the studio. If you see me, you present yourself."

"Servicing you?"

"We can call it whatever you want."

I used to do this all the time. I'd brought a dozen subs up for thirty-day stretches, and they were typically excited and thrilled. They were usually sucking my cock before I even told them where their room was.

"Can I ask a question?" she said.

"Yes."

"I didn't redline you sharing me."

"That's not a question. That's a statement."

"I didn't cross it off because I didn't think you'd let anyone else have sex with me."

"How strategic."

"Was I wrong?"

"You might have been wrong."

Her face fell. She'd miscalculated. I didn't want to hurt her, and I certainly didn't want to share her, but she had to accept the rules. She had to do this one hundred percent if it was going to work.

I asked myself if I enjoyed hurting her, and I answered yes and no at the same time. Then I asked myself if I was trying to scare her, and I got the same answer. My responses were tangled up in each other.

"Go to your room and get changed. There's a clock. The alarm is set for five p.m. Be at the base of the stairs before it stops chiming."

She didn't move.

"Yes?" I asked.

No answer. I picked a stack of mail off the side table, sorted through it, and headed out of the room. Still, she didn't move.

"Do you want to go home? I'm not going to ask you constantly. It's up to you. Or I can get frustrated with you and call it off."

She went up the stairs with her head down and her face firm. I watched her ass as she went. She wasn't going to last a week.

And yet, she only seemed scared when I was too brusque.

The more I embraced who I had been—who I was at the core—the more I saw the signs of submission. The downcast eyes, the still hands, the attention to my Dominant voice.

I flipped through the mail and paced the corners and edges of the house like a cat checking his territory. I hadn't been there in years, but I had paid for upkeep with the other two. Not much had changed. It looked like a normal house. The library with its dark woods and stacks of hardcovers. The piano in the corner. The Oriental rug. The hidden hooks in the floor and ceiling. The couch and long table facing the ocean in the open room. The TV room with its rustic furniture. And the kitchen, built for cooks with an island and a six-burner stove with a grill. When we'd had over a hundred people here, it had been really handy, and not just for cooking.

The entire back of the house was skirted by a deck that ended at a rocky beach, thirty feet from the high tide line. I stepped out into the cold and faced the water. I'd had a sub tell me the presence of the ocean and her Dominant in the same place made her feel infinitely small and powerless. She described it as the purest joy. Being under him, infinitesimal in the universe, yet cared for as if she was the most precious being in the world.

Her eyes had fluttered a little when she described the feeling, as if she was re-experiencing the high.

A grunt went up, carried by the wind, made anonymous and sexless in the gusts. It came from the studio. I walked to the other end of the back deck.

The studio building was painted white. The barn doors faced the main house and had windows at the top. On the side, another door and a small porch faced the ocean.

A plane of snow-covered grass tilted between the main house and the studio.

There, thirty feet away in the cold sun, were the residents of the studio. Serena, bare-assed and bent over a huge planter, one naked leg leaning on the edge, one boot on, pants pooled at the ankle. Stefan behind her, thrusting inside her as if he wanted to kill her.

I looked up. A railing above. The narrow balcony to Diana's room was just above me, facing the studio. She stood there, a flat, blurry figure against the darkness of the room behind her.

She was watching from her room. The edge of the porch wasn't in front of her by much, and it was possible she didn't notice me there. I couldn't read her from that angle, but she saw it, and Stefan knew it. She was the reason for the show.

Stefan put his hand on Serena's throat, leveraging himself against it. Pulling her up. Her face went red. I could see it even from far away. She'd redlined choking with me. Had someone pushed that limit? Or was this a first?

I looked up at Diana's window again. She was still there. Stefan's grunts carried over the wind, faster and more intense. When I looked back to Stefan and Serena, his hand was off her throat and her mouth was open wide as if she needed to inhale the atmosphere.

I checked Diana. Still there. Barely a shadow against the window frame. If she saw me, she pretended she didn't.

Serena cried out, barking, "Please!"

Stefan snarled something I couldn't decipher, and Serena's back arched in orgasm. He grabbed her ass with both hands and thrust hard and fast. He went tight, then loose.

When I looked up again, my wife wasn't at the window.

I'd be surprised if she showed up at dinner with anything but a request to go home.

Chapter 45

PRESENT TENSE – DAY ONE

The studio was visible from the office room. The sun lit a clear blue sky, warming the air enough to gently melt the last snow on the yard between the main house and the little studio where Stefan and Serena lived. By eleven, strands of dry grass and swatches of dirt came through the white tufts.

I didn't admit to myself that I was watching the studio, even as I looked over my laptop screen whenever there was movement. Diana's room was right above me. I kept it nondescript with white bedding and pale wood furniture. I'd had the door between our rooms left open so she could see my bed, which was higher with posts and beams that could be used for ropes and shackles.

She wouldn't notice the potential of the bedframe as much as she'd notice the blue-and-green quilt, the art on the walls, the Persian carpet. She'd notice how the décor showed our relative places in the relationship. To most subs, the subtle message was a turn-on. To Diana, it would be insulting.

Even the bed sheets made me think I was moving too fast.

I made a hundred plans for her body and mind at dinner, ranging from honest talks to unfulfilling fantasies, then dismissed them all. Having gotten her here, I felt the emptiness of my success. Still so much to do, and I couldn't decide how to do it.

Mostly because I didn't know what I wanted.

I thought I did, but I couldn't commit to it. I still straddled two worlds emotionally. My definitions were contradictory, and the shift had been too sudden. Was I half of a power couple? A Dominant with a submissive wife who didn't love him? Or a single Dominant with insatiable appetites? Neither? Some third, nameless monster?

I could only imagine what it was like for my wife. Except at the end of this, she could go back to being who she was. I couldn't.

At eleven fifteen, one of the barn doors opened. Stefan came out bundled in a wool hat and thick boots. Serena waited in the door, fully dressed in a burnt orange polo and brown pants. A narrow wood crate leaned on her hip. I'd seen Stefan transport his work, and that was a canvas crate. I stood and went around the desk, not even pretending to work anymore.

I watched as he backed a pickup truck up to the door. Got out. Kissed Serena on the cheek when he took the crate. She went into the studio and got another, handing it to him as he came back. He rushed to relieve her of the weight and wagged his finger at her. She didn't get far with the third before he took it.

When he closed the back of the cab, Serena got on her knees, right in the flat, wet snow. She kissed the top of his hand, then the palm. He patted her head and picked her up, led her into the studio, and closed the door.

As he drove away a few minutes later, I couldn't forget that he'd put his hand on her neck until she stopped breathing. That had been a hard limit. Yet the scene I'd witnessed was as warm and normal as any between a Dom and his sub.

I was making a problem where there wasn't one. Serena's lines had moved. Stefan was doing what Stefan did. Serena was a grown-up. She knew how it went. He was giving her what she needed.

Neither Stefan nor Serena needed fixing. If anyone needed fixing, it was Adam Steinbeck, walking across the slope to the little house on the west side of the property with his dress shoes crunching on the old snow and the salt mist freezing in his hair.

The guy with the love of his life biding her time to leave him. The guy who could only get her to spend thirty days with him by holding hostage everything she held dear.

That was who needed fixing.

As true as all that was, I didn't hesitate to knock on the side door. It had been painted since I'd been at the house last. A shiny flat red against the crisp white of the wood siding. A shadow passed over the glass, and Serena opened the door a second later.

"Hi," she said, only opening the door an eighth of the way.

"Hi," I replied. "Sorry to disturb you."

"It's all right."

"You're not supposed to open the door for me or anyone is my guess."

"I didn't know you were going to be here. You and your wife, I mean."

As if Diana and I were on anything more intimate than speaking terms. As if our marriage was more real than a thirty-day stay of execution.

"Are you going to invite me in?"

I was asking for trouble. Her ex-Dom asking to be in the house without talking to her current Dom first? Bad form. We were Dominant and in control. We shared submissives and put our emotions in a locked box. But we had so many ways of stepping on each other's toes. We could release a caged animal with a simple slip, much less an intentional breach of space.

Serena stepped away from the door and opened it wider. She knew what she was doing. It was possible I'd walked across the snow in dress shoes for a good reason.

Before I crossed the threshold, I looked back at the main house, up to the second floor, where Diana had been standing before.

She wasn't there.

Chapter 46

PAST PERFECT

Two days after I told Stefan to jerk off on his own dime, he split. Serena hadn't seen him at the house. He had a well-earned reputation and I didn't want her to be nervous. I wanted her to feel as safe as she ever had.

I waited another day. I let her heal, but not completely. I brought a dress back from the city and told her to wear it to dinner. I had flowers brought in. Willa cooked and set the dining room table for two. Everything shone. The tablecloth was stark white and the glasses were nearly invisible.

When she came down, she got on her knees, or she tried to.

"Stand," I said before she fell completely.

I held out my hand. She looked confused, but took it.

"This is your night," I whispered. "It's like your birthday."

"I don't know what you mean, Master."

"Tonight, I'm Adam."

She smiled nervously, looked me in the eye for no more than a flicker before putting her eyes back on the floor. "All right. Adam."

"You look uncomfortable."

"I don't understand. That's all."

"You came to me to lose your virginity, Serena. I'll take it how I see fit."

She nodded slightly. Started to say something. Stopped herself.

"Go on," I said.

"You worry me," she said.

"Why?"

"I don't know what to expect."

A submissive always knows what to expect within certain boundaries. I should have listened to the heart of what she was saying. When I pulled the chair out for her, I was pushing her limits. When I shut off my Dominant voice, I was exploring boundaries. I didn't realize it that night, but I was about to inadvertently stumble on my own redlines.

Chapter 47

PRESENT TENSE – DAY ONE

Presented with a choice in the moment of its making, I didn't think I was discerning one option from another. When I'd walked Serena up to her apartment in the Lower East Side, kissed her on the cheek, and thanked her, walking out hadn't seemed like a choice. It had seemed like crossing the last *t* and dotting the last *i*. I'd had a project with a start and an end and the end came exactly on schedule.

In the studio five years later, with the space scraped of the vestiges of its past and Serena in her polo shirt, I wondered at the choice. If I'd chosen to stay with her, if I'd given her a chip of my heart, would I have been able to give the entire thing to Diana the following week?

If I'd embraced Serena and given her the time she wanted, how would I have felt about Diana when she walked into the conference room with her father?

I shuddered to think of how easily I could have missed loving Diana. How the richness of my life with her would have been the reality of a parallel existence. One of a million lives not lived. A life created when my mind was blank as the subway rocked in the morning or during the last five tedious minutes on the treadmill.

How the fire of my current existence had been sparked on the kindling of a choice to shut Serena out.

"I saw you this morning," I said as Serena shut the door behind me. I didn't elaborate. She knew I didn't mean in the front, by the car.

The studio was painted bright white, from concrete floor to fifteen-foot ceiling. It was heated to over eighty degrees even though it was the dead of winter. Absolutely necessary when the occupants could be exposed and naked at any time.

"Yes. You did." Serena ran her hands along the white counter. The kitchen was part of the larger room, white and chrome. "Can I get you something?"

"Water would be great. Thank you."

She got a glass and went to the sink. She was never saucy or oversexed. She didn't flirt. Ever. Some of us found that very attractive.

Diana flirted. I made the comparison immediately and knew just as quickly that her clumsiness at it had been the attraction.

I took a few steps into the main room. Stefan's work was neat, precise, and bold. Tarps were down. Paints covered. The slop sink could have been used for surgery. I sat on a red chair that looked like a puncture wound in the white space.

"You'd never know how prolific he was from this studio," I said.

"I think cleanliness is part of the art."

"How many pieces did he take to the city today?"

"Seven. He has a show at Broome." Serena brought me the glass and stood in front of me.

"Sit," I said.

"I'm sorry. I didn't want to put on a show for you, but I didn't want to safe out over it."

I tilted my head toward the couch then slid a coaster out of the case and put my water on the glass table. She sat with her legs pressed together and her hands folded between her knees.

"I'm fine with it," I said.

"But your wife. Diana."

Serena. Mentioning Diana. Calling her my wife. In the architecture of my life, there hadn't been a hallway between these women. Now there was a thoroughfare.

"She's a big girl."

"She was the audience."

The room was so warm my glass already had beads of condensation on it. One at the top inched downward. Stopped in a no-man's-land of clouded frost. Stefan had wanted my wife to see him hammer and choke Serena. Blood rushed to the surface of my skin. The droplet curved a little to the left. Stopped again. I shut down my feelings on the matter.

"I'm not questioning your Dominant. I'm asking you." I looked away from the glass to her big brown doe eyes. "Are you all right?"

"Of course. Why?"

"Unless I'm mistaken, which I'm not, he cut your intake. You have bruises on your neck. Breath play scared you. That was your first redline."

"That was five years ago."

"Our basic fears don't change."

She set her jaw. "My basic fear has always been that no man would ever love me the way I am. We've been together for years, you know. He loves me."

She looked defiant and hard, as if she was challenging me to make the connection between our past and her fears. I wouldn't do it. If I didn't love her, it was because I wasn't meant to. There were no parallel realities. No imaginings created infinite worlds for every possible decision.

She broke our gaze and looked at her knees. I went for my glass. The drop I'd tracked fell another half inch, joined another droplet, and rushed to the bottom of the glass in a line, as it was meant to.

"I'm going to assume it isn't redlined now." I drank, put the glass back on the coaster. "Or I'm going to assume Stefan knows what he's doing."

"I'm glad you approve."

This was code for *I don't care if you approve.* She wasn't much more subtle than that.

"Don't be angry. Or be angry. It's up to you how to feel. Just know, if you ever get in over your head, which you won't, but if you do, you can come to me."

"What about when you get in over your head?"

She wasn't sniping. She wasn't throwing my words back in my face. Her voice was so tinged with regret, it cut right through me.

What I thought I'd hidden had always been exposed.

What I thought I owned had never been mine.

She'd been more perceptive and more in control than I ever gave her credit for.

I swallowed a hundred answers because they all came up my throat in a knot of competing desires. The desire to pretend I didn't know what she was talking about. The desire to confirm what she meant. The desire to tell her I was in as over my head now as I'd been then.

I'd come to the studio to protect Serena, and she'd turned it all around with a few words. The heat had its own weight, and it pressed on me, squeezing my lungs until they couldn't expand. The condensation on my glass was running in vertical lines that looked like a jail cell until two/three/ten drops met and—

A knock at the barn door.

The pressure released as if a valve had opened.

Serena started to get up, but I put my hand on her shoulder and walked across the studio to the big door. The island was dead in the off season, Stefan wouldn't knock, and Diana shouldn't trek across the yard to see Serena. It could have been Willa or Thierry. Or it could have been someone from the other side of the overpass who had noticed Stefan had left his beautiful girlfriend behind.

It had gotten dark in the few minutes I'd been in the studio, so when I opened the door into the bright white room, Diana squinted. She looked genuinely surprised to see me.

So much for her not trekking across the yard.

"Oh. Adam. Hi. I—"

"This building is off-limits."

She blinked in the light. Cold air swept into the studio.

Serena opened the door all the way so she stood in the frame with me. "Come in! It's freezing!"

Serena and Diana in the same room. Not just any room, but the back house of the Montauk property. On any other day, I may have been able to manage the collision of my worlds, but not that day. My sense of control was already chipped away in a situation where I was supposed to have the most control.

"No," I said to Serena, then I brought my attention to Diana, who was shivering. "We're going back."

My wife shot daggers out of her eyes. Who was I to tell her she had to go back?

"Thank you for the water," I said. "Give my best to Stefan."

"Sure." Serena stepped aside as I walked out, stepping into a crevice of ice-cold slush.

My shoes were soaked. I took Diana by the arm, gave Serena a last wave, and led my wife back to the house, along the widening path of yellow light from the open door. When it narrowed and closed with the click of the closed door, Diana pulled away and faced me.

"What was that all—"

"You don't belong over there," I said.

"Why not?"

"Can I ask why you were going there in the first place?"

She crossed her arms. Her breath caught the air in white frost and scattered in the ocean wind.

"Well. You saw." She gestured to the back house, where Stefan had fucked Serena for show. So Diana knew I'd been on the porch below.

"I did."

"I wanted to see if she was all right."

I tried not to smile. She and I had had the same impulse. But hers was born out of ignorance.

"So you know, it's not your place to question what her Dominant does to her."

"Whose place is it?"

It was no one's, really.

"Mine. That's why I was there."

She smiled and looked away, arms still crossed, nearly laughing. Her hair blew back from her face, exposing her high forehead. I didn't think I'd noticed for a long time how high it was, or what a beautiful arch her hairline made.

"What?" I asked.

"I don't understand this world you're in."

"How's that?"

"I didn't know you were there, but when I saw you, I thought you'd gone over there to have sex with her."

"I'm still married to you."

She shrugged. Was she jealous? There was no way of telling. She used to trust that I was faithful, and I'd never betrayed her. With the rules changing, was I about to see a different side of her?

"I figured she'd do things I don't." She let the wind take her hair to the side. "Things you need."

"Come inside," I said. "Willa put dinner out for us, and I'm sure it's getting cold."

I led her back to the house, up the back steps to the dining room. Willa had indeed left dinner out. Two silver circular warming plates crackled, surrounded by a full table setting for two. I took her coat, removed mine, ignored my cold, wet feet. I held her seat out for her. She sat, rubbing her cold hands against her thighs.

Lifting the cover of the first dish, I found tomato soup.

I ladled some into her bowl and stood directly behind her silently for more time than was normal or comfortable.

"Tonight," I said, "we start."

"All right." I heard the tension in her voice crack like an egg.

"Eat your soup."

"Aren't you having any?"

"No. Uncross your legs and spread them when you sit."

Slowly, her body shifted as she uncrossed her legs.

"Your ankles should be outside the width of the chair legs, and your knees should rest on the corners of the seat. The instructions are precise so I know you're listening. Now. Eat."

After a pause, she put her napkin in her lap. She picked up her spoon and ate. I split her hair in the back so I could see her neck, and I ran my finger over the length of it.

"I know what's in your mind," I said. "You want to ask if there's a way you should hold the spoon. Not because you care or want to please me, but because you want to assert my foolishness. My answer to that is, by the end of our time here, you may not submit in your heart, but you'll understand what it means. And you'll understand me."

I let her eat for a second before continuing.

"I know you think it doesn't matter. Maybe it doesn't to you. But it does to me. Maybe you'll understand why you stopped loving me, and maybe I'll accept it."

Her soup was almost finished. Diana ate quickly and efficiently. Always the first one done. It wasn't a competition. She didn't race. She had to begin and finish at the same time. It was how she attacked everything. If she didn't finish before she got bored, she didn't finish.

"What if you don't?" she asked.

"Accept it? I don't see that I have much choice."

She put her spoon down and wiped her mouth. "You might if you slept with that girl."

I yanked her chair out with a loud scrape. "She's not a prostitute." Diana started to look around to me, but I held her face fast in my palms. "I'm not defending her honor. I'm explaining how it works. Stefan owns her. I can't fuck her without his permission, and I won't anyway. I said before and I'll say it until you understand it. I'm married. I love my wife, even if she doesn't love me." I slid my hand down her throat, making her look forward. "Unbutton your shirt."

I felt her swallow hard against my palm before her hand went to her shirt buttons and she worked them open.

"You are not to go over there without me," I said. "Stefan

wants to fuck you. One, you're beautiful. Two, you're mine. Three, you're not in our world. He likes innocence. He likes resistance. He likes when people watch him defile something."

I pulled her bra up over her breasts, letting them escape. She gasped.

I let her go and stepped away, still behind her. "You're doing great."

"Thanks, I guess."

"You want to ask me 'now what.'"

"Kind of."

"I'll let you know." I waited, letting her feel her nudity and my presence behind her. I let her imagine what I was going to do. "Look straight ahead."

She stopped watching me to look ahead of her. I knew she could see me from the corner of her eye, but she didn't check me. She wanted to do it right. Maybe this was her way of getting it over with or maybe it turned her on. No way to know just yet.

"Stand up."

She stood, and I stayed behind her. Her hands trembled at her sides.

No way to know if this turned her on, except her posture, her scent, the red flush on the part of her lower back that led to her bottom. She might not understand why she enjoyed this any more than I did, but she did.

"Pull your pants down."

"Adam...?"

"You're using my name."

Long pause. She had no idea of the depths of my patience.

Instead of answering, she unbuttoned. Unzipped. Hooked her thumbs in her waistband and lowered it to her mid-thigh.

"Bend at the waist. Put your elbows on the table."

Her shoulders rose as she took a deep breath, and she bent.

"In my world," I said, "going across the yard to another Dominant's space without permission would get you my belt. It would hurt you, but it would satisfy you. You'd feel right knowing I was in charge. You'd be satisfied knowing I was here to relieve you of responsibility."

I placed my hand on her ass and slowly moved my hand down to her thigh. "Male or female, the more sophisticated and intelligent the submissive is, the more they need to get back to their primal urge to be dominated, and the harder it is to break them."

I moved to her other thigh and up the other side of her ass. "I'm going to spank you six times. Do you understand?"

"Adam…" She caught herself using my name, so I decided not to give her a hard time about it. "Last time. When you spanked me last time?"

"Yes?"

"The second one? I…" Deep breath. "I came."

Of course. The rigidity inside her. The stiffening of her spine. Remembering that night, I should have known she'd had a spontaneous orgasm.

I was glad she couldn't see me, or my face would have given away my elation. I could make her enjoy the month. It wasn't torture for her. More than simply being aroused, she was actually, really, unequivocally submissive.

It was better than I hoped for.

"Surprise will do that," I said, containing the emotion in my voice. "It's unlikely it'll happen again. But thank you for the warning. Because you're not coming tonight."

I pressed her lower back down so her ass went up. Her hands folded together, still shaking.

"Palms on the table," I said. She laid them flat. "And when you saw me, you didn't present yourself. Two more for that."

I could have invented a hundred more infractions if I thought she could take a raw bottom. I stroked it, running my fingers inside her crack and her folds.

"When did you get wet?" I asked. "When you pulled your shirt up or when I told you to bend over?"

She turned her face down to the table. "When you touched my neck."

I took a handful of her hair and yanked it until she faced forward. She yelped.

I smacked her ass hard, twice, and she yelped again.

"Hush," I said. "Not a sound out of you."

I slid two fingers into her. Soaked. Yanked her hair back again and hit her ass quickly four more times. The skin turned warm.

"How many is that?" I asked.

"Six."

Two more hard swipes on one side. The color. The perfect pink. My cock ached.

Three fingers in her, gathering juice, sliding up to her asshole.

Her cheeks tightened and her anus turned into pure hard muscle.

"No," she said.

"You don't get to say no. You get to safe out."

"Please."

Her voice came from deep in her gut, passing her lips as the size of a wisp and the weight of the world. I stopped moving. I was so still I thought my blood stopped flowing.

What about when you get in over your head?

I was running to my limits. I'd forgotten I had them. Again.

I blinked, I exhaled, blood flowed. I put my hands on her hips and kissed her lower back.

I still fucking love you.

"Go upstairs," I said. "I'll give you aftercare and tuck you in."

She stood up, looking baffled, hair screwed up, a red mark on her forehead where it had pressed against the table.

Still. I still love you.

God help me.

"That's it?" she asked.

"No ball gags and latex body suits tonight, darling."

She pulled up her pants and straightened her clothes with the efficiency of antagonism. She wanted to come, and badly. She opened her mouth as if to speak, shut it, and faced me.

"Go on," I said before she could say whatever it was.

She spun on her heel and paced out of the kitchen. Stopped. "Adam."

"Just go up."

"Are you all right?"

She wasn't supposed to ask me that. I needed to maintain the old rules. I needed those like I needed money in the bank and a house to go home to.

"Why are you asking?"

"You seem different."

"So do you."

She pressed her lips between her teeth and breathed deeply.

I didn't know what I hoped she'd say. But she didn't say anything. Not with words. Slowly, she turned and went upstairs.

I'd hoped she'd say something to release me from the purgatory I'd created for myself. Pinochle. I'll leave. I'll cooperate. I love you.

Standing in the space between the kitchen and the sitting room, watching her legs disappear up the stairs, I knew that of all possible answers, "I love you" was the most desired and the most unlikely.

Chapter 48

PRESENT TENSE – DAY ONE

I owed her aftercare. She didn't really need it. Eight slaps, even if I'd put my back into it, wouldn't require serious coddling. But I had to show her the routine so that when I accelerated the pain, she'd know what was coming.

I stood at the far end of my office, looking out onto the west house. I didn't turn the lights on. The only light in the room came from the moon and the headlights on Stefan's truck as he pulled up the drive.

I was technically giving Diana enough time to get undressed, then I doubled it. I didn't want to go up there and face her. I wanted to watch the empty space between the studio and me.

Stefan got out carrying a package, his slamming door muffled by the wet air. He went inside, hurrying in the cold. The lights in the studio flicked from moody yellow to starkly bright. The windows were set high in the barn doors, so I was spared the visuals.

If I went over there right now, Stefan would ask me to fuck Serena. He'd probably demand it, challenging me to refuse. She'd be a perfect sub for me, quietly taking whatever I dealt. Diana wouldn't care. I'd be one step further away from her, and she'd be a step closer to freedom.

I was a starving man offered a buffet, yet all I wanted were the crumbs my wife offered.

Sensing movement more than hearing it, I turned around. Diana was standing in the doorway. Cast in shadow, I could see the form of her body, with its familiar curves, through the gauzy white fabric of the nightgown I'd left for her.

She was supposed to be upstairs to get aftercare. She was supposed to do one thing I asked without argument. One fucking thing. She owed me nothing and that was what she was giving me.

"What are you doing?" I snapped.

"I was going to tell you I'm fine. Aftercare is optional."

I shook my head and turned back to the window. Worst sub ever.

"Did you love her?" Diana asked.

"No."

"Are you sure?"

Turning away from the window, I tried to read her, but it was dark and I didn't know what I felt besides completely alone. "Why are you asking?"

Arms crossed over her breasts, bare toes pointed, she took two steps into the room. "I think you don't always know what you feel. I think feelings make you uncomfortable."

"I don't need to be analyzed, thank you."

"Why are you looking at her window?"

"Because Stefan just got back."

In the dark, with her body no more than a silhouette shaded in moonlight blue, she shifted her posture, dropping her arms, relaxing her hips. "So?"

"Serena's very clear about what she needs and she knows he pushes limits. No one gets involved with him without knowing that. But she knew I didn't, and five years ago, she asked for me. So this?" I indicated the window and the building beyond. "I just want to watch."

"How long have they been together?"

"Long enough that it's not my business." I laughed to myself. "Long enough that they're bored with each other, from what Charlie says."

Not as long as me and you, and already they're bored. What does that say about us?

"You're a good man."

She was lying to soothe me. But I was immune to accusations of virtuousness, especially from a woman I'd taken such pains to lie to.

"Don't mistake me for the man I told you I was."

"I don't understand you. I don't understand all of this. Why you need to dominate women. No, I don't understand that, or why causing pain is even acceptable. But when push comes to shove, Adam, you've always done what was right over what was easy."

"You don't know what you're talking about. Especially when it comes to that girl." I pointed out the window again, and like a magic act, the lights went out, immersing me and Diana in moonlight.

Her silence wasn't space. It wasn't her waiting for me to finish. She wasn't thinking of what to say next. In her silence, she accused me of being a good man, and I wouldn't stand there and listen to that silent accusation without defending myself.

"She was trained by Charlie, and she came to me for thirty days to lose her virginity. She was nineteen. I want you to remember that when I tell you this story."

Silence. Dead winter wind from outside. My eyes adjusted to the low light and I could see the oval of her face and the shape of her breasts through the nightgown. How graphic could I make the truth of what happened? Because that was how she was going to hear it. She needed to be shocked out of the idea that she was leaving a good man with kinky habits.

"Two weeks in," I said, "I decided it was time. I'd fucked everything she had without breaking her virginity. She wanted me to. She begged me to. And I looked at her and thought she was so young. Why did this one thing have to hurt her? Her first time should be sweet. She should know how that feels before she started her life as a submissive. Because once she was fully in our world, there was no going back." I stood behind a wingback chair. "Sit."

Diana sat with her ankles together and her hands in her lap. I sat on the couch across from her. That was, of course, a stall tactic, and once she was still and listening in the way only my Diana could listen, I had to continue.

"I had dinner made. Right there in the dining room, I had candles and music. I got her a dress. She seemed nervous, so I did everything to relax her. Made conversation, all that. I kissed her and carried her upstairs. I was gentle when I touched her. She looked confused. But I figured she'd get it. Well, by the time I got my hand between her legs, she was completely dry. Not aroused at all."

"You're joking."

I smiled. Diana was easy. Always wet. Always ready.

"Nope. So I stopped and asked her what she wanted."

How was I supposed to describe what Serena wanted? Tell it like it was or sugarcoat it? I looked to my wife for the answer, but her expression didn't speak clearly.

"Took two hours, but she finally told me her fantasy. Her dream of her first time. She wanted to fight it. She wanted it to be forced. She wanted to know it was someone she trusted then wanted to forget about that trust. Her fantasy was that it would be a surprise and the more she resisted, the more it would hurt. She wanted the exact opposite of what I planned."

"She wanted to be raped?" Diana's voice was flat, as if she'd made a choice between disgust and emptiness. Or as if she was trying to wipe the shock out of her reaction.

"No," I corrected, "it was consensual. But yes, it would look like rape. Planned but a surprise. Staged but improvised. She needed to act it out in a way that felt safe. Everything but fear. She didn't want to be scared. I know it defies logic—"

"It doesn't."

It was my turn to be surprised. My Diana never ceased to prove she was perfect, and I wanted her more than ever.

You knew. You always knew there was submission in her.

Maybe I did. But I never expected her to acknowledge understanding it, even in someone else.

I leaned forward because I couldn't tell the next part in anything more than a whisper.

"On the way west, toward the general store on Breakfront Drive, there's a bridge over the creek. There's a narrow opening in the fence you can squeeze through and go under. It's a shortcut. I told her, if she was walking over to the general, never go that way. Take the long way. It's dangerous. But after that night when she was dry, I sent her to the store every day with an impossible time limit. If she didn't make it back in time, she was punished. She had to take the shortcut. I watched her. I knew she was safe from everyone but me.

"Twenty-eight days after she came to Montauk, I did it. We had a word I'd use, a dozen safety measures. She was going to fight as hard as she could and I was going to take her. So I did everything we'd talked about. I want you to imagine the most obscene, violent act. Your every fear."

I stopped there, because the act itself couldn't be captured in a few sentences. The dirt. The broken glass. Ripping fabric. Blood. Scratches. Her fist on my face. The sound of my palm on her face as I slapped her, pushed her against the filthy concrete. She was naked, skin marbled with black from being dragged on the ground. She spit at me and I spit back. Called her a whore. Wedged my cock in her tight, virgin hole, head to base in one painful thrust. She cried under me, spit and tears. When she screamed, I stuck my filth-streaked hand in her mouth. Four fingers down, pumping at her, asking if she liked taking it like a slut. Told her how tight she was.

I let go that day. I embraced my violence. Pushed her limits. When she came, I slapped her and her orgasm went on and on.

It took ten minutes to break her, and eleven to break me.

The deal was, I had to leave her there and come around the other side.

I could take care of her after that. I had blankets and broth. I had soothing music and all the words ready. As I crested the rise, I looked back at her lying naked on the concrete. I'd left her there. I was an animal.

I'd wanted to cry, but I couldn't. I wanted to apologize, but there was nothing to be sorry for. She needed me to be strong, and I felt as though I was made of brittle bone.

"I'd been developing feelings for her." Admitting that to Diana was almost as hard as admitting it to myself. "That was why I tried to make her first time gentle. I hadn't realized that until I looked back and knew those feelings were dead. I took care of her as I promised, but I was gone. She thanked me and told me it was perfect, but I never wanted to see her again."

I sat back because the whispering was done. She already didn't love me with a rabid indifference. Now I had no doubt she hated me with the same vigor.

"That's the man you think is so good," I said, satisfied I'd pushed her away forever.

She shook her head slowly, and all I saw was judgment and disappointment. I was immediately sorry I'd told her about Serena, then glad. I'd pushed her away purposefully. At least I could look at the divorce as something I had a hand in. I wasn't a whimpering victim. No. I was in control of my life again.

Good move, Steinbeck.

"And you met me the following week?" she asked.

"Yes."

She folded her hands together and tapped the thumbs, far away and deeply inside herself. Her eyes narrowed and her mouth tightened as if she was solving a math problem.

Did I just give her ammunition in the divorce?

I hadn't considered that.

Maybe it was time I was punished for the way I'd deflowered Serena anyway.

"Go upstairs," I said calmly. She finally looked at me. "Get in bed. Be at breakfast at seven. You'll get a stroke for every minute you're late or early. And next time I punish you, I won't be as gentle as I was tonight."

She stood and went to the door, brushing her finger on the molding. She stopped before walking across the threshold. She wanted to say something, but I didn't want her to say it. I only wanted to hear that she loved me again, and nothing about the story I'd told earned me love.

"Don't make me say it twice," I said.

She left. I heard her footfall up the creaky stairs. Saw her bedroom light on the last icy vestiges of snow in the yard. It flicked out, and the night was dark again. I waited, feeling the depth of my isolation. Once I thought I'd drown in it, I went to bed.

Having told that story for the first time, I saw myself through Diana's eyes and felt nothing but loathing.

Chapter 49

Stefan wanted anything I had. When I got a Mercedes, he got a more expensive one. When Charlie and I started talking about getting a piece of dedicated real estate for "away games," Stefan magically came up with a property he wanted but couldn't afford alone.

We'd met over a sub's body while I was still new in the scene. She was one of his. He never told me her name, so you'd think she didn't mean anything.

Well, I was young and stupid.

I liked making women come. I never felt as dominant as when a woman melted for me. If I could get them off six times in a night, I got them off six times. If I could squeeze in a seventh, I did. To me, the point of pain was pleasure.

The unnamed sub was in the Cellar, past a door separating public fuckery and a private party. I had an invitation. I met Stefan and some of the others, Dom and sub. Half an hour later, the subs were naked, tied, strapped, bent. Stefan's cock was in this particular sub's mouth. She was on her back, her head dropped upside-down, her knees strapped to two poles. She had pearly white lines all over her tits. I'd seen her in the half hour before it began. She'd been excited. She wanted a fantasy fulfilled. A gang bang.

I'd read the rules before I entered the room. There was nothing in there about not making them come.

So I fucked her. I was still figuring out what I liked and didn't. I hadn't gotten bored of the anonymity yet. I hadn't gotten frustrated with how careless it was. I fucked her, and I made her come twice.

The first time, Stefan didn't notice because he was busy with his own sputtering cock. The second time, he looked at me as if I'd taken a dump on his pillow. She was Stefan's. He owned her pleasure. Not me. I was only allowed to degrade her. That was what she'd come there for and that was what Stefan agreed to deliver.

Those rules didn't work for me. I learned that not every peg fit every hole.

So to speak.

Stefan learned… nothing.

"He feels shown up, mate," Charlie said, running his hands over the bare sheetrock in the new toy store. The one I'd visit years later to pick things up for Diana.

"If he wants a pissing contest, we can actually piss."

"There's no need. You both piss in different directions. But from now on, piss away from each other."

He'd taken the metaphor too far, but I got the point. Stay away from Stefan. I tried. I spent the next few years trying and failing. He went where I went, chasing me like a wronged alpha dog, and I just did all the things I needed to without looking back unless he nipped my tail.

Chapter 50

PRESENT TENSE – DAY TWO

I'd gotten up at five thirty and checked on Diana, making sure she was still sleeping. I didn't think I could bear to look at her. I left her a laptop with a note. She had to answer some emails and look at some résumés for Zack's replacement. Not that we could make any offers or execute a contract during the stay, but I knew she'd want to start thinking about it.

I hadn't slept, and I needed fresh air to wake the fuck up. I laced up my sneakers and went for a run.

It was still dark when I jogged the still-icy streets of Montauk. I took a left out the drive and headed toward the general store. Almost exactly a mile. Back and forth three times was a good run. My nose was cold and my hands were frozen into fists. The sky was getting a lighter shade of grey by my second lap and I had exactly nothing on my mind until my wet shoelace untied.

I crouched to knot it. When I looked up, I realized where I was. By the overpass. A steel-grey stream rushed along the tributary. It was colder than the October evening I didn't rape Serena but felt as if I had. I couldn't take my eyes off the spot, and my happy emptiness was filled with familiar questions.

What kind of person does that?

What kind of person enjoys it?

I didn't hear the truck slow down behind me.

"Working hard, Steinbeck?" Stefan's voice came from the road. He was leaning out of the driver's side window. "Or are you giving up?"

"You know what my grandfather used to say?" I finished the tie and stood.

"'More please, Mistress?'"

"If you've got nothing nice to say, you probably need to get laid."

He tossed me a water bottle. I caught it. Wondered if he poisoned it. Drank anyway. He got out of the truck.

"You don't like me." He crossed his arms and leaned on the cab. He had on a green doubleknit sweater and mechanic boots that were a dark wet black on the bottom part of the leather.

"What's the difference? I don't have to fuck you."

"We're staying on the same property for a month."

"You stay on your side and I'll stay on mine." I finished the water and tossed the empty back to him.

He caught it and put it in the cab. "Unless you need to ask my sub if she's all right. Then you come over. Make it when I'm not around."

"I'm not apologizing. You're the one putting on shows."

"No apology necessary." He waved as if he wanted me to forget what he'd taken the effort to bring up. "But you care. See? You proved it."

"I care. Fine. I have to finish my run."

"I'm going to the city next week. Few days at most. Feel free to look in on Serena for me."

"I'm sure she'll be fine."

Stefan opened the car door. "She's a good girl, but she needs to know someone's looking after her."

"All right." I was already looking down the road, ready to finish my run.

"If you fuck her—"

My head snapped around to him. "Married. I'm—"

"Whatever. It's permitted. But I own her orgasms. Don't force one."

The discussion was over as far as I was concerned, so I started down the blacktop. He passed me on the way to the general store.

He'd let me fuck his sub but not let her enjoy it. What a shit. I wondered if he was going to instruct Serena to offer herself. As if I'd be tempted. As if presented with an attractive woman, I'd have no choice but to cheat on my wife.

But he was doing nothing wrong. This was the world I was reentering. He was the one following the rules. Constant communication. Openness. Acceptance without judgment. Monogamy optional. I was the one living with abnormal vanilla-with-monogamy-on-top guidelines.

I wanted the old rules back and couldn't have them. I had never been so confused about what I wanted in my life.

I wanted Diana, and I was willing to do anything to have her, but maybe I'd made a mistake. We weren't alone. Serena and Stefan were wild cards, and they were too close. Too sealed inside a way of thinking that I used to share. I couldn't control what they'd do or say. They could poison my wife against me or tempt her with things I didn't want. They could scare her with their very presence.

I saw things through to the end unless the risks outweighed the benefits. In the case of the Montauk experiment, the risks loomed too great to ignore.

I got back to the house at six thirty, seriously contemplating putting Diana in a car and sending her home. Working the divorce out like adults.

Divorce.

I accepted the possibility at the same time as I rejected it. I'd never sit back and work out a divorce like an adult. I knew myself that well. Not while my heart beat for her. Not while she existed in the world.

But maybe there was another plan. If I'd gotten her this far, it was possible I could convince her there was another way to do this. Back home. In New York. Living together again. Falling into old patterns and then...

More of the same.

I got into the shower fully convinced Montauk was right, and equally convinced I'd made a huge blunder.

I made myself scarce the rest of the day, closing the pocket door to the office and staring at my computer screen. I told myself my absence was part of my domination of Diana, but part of me knew better.

I was ashamed of what I'd told her. I didn't want her to look at me.

Chapter 51

PAST PERFECT

Dinner soured in my stomach. Months to get a reservation at Metropolis for the company's anniversary dinner, and the whole meal had tasted like bark and bile. I threw the keys on the shelf and my bag in the chair.

Shake it off.

I'd never felt so distant from my wife. So much like a stranger. The patient had gone code blue. Our marriage stretched out on the gurney with the machine emitting one long beep and a flat green line.

Had it.

I've had it.

The front door opened before I could even fill a water glass. I thought she'd stay to finish.

"Adam." Diana closed the door. She had a run in her stocking. It accentuated the shape of her calf.

Somewhere in my heart, paddles rubbed together and a shock brought me back to life.

I checked my watch. "Did you pay the bill? I thought you wanted the cobbler."

"Kayti has her card. What happened?"

"I left." I leaned on the counter and drank my water. A nice headache was creeping up on me. I didn't want to fight. She didn't have to know I was upset.

"Because?" She slid her bag onto the counter and sidled up to me, taking my glass and placing it on the counter. The subtle bird pattern on her red satin blouse moved when she did, making the flock look as though it had taken flight.

"I had to manage something for Eva and didn't want to drag it into dinner. Everyone done with their alt-lit dissemination and social critiques?"

Shut up. Just put a fucking cork in it.

"The air went out of the balloon when you left."

Her hands under my jacket. Around me. Her lips on the line of my jaw. My bones were china and my muscles were stone. My lungs shrank to the size of fists. My dick was the only part of me aroused. The rest of me battled shame and rage.

With one hand, she slid my belt out of the loop. The other stroked me through my pants. "I thought you came home early to take me to bed."

Sure.

But no. I pushed her hand away.

"Zack didn't follow you out the door?"

She stepped back as if I were made of acid. "What?"

"The way you two look at each other—"

"I cannot even—"

"It makes me sick," I growled. I wanted to push her away. Wanted her to get the fuck out of my sight.

"He doesn't look at me, Adam. This jealousy is bizarre."

"Fuck he doesn't." I turned around and faced the sink. "And you."

"Me what?"

I rinsed the glass.

"Me what?!" She pushed me on the second word.

I put the glass in the rack. "You. That's all."

I pushed myself off the counter and walked to the door,

picked up my jacket, my keys, my fucking pride, and closed the door carefully behind me.

I paced the city for hours. When I got back, she was awake in bed, a book in her lap, under the cone of lamplight.

She closed the book. "Are you all right?"

On your knees. Hands behind your back. Right here.

"I'm fine. I'm just anxious. I don't—"

Open your mouth. Push the back of your tongue down so I can fuck your face.

"—I don't think you want Zack, but he looks at you like you're—"

You're so beautiful when you're tied down. I can control you with one finger.

"—a goddess, and it bothers me. Just fucking bothers me. I'm afraid to turn my back on that guy."

"He's not even on my radar." She said it as if I was out of my mind to even think she'd touch him.

I believed her. I always believed her, but I needed a cover story for what was really on my mind.

Submit to me, and I'll let you come.

Impossible fantasies. I held them down, tied them up, locked them away, only letting them breathe when I fucked her.

Submit to me, and you'll be happy.

I never thought of trotting them out, because then she'd know I was a monster.

Submit to me, and we will rule the world.

I'd die not telling her.

Chapter 52

PRESENT TENSE – DAY FOUR

Diana was getting more comfortable, and I was getting further away. After telling her what had happened with Serena, I'd locked myself off. I told her where to put her hands and legs. I gave her easy tasks to execute. I put my fingers in her mouth and corrected her posture. But I didn't have the space in my heart for more intensity. She knew about me. She knew what I'd done. She knew how ashamed I was.

I'd locked myself off before, but this time I knew I was doing it. You might call that progress.

I'd just gotten in the door after my run. Diana was sitting on the steps with her hands folded on her lap. She wore a short black dress that had been in the closet. Everything in the house made her body accessible, and this was no different. She pressed her knees together, but I could see the lace between her legs.

"What are you doing?" I asked.

"Waiting for you. I wanted to talk."

"About?" I leaned on the door and pulled the bow of my wet laces apart.

She watched me, weaving and unweaving her fingers as I worked my laces.

"We haven't gone this long without sex since the first time," she said.

"But who's counting?" I slipped off my right sneaker and worked on the left.

"Do you wanna?" She picked up her skirt, showing me the lace garter she'd put on for my benefit. She'd shaved herself smooth, and she crossed her legs just enough to hide herself.

I dropped my other shoe. "When I want your body, I'll take it."

A flash of rage rippled across her face. She didn't get the game. She didn't intuit the right way to act, and she didn't want to be there.

I was sweaty and loose, faced with an expanse of skin and a cunt hidden between crossed legs. My dick stretched my pants and begged for release.

She started to lower her skirt. I took the hem and I took one of her wrists and lifted it again.

I tapped her toe with mine. "Open your legs."

She did it. A saucy arousal replaced the flash of rage.

"Why do you think I haven't fucked you?"

"What you told me the other night," she said, and my back and arms went rigid. "I think you're worried that I'm—"

"Wrong," I shut her down. I didn't want to hear what she thought I thought she thought.

Ridiculous. She had no fucking idea what I thought. She had no idea what I was worried about, and as a sub, it wasn't her goddamn business. I shouldn't have told her. Part of me had wanted to drive her away by telling her about Serena's first time, but part of me couldn't bear the loss of hope.

"Hands on the bannister," I said. "Bend at the waist. Ass up."

Puzzled, she dropped her skirt.

The bottom step had a winding wood pole at the base that connected to a slightly flourished handrail. When I didn't change my instruction or add to it, she turned slowly and did exactly what I told her. She put her hands on it.

The anger that had started to spin inside me quieted. Not

because she did it right. She didn't. She could have been steering a bus. But I was slipping into a place where I was in control.

I put my hands on her waist and pulled her back until her arms were stretched. Kicked her legs open. Pressed her lower back down until her ass was up and the skirt slipped away enough to show me the snaps on the crotch of her underwear.

"So," I said. "You want to fuck?"

"Yes."

"Are you getting yourself off at night?"

"It's not satisfying. Not all the way."

I flipped her skirt over her ass and pulled her damp panties to the side. My God. That cunt. So beautiful. I could smell the bouquet of her sex.

"Show me what you do," I said. When she took too long, I egged her on. "Come on. Let me see."

Her hand left the bannister and crept between her legs. "Can I say something first?"

I went around her until we were face to face. "Yes."

Her eyes were huge and clear. Her lips enunciated each syllable, letting them roll around her mouth as if they were surprisingly delicious. "You are filthy."

She wasn't disgusted. She was turned on. And she didn't take a second to wait for me to react to her comment. Her eyelids fluttered. Her lips parted. Her cheeks flushed. I'd intended to watch her fingers move over her cunt, but her expression was everything. It was complete submission to desire.

I bent to get close to her face.

"Look at me," I whispered. She opened her eyes, grimaced, loosened. "I haven't taken you yet because the next time I do, you're going to submit to me. After that, you're going to compare every man who fucks you to that one time, that first time I owned you. Every guy you bring home for a night. Every man you date. Every one you think might be more than a fling. You're going to compare every fuck to that first time you submitted completely, and every one of them is going to come up short."

Her breath got shallower and her body jerked below the waist. Her fingers gripped the bannister.

"You have to be ready. You have to earn it. I have to be sure I want to give it to you." I took her chin. "Look at me. Eyes open. Good."

A crackling sound came from her throat. I knew her so well. We'd cut our bodies into matching shapes for years. She was going to come. Having her jaw in my hands, I couldn't resist. Not another second. I kissed her while she moaned her orgasm into my mouth. I used my tongue to seek out the taste of her soul. The corners and crevices of her body, the hard and soft, slick and rough, feeling her throat vibrate with the last of her release.

She knew me. She knew the ravaging of Serena ate me from the inside. She knew telling her about it was why I'd shut down, even if I'd told myself another story.

I pulled away a few inches, leaving my spit on her face and my taste on her lips. I had another few weeks with those lips. I could enjoy them as much as I wanted and choose not to worry about our future.

"And yes," I said. "You're right. It was about what I did the last time I was here."

She stood up straight. Her skirt dropped and her right hand was shiny and wet. "Why couldn't you just say that?"

I took her by the right wrist and put her finger to my lips. I sucked it clean, tasting her. She had the same look of awed arousal as she'd had when she told me I was filthy. I dropped her wrist.

"Come to breakfast," I said. "Let's just sit."

I walked across the house to the breakfast table. She padded after me, washed her hands, and sat with me. The hot dishes were already out. Coffee made. Settings laid out. I put eggs and potatoes on her plate.

"Eat," I said.

My wife could pack it away. She'd eat a man out of house and home, but she took a smidgeon of egg and put it on a single sliver of toast.

"That's it?" I asked when she sat.

"Yeah, why?"

Normally, I'd shrug and say, "Nothing," but I wasn't feeling normal. I was feeling like a man who knew a woman better than he had the right to, and I was feeling the need to take care of her. "Because it's breakfast and you're always starving in the morning."

She shrugged and pushed her eggs around.

"That was fun," she said without an ounce of fun in her voice.

"If you're miserable," I said, "just say it."

"I haven't said it."

She had said it. She'd said it in writing and to my face. I'd believed her but hadn't understood it until the breakfast table in Montauk. I hadn't seen the depths of her sadness until that morning, when I told her to finger herself but didn't fuck her.

"You have." I put milk in my coffee to give myself a second to think, but it was too long for her.

"I don't know what to do. I kept hoping these past few months that if I dropped enough hints, you'd catch on and say, 'Yeah, I want out of this marriage,' but you never did. And I thought a clean break would be best. Then this…" She drew her hand over the scene we'd found ourselves in. "I came here because of McNeill-Barnes. I admit it. But a part of me thought if I came, the breakup would be easier for you. I figured, 'How bad could it be?'"

"Has it been bad?"

"No. Not really. I see…" She stopped herself, looked out at the ocean. "I see the appeal. You kissed me back there and…" She put a chunk of eggs in her mouth, eyebrows knotted as if looking for a word. "You haven't kissed me like that in all five years. I mean, ever. And then I think of all the times you seemed so far away. The time we took a vacation in Ojai. We talked about work the whole time, and when we were in bed together, it wasn't… something was off. Were you here? In this house?"

"Yes."

She nodded into her lap. "Were you with someone else? In your mind?"

"Yes."

She blinked. A tear fell. Then another. I hated hurting her, but I couldn't lie. We were past that.

"It couldn't be you," I said. "Do you understand that?"

"I do. I really do. You told me that story, and everything clicked into place. You love me. But why? Because we're a great team and I'm never going to ask you to rape me? I'm safe. You can take that side of yourself and pretend it doesn't exist. Put it where it can't hurt you. But all that time, it's beating down the doors to get out, and it ate at us. It ate us alive. Adam, there is no *us*. There never was an *us*. I loved a man who didn't exist, and you loved me because I wasn't in your world."

She covered her face with her napkin, and I was glad. I didn't want her to read me. This whole project was a mistake. If I hadn't been sure about it before, I was sure now.

But I didn't know how to give up. Even as I told myself I'd had no business bringing her to Montauk, I told myself there must be a way to get her back.

Diana wasn't a blubberer, but she was sobbing quietly into her napkin. I got up and put my hands on her shoulders. She pushed me away.

"Stop it," I said. "We're going through this together."

"No, we're not. I've never lied to you. I loved you honestly."

She wrenched herself out of her chair, standing and running away at the same time. I caught her three steps away and yanked her to me.

"Let go!"

"No. Listen."

"I don't want to listen." Her face and mouth were painted with spit and tears. I'd pushed her, and now I'd gotten exactly what I'd asked for. The truth. "I'm sorry you did that to her, and I'm sorry she liked it. I'm sorry you felt like shit about it. I would have been there for you. If you'd just trusted me, I would have been there for you."

I couldn't bear it. She was right. Every word was right. I'd asked her for trust I'd never given her. Instead of letting her go, I pulled her closer, trapping her in the circle of my arms. I knew it was the last time I would. I knew that once we left the kitchen, we would change.

I was the architect of this marriage and divorce. I was the catalyst. All she'd done was what I'd pushed her to do, then she took the blame for it.

"It's easy to say now you would have been there for me." I squeezed her shoulders.

"I would have."

Monday morning quarterbacking. Pure bullshit, but she believed it, and that was the important part.

"When I'm sleeping next to you, some nights, do you touch yourself?" I asked.

"Yes," she exhaled.

"I know," I said softly into her ear. "I'm not always sleeping. I feel you move the tips of your fingers. I feel you trying to stay still. I feel your muscles tighten."

She swallowed hard.

"I didn't give you what you need. That changes today. I know you throb for it. I know you need it. Let me tell you something, my wife. For the next twenty-six days, I own every single one of your orgasms. If I don't take your pleasure, you don't have any."

She touched my fingers, and I put her hand back in her lap.

"Can I tell you something?" she asked.

"Yes."

"You're really sexy when you're bossy."

"Now you tell me."

Her shoulders hitched with a silent laugh.

"Tonight, we'll reconvene." I kissed the back of her neck, taking in her scent of orchids and oranges.

"I need to go for a walk," she said. "Alone, if you don't mind."

"The general store is open from ten until two. Don't take the shortcut."

She stood. "Tonight then."

"Seven sharp. Winter clothes are in the closet, in the drawers."

She took a step then stopped herself. "Tonight?"

"Yes?"

"I'm looking forward to it."

She skipped away, and I stood in shock.

Chapter 53

PRESENT TENSE – DAY FOUR

Diana knew how to get to the general store since there were no turns, but I followed her anyway. The town was dead in winter. Year-round residents were known for hunting and drinking. I was a city boy, and I didn't trust the miles and miles of desolation and empty houses.

She trudged along on the side of the two-lane blacktop, head down with a Manhattan tempo. As if she had a meeting to get to or a train to catch. Storm clouds gathered over the horizon, dark grey eating the lighter grey. It would be light and charming. A little snow cover adding to the romance.

She stopped at the underpass, looked at where I'd taken Serena five years before.

What did she think? What was on her mind? Did she really hate me for lying about it, or was the act itself repellent? Maybe both?

She was stepping away from the fence and the icy stream when a truck pulled up. I heard the crackle and roar of it before I saw it. Stefan's truck. I chided myself for thinking he would stop, then I was surprised when he did.

That motherfucker.

He was talking to her.

I couldn't make out what they were saying past the treeline, but she laughed at something he said. Some other shit came out of his mouth and I saw in his rearview mirror that he was smiling. Entertaining her. Charming her.

Oh, fuck this.

Fuck no.

I stomped across the street. As if he could sense my decision, Stefan said good-bye and drove away. I was left exposed in the middle of the road, no truck to block my stalking from Diana's view.

"What are you doing?" she called.

"Following you. It's not safe."

"Then why did you let me go alone?"

"You wanted to. Listen. This is…" I looked down the road. He was a speck in the distance. "Don't talk to him. That's all."

"Why?"

"Because I said so."

She jammed her hands in her pockets, looked toward the general store, then back to the house. Didn't move.

"What?" I asked.

"Either you let me in or you don't. Either you tell me about this other life or you shut me out. You can't have it both ways."

"And if I let you in? Then what? Miraculous healing and a joyful marriage? Is that what you're promising?"

Her breath came out in a long cloud of contradictions. In and out. Desire and repulsion. Thoughts and feelings. Yes and no.

I didn't want the answer. Both would hurt.

No, I don't want our marriage.

Yes, I do want it.

One was a knife, the other was a hope I didn't trust would outlast her curiosity.

"Come on," I said, leaning toward the store. "I have to get gas for the generator. The power always goes out when there's a storm."

"I'm just going to go back, I think."

I let her think she was walking back alone, but I followed to make sure she was all right.

Chapter 54

PRESENT TENSE - DAY FOUR

I caught Stefan outside the studio. I had intended to be easygoing but firm with him, and instead I fucking lost my shit. "Stay away from my wife."

"Whoa, there."

"Don't talk to her," I continued. "Don't smile at her. Don't try to do the Scandinavian charm shit."

"I was offering her a ride."

"Stay. Away."

"You forgot. Five years and you forgot that we look out for each other and our subs. We are a village. That's why you go to Serena to check on her and I'm not in your face. I'm grateful. I know you'll make sure she's okay."

Trust this asshole to play the community card and be the bigger man all in a few sentences. I didn't want her near this logic. This was the exact logic that led to sharing subs, to pushing their pain, to situations that could only be rectified with bullshit contracts.

I didn't want this for her. I didn't want it for us.

"It's not going to matter," I said. "I'm sending her home."

"When?"

"Tomorrow."

"I can take her if the truck's ready."

"What's wrong with it?"

"The radiator. That was what I was telling your wife. I'd give her a lift back to the house or as far as the truck would make it. Not far actually, but far enough."

That was why she was laughing. They were joking about the truck. But he was still trying to charm her, and I was still sure he wanted to fuck her.

There was no way she was getting in a car with him all the way to the city. Stefan was good. Very good. The thought of anyone with Diana boiled my blood. The thought of Stefan with her added fear to the rage.

"I'll have Thierry take her tomorrow."

He shrugged. It was a little too fine with him. His smile was shot through with cockiness, as if all my avoidance was useless.

The air was cold and dead calm. The sky was flat cirrus with crystal blue holes. Pre-snow weather. I had to go back to the house and tell Diana she was leaving, and she was going to ask why.

I wasn't going to lie. I was done with lies.

She was in the library with a book, bare feet tucked under her. The diffused light from the window caught on her stray hair.

"Hi," I said when I came in. She faced me. "What are you reading?"

"Steinbeck, of all things."

"Really?" I sat on the arm of the couch next to her.

"I was looking in the stacks, wondering if things would have been different if I'd changed my name. Would it have been harder to leave you? Was I not really committed? And then I came upon this." She held the cover up long enough for me to see *Travels with Charley*.

"'A journey is like marriage,'" I quoted. "'The certain way to be wrong is to think you can control it.'"

"He was married three times." She closed the book.

"That doesn't make him wrong. So." I bent my head forward, putting my hands on my knees. I couldn't face her when I said it.

When I looked at her, I wanted her. I needed to be stronger than my desire. Tougher than my love. "You should go home."

"What?" Was she just surprised? Or was there a tinge of disappointment? And was the disappointment over an easy handoff of the company? Or the fact that I was giving up? "Why?"

"I feel better. I feel like we cleared a lot of air between us."

She seemed pensive. I could guess her next questions. Would she still have an easy out for McNeill-Barnes? Was I going to work with her? Did she still get the loft? But none of those questions came.

"Thank you, I…" She caught herself. "When are we going?"

"You. You're going. Thierry will take you tomorrow."

Her head shook slightly as if she was thinking "no" but didn't want to say it. "You're quitting? It hasn't even been a week. And you're staying and I'm going?"

"I need time, Diana."

She crossed her arms and thought for what seemed like a long time.

"Speak," I said.

"I'm leaving tomorrow. Stefan's leaving on Friday. You're staying. And this means you're in the house alone with her?" She jerked her thumb in the general direction of the studio.

"Yes."

"Yeah. No." She stood, clapped her hands as if getting dust off them, snapped up the book, and tapped it on the heel of her hand.

"Yeah, no what?"

"This woman fucked with you so badly you married someone totally wrong for you. She did a number on you. And now, look, I'm not trying to tell you how you feel, but you're vulnerable. I know what me asking for a divorce has done to you even if you don't show it. You're an open wound. Still handsome as hell, but hurting. You're primed to get involved with her again, and she's going to drag you right back where you were." She slapped the book back into its place. "So no. I'll go back with you when you're ready to go back."

I didn't know what my expression revealed. Shock. Disbelief.

Denial. Insult. I didn't try to hide any one reaction because they all came up at the same time with equal measure.

"Wait." I held up my hand. "Are you jealous?"

"No. Of course not."

"You want to stay and make sure I don't sleep with her."

"For your own good."

"For my own good?" I added frustration to the list of emotions. How did I lose control of another conversation?

"I'm not trying to emasculate you," she said without a hint of irony.

Impossible. She was impossible. Was she always such a pain in the ass?

"Thanks for that. You're a fucking gem. I brought you here and you don't fit. You don't want to be here. You have no interest in helping me get my footing, and honestly, I don't blame you. I've never felt as completely fucked in the head about making a deal as I do with this one." I put my hands on the arms of the chair and leaned into her. I needed to take up her entire field of vision. "You know me. I see things through to the bitter end. This is the first thing in my life I've wanted to quit. Can't you respect that?"

"I'm staying."

She was staying to torment me. To expose all my raw nerves. To drag this boneless half-dead shit out into the street.

Well, torment worked both ways.

"Stay. But it's your choice to be in my house. The contract stands. You're my sub. You will kneel when I say kneel and bend when I say bend. Your body is built for me to fuck anywhere I can fit my cock. You have no pleasure I don't allow and it comes with pain. Do you understand?"

I designed the speech to scare her away.

Instead, she swallowed hard and said one word. "Fine."

"See you at seven."

Chapter 55

PAST PERFECT

Reservations at Metropolis were about as hard to come by as a virgin in a whorehouse, a parking spot in midtown, an honest banker—pick your analogy.

Our production director, Georgette, had managed to get us a table for the three-year anniversary of the McNeill-Barnes reboot.

I'd started the evening lighthearted at the round table of eight. Me, Diana, Georgette and her husband, Lloyd, Zack, Kayti. We had a lot to be grateful for. The company wasn't just treading water. It was swimming with the sharks because of what Diana and I had done. She sat across from me in a bright red satin blouse with a subtle bird pattern. When she moved, the birds took flight. I couldn't stop looking at her, seeing how those birds would look with her on her knees.

We were a few bottles of wine into the meal, laughing too loudly and complaining too good-heartedly about the dire fate of publishing. How good books got buried and shit sold like hotcakes to starving men.

"Case in point," Zack said, pouring another glass. "The Books That Shall Not Be Named."

"Glorification of abuse," Georgette slurred.

Zack tried to top up my glass, but I put my hand over it.

"Do you know what my wife would do if I told her to get on her knees and suck my dick?" Georgette's husband—Nick? Ned?—jerked his thumb at his wife.

"Give you five bucks for a hooker?" she said, and the table went wild with laughter.

I tried to smile.

Kayti held up her hand. "I read them!" Everyone went *ooh* and *aah*. "Hot. They were hot." She fanned herself with her napkin.

"How is getting spanked arousing?" Georgette asked as if she were a reporter on a crime scene.

"Because he's looking at your butt and you know… the other stuff. You're totally vulnerable. It's you and this guy and you can't see him. The tension of it. The anticipation. And the sting is more like… it sensitizes everything. I can *feel* more." She turned red and sat back in her chair. Put her glass near her lips. "Frank and I did a little experimenting."

The discomfort was broken by laughter and chatter about the Books That Shall Not Be Named.

"He was a stalker."

"Creepy."

"Barely consensual."

"But why?" Diana spoke for the first time since the conversation started. "Why read about that? Why invite it into your mind? We've spent a hundred years fighting for equality, and we still get paid less than men. Now we're supposed to let them beat us in the bedroom? How are we supposed to progress when we're saying abuse—literal physical abuse—is a turn-on? Not just acceptable, but desirable?"

Was she asking the table or asking herself?

I didn't know what I expected out of my marriage. I wanted her to bend for me, and I was terrified she might. I wanted to welt her skin and make her scream and beg. I wanted her to want to please me, to give me her body and soul.

If she did let me take all of her, I'd do what I did with every other sub I'd known. I'd throw her away. I loved her too much for that.

But even as I understood that truth, I couldn't let her comment go unanswered.

I leaned toward her with the full force of my intention. I needed her to hear me. Needed her to know that even if I wasn't going to ever tell her why the discussion was personal to me, she was going to know I believed what I said.

"You don't realize this because you're married to me, but most women don't have satisfying sex lives." I must have managed to keep the disappointment out of my face, because most everyone at the table laughed and hooted. "For most women, the fantasy that your husband might actually care about your pleasure is unfortunately just that. A fantasy. So given a novel about a man who loves you, wants you, would give up everything for you... and on top of it pays attention to your needs above his own? I think a little spanking under those circumstances might be a turn-on."

"Now bend over!" Georgette's husband cried, and everyone bellowed except me and Diana.

We were locked over the distance of the table. She had a response. She was waiting until everyone quieted down.

I didn't want to hear it. Couldn't. I didn't know if I'd hate my wife or myself more.

Pretending I had a phone call, I excused myself from the table. I caught a cab and went home.

Chapter 56

PRESENT TENSE – DAY FOUR

"Hello?"

Her voice came from behind me just after seven o'clock. In the window, I could see the studio lights go on and Diana's reflection from the doorway.

"You're not on your knees," I said without turning around.

"I just wanted to know if I should make us dinner."

I hadn't even eaten lunch, but I didn't answer. I wouldn't until she did what she was supposed to do. The whole scene was getting turned up ten notches. She had to go. She had to beg me to get out of the house.

"Adam?"

"Third time you used my name." I typed complete gibberish into the laptop at a thousand miles a minute. "Now you can take off your clothes and get on your knees. Delay again and you're going to be crying before I even get out of this chair."

Again, she surprised me.

She dropped to her knees without a word, holding up her red journal with a page marked with a ribbon.

I spun in my chair. She hadn't undressed and I should mention that, but I couldn't take my eyes off her bowed head. "You want me to read something in here?"

"Yes."

I took the book and ran my finger along the edges of the pages, opening it. I flipped through dozens of sheets full of questions and landed where the ribbon was marked. There was only one question printed in the center of the page.

What if I like it?

I closed the book. Rapped the soft cover over my knuckles. Fast. The same speed as my heart. She was open to this. Not just as a sacrifice or a kindness, but as a path to her own self-discovery.

Some new hormone pumped through my veins. As powerful as adrenaline without the fight or flight. More with the power of "embrace and accept." A tingling desire to run into this particular trouble. Anticipation cling-wrapped tightly and ready to bust.

And still, I wanted her to go. And stay. And go. Make this so hard she'd run like she always did.

I closed the book. "Take off your clothes. Don't do a strip tease. Just get down to your skin."

I sat back down with my back to her and pretended to work. My fingers shook. My heart felt like an alarm going off. I'd filled her closet with things that were easy for me to remove, and lingerie with straps and hooks. She pulled the T-shirt over her head. Slipped out of her bra. Slipped off the skirt.

"Leave the garter," I said with my back to her.

She stopped and stood, straight and nearly naked. I twisted around. Only then did she remember to get on her knees.

Now what?

Make her want to leave.

I shut the laptop and got in front of her. "Hands behind your back."

She did it, big broken-glass eyes turned to mine. Lashes black as a lie. Lips round and full with a knife of an opening between top and bottom.

Run away, huntress.

I was hard, and my cock was one inch and two layers of fabric from those lips.

She looked up at me and opened her mouth. She was doing what she thought I expected. Wanted. Needed. And she was right. She was giving me the gift of her submission as much as she knew how. Tonight. Now. Maybe this was the last of it. I didn't care.

A shot of gratitude cracked my frustration, disassembling the pieces of it and building a foundation for the authority I needed.

Deliberately, with a purpose to every movement, I unbuckled my belt, undid my pants, and took out my cock. I put it against her bottom lip. Her tongue flicked out, catching the place where the head met the shaft. She reached for it. I grabbed her wrist.

"Open your mouth."

She parted her lips then opened a little more.

I took her jaw roughly, pressing in her cheeks. "What's your name?"

"Diana," she said around my fingers.

I stroked my cock, putting the tip on her lower lips but not entering her. I'd been pent up for days, so it didn't take long for me to shoot my orgasm into her mouth.

Her eyes were shut tight and her nose was wrinkled.

"Swallow."

She shook her head.

"Do it."

She closed her mouth and swallowed. I brushed my thumb on her chin, collecting the last white drop. I put my thumb in her mouth. After a pause, she sucked it clean. Fuck, she was hot. Even in her resistance she was hot. I was about to get hard again.

"Now," I said, buttoning my pants. "Go over to the couch and bend over it from the waist."

She started to speak, but I put my finger over my lips. I didn't want her to say anything. She wouldn't last another day, and I wanted to enjoy every moment before she stormed out.

She stood and went to the end of the couch then bent at the waist.

I kicked her legs open. What a sight. What a beautiful sight. I'd been fucking that cunt for five years and I never appreciated how gorgeous it was.

I took her left hand and put it on her ass. "Open it. Spread out for me so I can see my options."

"Wait—"

"Hush." I took her other hand and put it behind her, using her fingers to spread her ass and thighs apart. Beautiful. Pink and glistening. "I'm going to ask before I check. Are you wet?"

"Yes."

Without prelude, I put two fingers in her.

Yeah. Wet.

"Do you want to come?"

"Yes."

"Yes, what? Is that how you were raised?"

"Yes, please."

I ran my finger along her seam. "When did you get wet? When I came? When you got undressed?"

A third finger disappeared inside her. She groaned and pushed against me.

"When you stood in front of me."

The moment I stood in front of her was the moment I exerted physical dominance. I hadn't expected that answer and I had to hide my surprise by stroking her clit.

I was incapable of loving a submissive. Or was I?

I'd gotten behind her intending to make her come then take her ass for a long, long time. I'd intended to turn her desire to please me against her. I knew if I took that tight, virgin hole, she'd leave. I'd kill all the beauty of her acceptance and turn her against it.

With all four of my fingers pressed on her, she moved her hips with me as I rubbed, then flicked, then rubbed her hard clit until she raised her ass and buried her head in the cushions. I slowed down, extending her orgasm until it drained her.

My fingers were soaked. I could lube her ass with her own juices and fuck it until she begged to go home. My cock was ready.

I put my wet finger against her asshole, pressing just enough. She clamped down.

"Please," she said softly. "I know I didn't cross it off…"

"Hush."

I circled my finger around it. I could do it with only a little pain. Her hurt would be only emotional, and she'd go home.

"What would you do if I insisted?" I asked, gathering more lubrication and drawing it back up.

"I don't know."

One finger. Pressure. Circles. Pressure. Circles. She loosened up.

"Would you leave?"

"Yes," she said as I put more pressure on her ass. "No. Maybe. I…" She didn't finish.

"What?"

"I trust you."

I thought she'd reveal some core dishonesty with herself or me, but she only ever spoke the truth as she saw it, even if one of us was hurt by it. Maybe it was about time one of us was honest.

I pushed inside, sliding against her own juice. One finger, all the way in.

Every woman has a vowel. Diana's was O. The sound came in a long moan, beginning when my finger entered her and continuing until I couldn't go any farther.

My cock throbbed.

"Do you trust me?" I said, pulling out the finger.

"Yes but—"

Two fingers, all the way in.

She bucked. I took a fistful of her hair and pulled her head back so she could see me.

"If you trust me, there's no but."

"Okay. Yes."

"How does this feel? When you stop worrying about it, how does it feel?"

230

A smile teased her mouth. "Good, actually."

Diana had arrived. She was still bratty and demanding. She was still barely a novice, but something in her bones had submitted, and the rest of her body liked it. I hadn't expected that, yet I knew it would happen. I held one reality in each hand and balanced the contradiction. Now to balance her and keep her off balance at the same time.

This, I could do. This was my game.

Fuck Stefan, we were staying.

I kissed her lower back and took my fingers out of her. "Let's wash up and eat something, huntress."

We ate dinner, listened to the radio, breathed the same air until bed. I pulled the covers over her and kissed her cheek.

"Stay," she whispered, eyes drifting closed.

"Not tonight. Sleep well. You're going to need it."

I planned the rest of the week in my mind, running through the days and hours.

The only things that could interrupt were work and the pair in the studio. Another week of slight contact. Comfort. Building trust. She said she trusted me, but she didn't even know what that meant.

I had something to do besides feel sorry for myself. Diana's submission was my distraction from Diana's betrayal.

The windows shook with the wind with a *tick tick tick* of driving snow and the sky glowed the flat orange of snowy nights.

I wanted her to go.

I wanted her to stay.

I wanted her on my terms.

I wanted her on any terms.

I wanted to be cured of the disease of love.

I wanted to be cured of want.

Diana

Chapter 57

PRESENT TENSE – DAY SEVEN

How long has it been?

A week. He hadn't slept next to me. He hadn't put his dick inside me.

Is that true?

We hadn't had intercourse, and night seven would be no different.

What is he trying to prove? That I want him?

I did and I didn't.

Am I a monster?

I asked my journal questions, but they were beside the point. I knew what he was doing. Keeping me off balance. Making me pay attention. Showing me his attention.

Adam was gone, the storm beat the windows, and I could still taste the flat bite of his come on the back of my tongue. He'd just taken my mouth as if he owned it, instructing me how to please him.

Instead of being irritated, I was grateful. If you're going to give a man a blow job, it should please him.

Doesn't he wonder if I'll use the skill on another man?

I'd expressed myself in questions since a journaling class in college. It felt less like talking into a void and more demanding the void to fill itself. It also kept me from getting lazy. I may have known the answers, but posing questions meant I never took them for granted.

What do you want? Do you want him?

Him, no. Still no. His body? The one he'd barely used to touch me? The one that hadn't fucked me since Manhattan? Only delivered orgasms that were powerful, but somehow left me wanting him more?

Even when we sat together, talking about McNeill-Barnes, I wanted him. Even when we signed payroll checks across the table, the tension in his fingers as he held the pen, the veins in the tops of his hands, the way they moved in and out of me…

What do you feel?

I still felt like a monster. I wasn't some careless, unfeeling, heartless bitch, but if you asked me, "Are you a good person?" I'd say I wasn't.

I'd married young because I fell in love young. I married a man with a strong jaw and a heart shaped for me to fit inside. I couldn't resist him, and I admit, in the back of my mind, I thought, "You're young. If you have to bail, you bail and your life won't be over."

So maybe I was a monster.

He just got so far away. I called for him and his body came to me. He showed up physically. But the *him* inside? He was elsewhere.

I shouldn't pretend I understood him, or me, or why I married him besides the fact that I loved him. I loved him so much that when I stopped loving him, it was as if I'd lost an arm or a leg. Not loving him hurt me. I didn't leave to find someone else. I left because he was there, every day, reminding me I'd lost something I cherished. I could deal with the hole in my life if he wasn't there at the edge saying, "Look at this hole, how deep it is, how wide, how empty. Look how our hearts fit into it so well."

I carried guilt and shame. I couldn't even face him because he didn't see the hole. He didn't think it was a hole. He thought it was… I didn't know what he thought it was. He didn't even see it as a hole. He didn't see it at all. He just created it.

I needed out. I only feared the divorce. I was a bad finisher. I was afraid that if he dragged it on, I'd cave and give up anything worth having.

He'd offered the impossible. A cheap ride. An abrupt fall into the heart-shaped hole. I'd heal sooner, start almost immediately the life I didn't know how to imagine and I wouldn't have to risk much more than a month.

I'd have to have sex with him. Probably a lot of sex. I could do that. I wouldn't have married him if I didn't enjoy his body. But I didn't want him to take me to Montauk as a strategy to get me back. I wanted to be clear with him that if he was trying to get me to love him again, he should rescind the offer.

I must have looked like the biggest bitch in town, but I was already hurting him. If I made it worse by being dishonest, I wouldn't be able to live with myself.

Is that what it means to say, "I care about you, but I don't love you"? Is it another way of saying, "I don't love you, but hurting you makes me feel shitty about myself"?

Why do you turn everything back around on yourself?

My therapist, Regina, always tried to boost me without blaming, but when I told her about the club, she spun it fearlessly.

"Maybe you knew," she'd said with a glint of satisfaction, as if Adam's admissions were her victories. "Maybe you always knew he wasn't what he said he was."

I never told her I'd had an orgasm when he spanked me, or that, at the Cellar, the paddling on the other side of the glass turned me on. I denied it to her. I said it was disgusting. I said, with real conviction, that it undid decades of women's progress and legalized domestic abuse.

Once I decided to join my liar of a husband in a house he'd never told me he owned, I couldn't face her.

I told myself it all happened too fast, but I'd canceled our last appointment before the trip, telling her I was taking a vacation.

The fact was, I didn't want to tell her about the offer. I didn't want to tell her I was curious and that I trusted my husband. He'd lied. He'd kept the house and a huge chunk of his past from me. He'd pretended to be a different man than he was, and I couldn't ever forgive him for that. If there had ever been a chance we'd get back together, his lies ruined it.

But I trusted him with my body.

Crazy.

I was crazy.

You ever going to grow up?

I put my hand flat on the paper, covering all the questions. I usually asked about the world around me, but the past few month's entries were filled with questions about who I was and what I wanted. I had four pages that asked only one question.

What do you want?

The previous night. In the kitchen. On my knees in the middle of the room with nothing but the gauzy nightgown covering my hard nipples. Out the window, ocean made an eternal meal of the shore.

His feet came toward me. He was fully clothed and I was practically naked. He stood so close I could smell his cologne and the dry cleaner's softener on his suit. His erection stretched his pants. It was right in front of me like a loaded gun.

Why did it turn me on? Wasn't he just standing still?

But so close and for so long. The anticipation. The unknown. I stopped writing when I came to the part where he took out his cock. I'd always admired it, but it wasn't just my husband's penis. It was an instrument of domination.

My domination.

My pussy swelled remembering it and I stopped writing, laying my hand on the page like a starfish. He hadn't let me touch him last night. My hands had been behind my back, each hand grabbing an elbow. After telling me how to please him, how to push the back of my tongue down, how to open my mouth and not close my lips around him, how to take it instead of give it, he came down my throat.

Do you want him to use you? Insult you? Do you want to give up control of what your body's used for?

When I thought of it that way, that he used my mouth to come in, I was mad. Sure. I was better than that, but my god… I was turned on.

What do you want?

Chapter 58

PAST PERFECT

After my mother died, I thought my father would leave their Park Avenue co-op. It was too expensive and too big. Every scrap of wallpaper, every deeply-hidden dust bunny, every swatch of fabric on the upholstery or drapes held a memory of her.

I'd fought with him, cajoled him, shaken my fist at him. He had to move. Start a new life. Instead, he got so depressed I had to leave college and run the business for six months, then forever.

But when Adam and I got rid of our baby because its life was going to consist of a few days of extraordinary pain, I was glad Dad still had the apartment. I needed familiarity. I'd left my first day back at work after two hours, saying I was going home. I didn't clarify where that was.

"What do you want?" Dad asked, turning off the heat on the whistling teapot.

"I want a normal baby. And I want to stop bleeding." I was hunched on a chair, hugging my knees. My tear ducts hurt because they wouldn't stop production for five freaking minutes. They'd been at it all damn day.

"No, I mean what kind of tea do you want?"

"Chamomile."

Dad got a box down from the cabinet. He'd put his oxygen back on when I arrived in tears. I knew I was stressing him out, but I didn't know what to do about it. I needed him.

"Did you call Adam?" he asked, pouring.

"He'll find me."

He would. Eventually. Once he took his head out of the ledgers. After he realized I wasn't at our SoHo place because we'd started talking about the baby on the couch, and sat on the balcony applying for school waiting lists, and named her while listening to the cars out the window. And because I wanted him to come and get me, dammit. I didn't know why and I didn't have to explain it. I needed him to ride in and scoop me up without me giving him instructions on what color the horse should be or how shiny his armor needed to be. He needed to figure it out.

"You should get checked," Dad said when he put my teacup on the table in front of me. "If you have the same thing your mother had."

"I don't. They tested me. Not yet."

He sat and pulled his oxygen tank close to the seat. "Then you can try again."

I nodded into the hot liquid. "I can."

Gilbert, Dad's helper/housekeeper/butler/whatever poked his head in from the back stairway.

"Mister Steinbeck," he said, and opened the door. Dad took his mask off. He hated looking weak in front of my husband.

Adam stood in the frame, looking at me. Disappointment? Pity? I was too blind with sadness to see what was on his mind. But his armor did shine, and his horse was a fine white stallion.

He scooped me up and took me to the couch, placing me on his lap while I cried. He told me it wasn't my fault. It wasn't meant to be. He said a lot of things that didn't mean anything.

The couch faced the window that overlooked Park Avenue. There was nothing out there. Just the building across the street, a polygonal-shaped night sky, a barely visible reflection of us on the couch. But he looked out it. Not at me. He shushed my tears away. And when his hand got tired of cupping my shoulder, he patted it absently, as if comforting a child who had dropped his ice cream.

I stopped crying.

He shushed.

He stared.

He patted my shoulder as if I were a puppy.

And that was the beginning of the end for me.

Chapter 59

PRESENT TENSE– DAY EIGHT

Stefan stood in front of the stove, where a teapot hissed. Serena sat on the counter in a sage-green polo and a skirt hiked up to her waist. The corners of the tea towel on the counter peeked from under her. Her legs were spread so wide, one rested on the edge of the sink, and the other on the kitchen island with another tea towel under her heel.

She had one hand behind her for balance. The other was between her legs.

I stopped short. I couldn't go in there.

They'd come back the previous night. The motion-sensor light had woken me up briefly.

"I think it's boiling," she said.

"It's not whistling, pet."

She squeaked. I saw the game. She couldn't come until the teapot whistled for no other reason than her Master said so. The scene was disturbing and probably the sexiest thing I'd ever witnessed. I took half a step back. I didn't want to disturb what was happening, but I couldn't walk away. The tension held me. I had to know if she made it. I wanted her to succeed.

"Let me turn it down," Stefan said playfully, turning the knob to lower the heat. He got two cups with excruciatingly slow movements and placed them on the counter.

"Please," she said. "I need to slow down."

"Don't be silly. You can hold it."

"I think the whistle is broken."

He pulled two teabags from a box and swung them into the cups. "It's not broken. Do you want the pekoe or the jasmine?"

"J-J-Ja—"

"Don't you dare come."

His voice was so firm and direct, I probably would have obeyed. The cups ready, he stood in front of her and watched her play with herself.

The teapot whistled.

Serena's head leaned on the cabinet and her ass came off the counter as she opened her mouth and came onto her hand. She didn't cry out or make a sound, but with her mouth open, it looked as though she screamed the sound of a teapot whistling.

When she put herself back on the tea towel, Stefan turned off the burner.

"I knew you could do it," he said, pouring the tea.

She hopped off the counter. "Thank you."

He looked at her with pride and warmth, placing the mugs on a little bamboo tray. "Wash your hands and meet me in the gym."

I stepped into the shadows when he walked out the back door.

"I saw you," Serena said, still rubbing her hands together under the tap. "Diana. It's not a big deal."

Shit. The crust of my shelter cracked and fell away. I was wet from what I'd seen and the object of my arousal could see right through to it.

I stepped into the kitchen. "I was rooting for you."

She shut off the water and dried her hands. "He makes it harder every time. Sometimes I come too soon on purpose."

"Why?"

"He punishes me." She flicked her hair behind her shoulder.

"How?"

She picked up her skirt a few inches. Horizontal welts healed over her soft flesh. She drew a finger over the length of one, then dropped the hem.

The night I came home from the Cellar, I attacked the internet for fifteen minutes before I freaked out and shut the laptop. I'd seen pictures of caning marks, and now, in front of me, was the real thing.

I'd thought a lot of things when I went to the Cellar and when I saw the pictures. My husband was part of that world, so I wanted to understand it. Instead I felt sorrow and anger. When I saw Adam after that, I added betrayal to the list. And with Serena right in front of me, I had to sweep it all away. I couldn't dismiss a living, breathing woman who clearly had her own will in the matter. I was curious.

"You don't get it," she said, half statement, half question.

"No, I don't get it. I wish I did."

She leaned on the counter and put her hands behind her on the edge. Was she getting more comfortable or ready to launch? "What don't you get?"

I didn't get myself. I didn't get why I'd let Adam use my mouth for a sperm receptacle, and I didn't understand why I liked it. "Pain. Punishment. Degradation."

She cocked her head to one side, puckered her bee-stung lips a little, paused as if deep in thought. "My mother wanted me to be a lawyer. She worked so hard. She had three kids and I was the 'smart one.' So I got to go to private school, and she had enough money to send one of us to college. That was me. I got to go. I got my own room so I could study. When I fucked up, she didn't yell at me or punish me. No. She'd say it was all right and she trusted me to fix that B-plus next semester or it wasn't a big deal about that dent in the car. But she'd get all pent up and on edge and she'd yell at one of my brothers for something stupid. I think she was scared of me."

She ran her finger along the edge of the counter, seeming pensive. "And when Mom got sick, it was all on me. I thought I'd break until I found Charlie. Have you met him? He has this old cane he uses?"

"Australian?"

She nodded.

"He came to our wedding."

"He was my first Dom. The first time he told me to bend over his desk and pull my pants down, I was so relieved. I knew I was going to do what he told me, no matter what. No matter how much it hurt. It was like I'd been chained up my whole life and I was free." She looked at me, letting her hand fall from the counter. "Do you get it now?"

She was so vulnerable, I didn't want to cut her down. I wanted to pull her up, but it was hard to pull up someone when you were being dragged down yourself.

"I don't know your parents. I don't even know you. But it sounds like a story you're telling yourself so you have a reason to let men hurt you."

A little smile curled her mouth, and she tried to hide it. "They say masochists and submissives have different brains. Our violence centers are entangled with our pleasure centers. If that's the case, then why deny it? I could be telling myself a story, sure. But if I was wired that way from the beginning, then the story is still true."

Did getting turned on when he spanked me or came on me mean I had a different brain?

"I've been with a few Dominants," Serena said. "Women and men. Your husband can deliver pain better than any of them."

He hadn't delivered pain. A few spankings and a little bondage. But it had been all about me doing what I was told. He'd been all about control the first week, and somehow, I thought that was going to be the last of it. I'd let myself forget the pain part.

"And Stefan?" I asked.

She dropped her voice to a breath. "We've been together a long time."

"Serena." Stefan's voice was taut and deep, making a paragraph-long statement in one word.

She fell to her knees, then her hands, putting her forehead to the tile and her ass up. I backed away.

"It was my fault," I said. "I was keeping her."

"Really," Stefan said with a grin, coming into the room. "I thought she was looking for an excuse to get punished." He put his foot on Serena's upturned ass and gave it a little push. "Is that true, pet?"

"It was my fault," she said to the floor as he rocked her back and forth with his foot.

"Was she entertaining you?" he asked me.

"We were talking. That's all."

"About what?"

His manner was subtly threatening. I didn't like it. The warning was deeply sexual, a promise of something he dared me to enjoy. His ego put me off more than the menace of his manner. It insulted Adam, and I couldn't call him on it because he didn't actually say anything I could pin down.

"She can tell you if she wants," I said with my head held high. "She's a big girl."

"She is. I was about to take her into the gym to reward her, but now I have to punish her."

Did the mention of punishment make Serena feel free from the kitchen floor? Were her chains unbound? The stress released? Had she really wanted to be punished?

"What are you going to do?"

He regarded his sub. "What do you think, pet? What should I do?"

"Whatever pleases you," she said.

"Why does it please you?" I interjected. I wished I hadn't asked, but my curiosity got the best of me.

"The world's a crazy place, Mrs. Steinbeck. Except when she's under me. She makes it sane. Right, pet?"

"Yes, Master."

"Come, then." He stepped back, giving Serena room to turn and crawl toward the door. Stefan bowed to me. "It's been a pleasure. Regards to your husband."

I was left alone in the kitchen, shaking.

That's what you do when you come face-to-face with your fears, and the fears draw you in like a warm cocoon lined with thorns.

Chapter 60

PRESENT TENSE - DAY TEN

*Where is Adam? What will he do today? How much do I love that mouth
of his?*

I froze writing the word love.

I never scratched out anything in my journals, but I scored a
big, dark i over the o.

The days and nights had passed pleasantly enough. I let him
order me around in bed and it was nice. We worked some days the
way we always did when we were away. There was very little work to
do actually, since we'd put a stay on all new business for thirty days.

> *D—*
>
> *The sales staff wants to know why they can't chase new accounts?
> Lloyd keeps talking about status quo? They're all saying you're
> getting a divorce and I'm like... no way. Right? That's crazy! Can
> I have the official word from you guys? They're making me nuts!!!*

Kayti's email had been sent at two in the morning. She'd be at
her desk in an hour, and I needed to answer it. We'd expected this to
happen and had prepared a statement. It was a noncommittal stall,
but it said enough to hush everyone for a couple of weeks.

Adam was outside, wearing a sweater against the cold, talking to Stefan.

I didn't want to bother him. That was what I told myself. I couldn't bother him with the fact that the prepared statement was two tons of horseshit. No matter how much I was enjoying this month, I couldn't go back to him. Not with the way he was. I couldn't love Manhattan Adam again, and Montauk Adam would be dead in two and a half weeks.

And fuck him for that.

> K—
>
> *We are getting divorced. It's amicable, but we need to work some things out. Don't panic. Don't tell anyone. Let the rumors be rumors for now. I'll be back in a few weeks.*

Adam and Stefan shook hands and parted.

I hit Send and shut the laptop.

Why are you hiding it?

Because telling Kayti we were splitting up wasn't up to me. It was up to *us* and I'd done it anyway.

The front door opened. Boots off.

He appeared in the office doorway with cold-bitten cheeks and ears. "Stefan's going to the city for a week. I'm going to help them load up."

• • •

I tried to help load the crates, but the men shooed me away, so Serena and I stood by the barn doors. Hot tea boiled on the stove. Adam had his sweater sleeves pushed up to the elbows so when he lifted his side of the crate, I saw his forearms tense and bulge.

"It's going to get cold in there with these doors open," I said.

Serena stomped snow off the fur of her high-heeled boots. "And the furnace has been acting weird. It's going to take forever to get warm tonight."

"You'll be in the city anyway."

"I'm staying here."

I didn't know what my expression said. Maybe it asked why, or showed a little shock I didn't feel. Maybe no matter what my expression said, her answer would be the same.

"For a whole week?"

"I had a very busy fall. I need the rest. The ocean. Manhattan stresses me. Besides, my Master said Adam would take care of me while he was gone."

Stefan slapped the back of the truck closed.

Maybe my eyes went wider because of gunshot sound and not because my spine turned to ice. Because when she said "take care," she said it with the lush depth of pictures and smells, and her expression— all fluttering eyes and bitten lip—implied more than a pat on the head. His hands on her. His lips. Her eyes looking up at him and his body pressed against hers, naked, loving, rough, and passionate.

Can't he do what he wants? Didn't you leave him?

I felt Adam near me more than saw him, because all I could see were Serena's eyes, the sex in them, the anticipated satisfaction. When his earthy scent mixed with her pleasured smile, I panicked.

I met up with Adam as he approached. "Kayti asked if we were getting divorced."

He cocked his head at my timing then nodded. "Did you give her the statement?"

"I told her."

"You told her what?" He raised an eyebrow.

"It's amicable. I told her it was amicable."

His face gave away nothing. Only the length of time it was frozen told me he was hiding his thoughts from me. I decided it wasn't a big deal. It was my news as much as his and if I wanted to tell my assistant, I could tell her.

That didn't wash, even in my own head.

Adam pulled his glove off one finger at a time. I couldn't tell how much of his expression was hurt and how much was anger. "That wasn't what we agreed."

"I know but—"

"Go to the truck. Put your hands on it."

Serena waved Stefan over. Said something in his ear.

"I told her not to tell anyone," I said defensively as the couple stood at the barn doors, watching.

Adam's voice didn't change. "Bend at the waist. Feet apart."

He slipped the glove off and started on the other. I didn't move. When the glove was off, he regarded me fully. Hours and days passed. I made no move to the truck.

"I wonder how many more times you'll betray our agreements." He put the gloves in his pocket. "One, we don't talk about the split until we know who the company is going to. It affects our relationships with vendors and buyers. Two, you do exactly what I tell you for thirty days or I treat you like an adversary."

A lump of culpability grew in my throat. If he wanted to make the divorce ten times more difficult, my impulsivity with Kayti had just made it ten times more possible. I looked like a liar unworthy of trust. I wouldn't be expected to fulfill the terms of any deal.

I glanced at Serena and Stefan, who were still watching.

"Put your hands on the truck. Bend at the waist. Feet apart."

I walked to the truck, heart pounding. Palms sweating even in the cold.

From behind me, he said, "Undo your fly. And don't spread your feet so far I can't pull your jeans down."

He was going to punish me.

He was going to punish me in front of people.

I was turned on and sickened at the same time.

Facing the truck, I wrestled my clothes for my fly. I felt them watching. Heard them step closer. My nipples got hard. My heart felt small and tight, constricting into itself. My breath came in sharp white clouds.

Adam came astride me. I couldn't look at him. My body had gone rigid with fear.

He let out a long breath.

"Go upstairs. Now."

I ran.

Chapter 61

PRESENT TENSE – DAY TEN

I made it upstairs, buttoning my fly on the way, and couldn't go into my room. I stood in the doorway and couldn't. Just couldn't.

Its plainness offended me. It's not-mineness. Nothing about it reflected me or my personality. It could be anyone's room.

The same could be said of the house. Not mine.

The same of my husband, whoever he was. Not mine. He wasn't even the man I'd married anymore. That guy had slowly faded into memory. I missed him and never wanted to see him again at the same time.

I sat in the hallway with my back against the wall between our two rooms. Adam came up the stairs a few minutes later with two mugs in one hand and a bowl in the other.

He put one of the cups by me and sat across the hall.

"You're an asshole," I said before he'd even settled in.

"Not going to argue."

"Am I in 'trouble' for not going in the room?" I didn't sound as sarcastic as I thought I would. The tea was warm and a deep amber. I sipped it. It was scalding hot and he'd sweetened it the way I liked.

Maybe he wasn't one hundred percent stranger. At least where tea was concerned.

"I said upstairs." He rooted around the bowl and came out with a walnut.

"Nuts? You brought a bowl of nuts?"

"We didn't have lunch, and they were all I could grab. Want one?"

"Sure."

He cracked the walnut between his palms, crushing it just enough to keep its shape while making the nut accessible. The sound reminded me of a time long ago when I was pregnant and he fed me walnut meat out of the shell.

"What happened out there?" I asked.

"I lost my shit."

He tossed me the cracked nut. I picked through it for the meat, leaving the shell pieces in a little pile beside me.

"Why did you stop?"

"Your face. You weren't ready. When I saw that, I knew I'd gone too far. Then I realized the thing I really owe you an apology for." He used a small hand cracker for a hazelnut. "Business is business. I think telling Kayti was incredibly stupid, but it's business. Tanning your ass for it would have been a mixed message."

The last compartment of the nut was trapped behind a sheet of shell. I broke it and picked out the last of the meat. I really was hungry. "Can you break me another?"

He sifted through the bowl and came up with a walnut.

"You think it was stupid?" I asked. "Why?"

"Because first"—he crushed the shell in the heel of his hand, smashing it to dust and shrapnel—"before the divorce is public knowledge, you and Lloyd need to instill confidence that you're not going to go into bankruptcy without me."

The nut couldn't be tossed across the hall. With his palm up so he wouldn't drop it, he shifted to sit next to me. I put my hand out, and he dumped it in.

"It's funny," I said, picking out the good stuff. None of it was caught in the little compartments, so I made quick work of it. He cracked me another, crushing the compartments again. "I thought you were going to say something else."

"I can't imagine."

"I thought you were going to say you wanted to see how this month panned out."

"It's going to pan out." He held out his palm. I picked the nut from it. "You need to get ready to own that company completely again."

The nut stopped in the middle of my throat, and I had to make an extra effort to swallow. I was still confused and a little angry, but when he said he expected to give McNeill-Barnes back, he was saying he expected us to make it thirty days and part cleanly. Exactly what I wanted. Right?

Your head's all fucked up. You should want to leave him now more than ever.

When I got that thought out of the way, I was left with satisfaction. Not over getting what I wanted, but that he had faith that I could make it. I craved his approval like never before. So like a child, I asked for it.

"I feel like a failure at this," I said.

"You're not."

I faced him, seeing his profile against the hall window. His jaw moved as he chewed, and the line of his neck rolled when he swallowed.

"I bet Serena would have taken her punishment even if it was business." I hoped the statement would seem like a random musing, but I sounded petty in my own head.

"She would have screwed up the business to get the punishment. What I saw there, outside, was that you were willing to do what I told you no matter what."

"If you hadn't stopped, what would you have done?"

He faced me and took my hand. "You want to know?"

"Yes." The word caught in my throat.

"I would have pulled your pants down, right outside with them watching. I would have made you choose between my hand for twenty, or the belt for ten."

His voice came in three dimensions, putting me back in the scene. The cold. The watching eyes. The tingle of pushing against my own will to do his bidding.

"Your hand. I redlined anything but your hand."

"Twenty takes longer. They'd be watching you longer. Watching me punish you like a child. Seeing your pain and seeing how much you liked it." He brushed his lips on my cheek. "For the length of twenty strokes, they'd see you'd do anything for me. Ten on your ass and ten on the backs of your thighs. Then I'd make you come."

I found myself shifting my hips so my clit rubbed on the inside of my jeans. My fingers pressed against the floor as if I could leverage myself against it.

And still, he kept on. "Hands still on the truck. Ass up in the cold. I'd finger you when I was done. You'd come for me and they'd see who owned you. So. Hands for twenty or belt for ten?"

"Hands. Still hands."

I wanted it, and didn't. The witnesses had turned me on and frightened me at the same time, because I wasn't sure what they'd do. But I could trust Adam. By sending me upstairs, he'd earned more trust than I knew I was capable of.

"Open your fly," he said in that voice. The voice that didn't have room for "maybe she won't."

"What's happening to me?" I asked myself more than him. Neither of us had an answer.

"Pull your pants down to your thighs and get on your hands and knees. I'm going to punish you just because I feel like it."

I unfastened my pants and arched my back to pull them down. Then I rolled to one side to get on my hands and knees on the hallway floor.

He was going to punish me. My whole body begged for his hardest touch.

Behind me, he slid his fingers in my crack, between my folds, putting two fingers inside me. It didn't feel like punishment.

"Were you wet when you came up here?"

"Yes."

With his free hand, he pulled the hood of my clit away, then he stroked the sensitive, nerve-bundled skin with his wet hand. "Do you want to come in this hallway?"

"Yes."

"Don't. Not until I say."

He rolled his finger across my most sensitive parts, slowly gathering pressure and pleasure. I dropped my head, breathing heavily, and when I groaned, he knew I was close and slowed down.

"Can I come?"

"Can you come what?"

"Please. Let me come please."

"No." He took his hand away. "This is your punishment." He slapped my bottom once and stood. "Let's eat something. I'm starved."

I pushed myself off my hands. "You can't leave me like this."

"Yes, I can. Not all punishment is pain. And for telling Kayti, you need to be punished."

He held his hand out to help me up. I took it and got to my feet.

"I don't like this." I pulled up my pants.

"You're not supposed to." He kissed my cheek and went downstairs, whistling.

I shouldn't have told Kayti. It was a monumental blunder, yet he was whistling as if it didn't matter.

As if he knew—no, not just knew. As if he accepted and embraced the fact that he'd no longer be running McNeill-Barnes. As if he'd be signing it over to me when this was done.

Why aren't you overjoyed?

Chapter 62

PRESENT TENSE - DAY TEN

He was fully dressed, standing over me at the edge of my nondescript bed, smiling, with an erection stretching his pants. After the walnuts in the hall, lunch in the kitchen, a nap, and a languid dinner, he'd told me to put on a nightgown. I'd spent the past few hours on the couch watching a movie with my head in his lap. It had felt normal, but it wasn't. Whenever I'd tried to close my legs, he opened them as if he was going to let me come, then he didn't. I couldn't have repeated a single thing from the movie. All I could think about was sex.

When the movie was over, he'd told me to go upstairs and get ready for bed, then he watched me brush my teeth and hair. He had me leave the door open a crack when I used the toilet, and made sure he could see me wash my hands. He only left long enough to get a wooden box the size of a stepstool. He placed it under the bedroom window and told me to remove my nightgown. I knew for sure he was going to release the bursting tension between my legs, but I was wrong.

On the bed, with him over me, my nakedness became the whole of my existence. I was aware of every single square inch of skin. His eyes zigzagged over me in swaths, leaving scorched lines behind. My body was crisscrossed with burning lines of his awareness. He set the space between my legs alive. The engorged, unsatisfied throb that begged for release.

For a long time, he didn't say anything. Not with his mouth. He took something from the box under the window, closed it, and turned back to me with black straps dangling from his hands.

I closed my legs.

Gracefully, with a precisely measured pace that was definite, not reactionary, like he was catching an orange rolling off the counter, he opened them.

Who was this man? This competent, commanding man with no interest in what I wanted or what we'd established as an expected routine. Who was this man, this presence? And what was his agenda?

He sat on the edge of the bed and ran his hand along the inside of my thigh.

I went from solid mass to fluttering energy. "Finish me," I groaned.

"Diana," he said, "you've never finished anything in your life, and for the past five years, I've let you get away with it."

His hand moved to my other thigh without pausing, and I was convinced my pussy's gravitational force could have pulled him in up to the elbow, releasing an orgasm that would snuff out the universe, but he smoothly laid his fingers on my skin and stroked it.

I squeaked. I'd never been so close to the edge of orgasm for so long.

"I can finish. I want to finish." I sounded as if I was begging, because I was.

"We have different definitions of finish, and yours doesn't count. Not in this house."

When he took his hand off me, my body jerked to get closer to it.

"What do you mean I don't count?" I objected. "That's—"

"No talking." He stood and faced me. "Or I *will* gag you."

He knew damn well I'd redlined that. Was it possible the

redlining meant the item became optional after a certain point? Was it a test? I read the contract carefully, but did I miss it?

"But—"

I ate my words. His glance at my closed knees quieted me, and I opened them again. Not because I was afraid he'd gag me, but because I didn't want him to want to. I wanted to do it right. To finish this thing his way, no matter how psychotically aroused I was.

"You were going to say something about not counting?" he asked.

I nodded.

"That hurt your feelings. It offended you. Is that right?"

I nodded again.

"This is a game. It's a bedroom game. A Montauk game. We've been business partners for five years. Have I ever made you feel like you don't count?"

My answer was obvious to both of us, but he waited for it, fingering the straps while I stretched naked before him. I didn't feel threatened. If I could dig out a single instance when he didn't treat me like an equal, I was safe to mention it.

"No."

"If the game is too much for you, opt out." He stood over me, exuding a stillness the room revolved around. "But you know I won't push where you won't go. Right?"

I could have said yes. I could have said no. I could have continued the discussion or freaked out or honestly, with the frustration of the orgasm banging at the door, I could have cried and begged. But my voice would be sharp. Even a whisper would have cut through the moment and severed desire from time.

He'd asked what I thought. I wanted the answer to be more than simple, and less that complex, because in throwing it back to me, he made me look at not just what I wanted, but what I needed.

I gave up. But not really. I wasn't throwing in the towel and abdicating. I didn't want to say, "Forget it, I'm out." I wanted to say, "Forget it, I'm in."

So all I did was spread my legs a little wider.

He bent over me, taunting me with the straps in his hand. "You want to come. I understand. You think that's finishing." He gently grasped my right arm. "It's not. Not to me. To me, you're finished when I say. For any reason. And it's going to seem arbitrary. It's not."

He leaned over to get to my left wrist. His body was a hard mass hovering over me, blocking my view of anything else. Like a mothership descending over Manhattan, covering the sky. I let my arms drop and blood flowed back through them, even as it continued to heat my clit.

"P—" The first sound of supplication. The beginning of *Please*. But I didn't finish. I didn't want a useless orgasm. I wanted to do what he wanted, to see where he was going. I trusted him. I trusted whatever he had in mind. It wouldn't be a throwaway climax, but something else entirely.

He centered his face over mine, close enough to kiss. "How old are you?"

He didn't seem to be doing anything rough enough to warrant safe questions, but I answered.

"Twenty-eight."

"Where do you live?"

Where did I live? He'd asked this before, and I still didn't know the answer. "In this bed, in Montauk, in a cottage in snow."

"Do you hate your husband?"

"I never hated him."

"You're about to."

He sat up straight, his eyes between my legs more substantial than warm fingers. He put his hands on either side of my labia, thumbs pressed into the muscle and skin of my ass, fingers in my upper thighs, pressing me open. My legs pivoted outward to the point of discomfort.

Maybe now. Maybe now he'd release me.

Touching me more than he had to, but not where I wanted him, he placed my right arm at my right thigh and snapped one of the straps off his shoulder.

"I'm saving your orgasm for"—he shrugged—"tomorrow, earliest."

"Tomorrow?"

He answered with a stern look and strapped my wrist to my thigh. The nylon weave dug close to my pussy, so close, yet not close enough. He crossed the bed to do my left wrist and thigh.

"I can come both times." I didn't know what I was even asking for. A second ago, I wanted to accept whatever he dished out. That was before "tomorrow, earliest."

"All orgasms aren't created equal." His hands were efficient and businesslike even as my body craved his intimate touch.

He stood. I wiggled, and it came to me what he'd done. Wrists attached to thighs, my legs spread, the storm picking up speed outside the window. I wanted to curse him and please him in one breath.

Adam stood at the foot of the bed, arms crossed, feet slightly apart, his erection outlined in his pants.

"I can't sleep like this," I said. But what I wanted to say, what was flooding my mind, was the sight of his dick and his complete control over it.

He bent at the waist, grabbed my ankles, and pulled me forward until my head rested flat. "Yes, you can sleep. On your back or you can roll over. I'll keep it warm in here in case the blanket falls off. You can sleep knowing you're doing exactly what I'm telling you to do."

"Why would you do this?"

"Because I can."

I'd thought the question would cause reflection, but he relished his answer. That much was obvious.

"I thought this would be different."

Did he smile because he'd surprised me, or because he'd tricked me with my own expectations?

"You're a creative person," he said. "You'll figure out how to get yourself off. After you do, it's your choice to do it or not."

He put his knee on the bed, then his fist pressed the mattress. He thrust forward until his breath cooled the juice on my cunt.

I groaned when his lips found my clit. A quick peck. It was a groan of hope that he'd changed his mind. His eyes made contact with mine as he kissed it again, more slowly, then he kissed where labia and thigh met, near where the strap dug in, checking my reaction.

I thrust my hips into him, but he backed away in reverse. Face, then fist, then knee, until he was standing at the foot of the bed again. With his arms crossed and his erection straight, his attention was riveted on me.

"Can I ask you a question?" I asked.

"Yes."

"You know what I want before I say it. I feel like you're reading my mind."

"I know you. You're my wife."

"Why didn't you know what I wanted before? When I needed you?"

He stiffened, tightened his lips. "Like when?"

"After Lenore."

"You mean Olive?"

"When you came to my father's house and brought me to the couch. You were a million miles away. You were phoning it in."

Did an ounce of his dominion over me leak? Did it fall off him? Any of it? Did I crack his armor?

"I was scared." He stated the fact without losing his dominance. No crack appeared.

"Of what?"

"Of having no control. Of failing. Of you. Everything. And I'd given up the one thing that makes me fearless. I was trying to be what you wanted, but as we now know, I can't be that." He picked up the blanket. "Be good." He threw it over me. "I'm in the next room if you need me. Otherwise, I'll be back in the morning."

He shut off the light and closed the door.

It hadn't occurred to me that he'd be frightened of anything, and if he'd told me that before he told me about taking Serena's virginity, I wouldn't have believed it.

Maybe that was my failure.

Chapter 63

PRESENT TENSE - DAY TEN

The snowflakes were dry clusters floating down with the speed of feathers. Some landed gracefully on the windows and dissolved into tears. I drifted into sleep like one of the clusters on the hot pane, condensing and warming into a dream where my husband drew a white feather over my cleft over and over and the white light of my orgasm flicked on but stayed dim. My wrists were strapped to my thighs even in the dream, and I strained against them.

I woke to a light from outside.

The motion sensors outside the studio had gone on. There were no clocks in the bedroom, but I guessed an hour had passed. The torture between my legs had abated a little, leaving me with only raw potential. Desire had crouched back into the corner but was ready to spring.

Why would the light go on? A bird? A cat? Too much snow?

Or Serena crossing the yard to fuck my husband?

I trusted him, on the one hand. On the other, the rules of this game constantly surprised me. I'd thought controlling me for a month meant he'd constantly fuck me. I'd thought I could just shut down my mind and heart.

I'd left sharing on the list because he wouldn't share me.

But what if that meant I was sharing him as well?

It shouldn't matter. I'd left him. I'd sent him packing with a note on the counter. I'd assured him repeatedly that I wasn't coming back, ever. That I didn't love or want him.

So I should be fine with her coming over here and letting my husband kiss and touch her and—

A split second passed between the light flashing on and me realizing I wasn't okay with this. No. Not at all.

Wait. Stop. If you're not okay with it, you have to stay married, and all this trouble will be for nothing.

Right. I was fine with it. Totally fine. I just wanted to know. Wanted to see if she was coming across the yard. Had to know. My curiosity was a living thing that needed to be fed.

I wiggled out from under the blanket, dropped a foot to the floor, and wrenched myself to standing. It was hard to balance without my arms, and I was bent halfway, graceless, unselfconscious as I put my knee on the bench by the window and looked out.

Serena wasn't coming to fuck my husband. She wasn't even close to the main house.

She was in her own damned doorway, but Adam was standing in front of it, talking to her. He'd gone across the yard. She stepped out of his way, and he went into the studio. She closed the door.

A back-breaking rage filled my heart. A righteous, sour, powerless rage.

I put my forehead to the cold glass. My face twisted, muscles tightened, breath left me. I sobbed.

The motion light went out.

Didn't you ask for this? Didn't you want to be free of him? Why aren't you happy?

Not like this. I wanted it to be easier at the same time that I knew the easier it was for me, the harder it was for Adam. As if pain was a zero-sum game. As if there wasn't plenty to go around.

My face was crusted and wet. I couldn't wipe my nose or my

cheeks. I yanked at the straps, but they weren't built for me to remove. They were designed to put me under his power.

While he screws the submissive.

Fuck him. Fuck Serena. Fuck this whole deal. I wasn't cut out for it. I enjoyed this shit up to a point, but he was crossing a line. All the lines. He was supposed to be in the next room while I was tied up. He said he'd be here, but instead he'd run off to give her what he wouldn't give me.

When I thought of them fucking, my body flooded with petulant and dissatisfied arousal. I couldn't think. Couldn't even be mad because all I wanted was release.

My eyes adjusted to the light, and I scanned the room. The bed's footboard was a low bar across two higher posts. It would do.

I slung my leg over it, nearly falling until I got one knee on the mattress while I leveraged myself against the foot on the floor. I rested my shoulder on the post and lowered my wet pussy against the smooth wood of the footboard.

I sucked air through my teeth. It was good. All good. The friction built tension for a release I had control over. I jerked my hips over the surface of the wood, sliding half an inch one way, then the other, the post biting into my shoulder as I pushed against it.

I fucked the footboard like an animal, back and forth quickly with only one goal.

Finally.

The wood got warmer as the hood over my clit rubbed back and forth, sending blood between my legs, swelling it. My eyes closed and my mouth opened. I rode the bed until my back arched and I came with a long, angry grunt.

Because fuck him for giving her an orgasm and not me. And fuck him for touching her and loving her when he was still married to me. And fuck him for tying my wrists to my thighs and not being where he said he'd be. And mostly, fuck me for leaving him and expecting him not to fuck a beautiful and accessible woman.

Fuck me and my inability to love him.

Chapter 64

PAST PERFECT

My mother said I was the best daughter in the world. I spent my adolescence telling people she made me the man I grew up to be. They laughed and she made her pissed-off face. I joked about it until she was too sick for anger or anything else. She couldn't do much more than breathe in that last month. After three months of shitty prognoses, I was still surprised when the cancer beat her.

I skipped the funeral. I couldn't bear the line of New York's luminaries telling me how sorry they were. How they knew how hard she'd fought and what a fine patron of the arts she was. I couldn't bear another story illustrating her wit and intelligence or another friend I barely knew asking me if I needed anything.

I needed my mother back. I was twenty. An adult for all intents and purposes, and a child who needed her mother.

So I went to the Met instead of the funeral. I wanted my mother, so I looked at art. That was where she lived in my heart.

When I was twelve, she'd taken me bra shopping at Bloomingdale's. I was coy and embarrassed, but her businesslike manner and loving touch made the reality of my budding sexuality bearable. With a little brown bag full of A-cups, she took me to a special exhibition at the Frick. The Fifth Avenue mansion housed great Old Master paintings from a private collection. Mom had been on the board for a while, before every body part that made her female betrayed her.

On Bra Day, the Frick exhibit held Impressionists inspired by Old Masters or somesuch. We made small talk, and she stopped me in front of a particular painting and told me about men. I hadn't been ready to hear it, but I remembered it.

On the day of her funeral, I didn't go to the Frick. I went to the Met to see the same painting. I'd noticed it was on loan from the *Musée de Orsay* that summer, and in some crazy fantasy, I thought Mom would get well enough to see it again with me. She died instead.

The doctors had told me that as soon as I had children, I had to have my uterus, ovaries, and cervix removed. They stopped short of recommending a preventive mastectomy.

Why is the feminine so volatile? Why don't we get arm cancer? Cancer of the nose? The eyes? Why does femaleness kill so many of us?

Bra Day.

Funeral Day.

Eight years apart and spun together like loose threads in the sewing box.

On Bra Day, Manet's *Luncheon In the Grass* was probably the first meta-painting I ever saw. Two fully dressed men sit on the grass, picnicking with a naked woman. Behind them, another woman wears a diaphanous white gown. The light and proportions tell the story on an intellectual level. It's a painting about painting, where an artist and a friend step onto the canvas to discuss the image of the naked women bathing.

"What do you think of this?" Mom had asked, flicking her wrist toward the painting. It was one of many, and I didn't know why she was stopping in front of it.

"The lighting is weird," I said, clutching my bag of A-cups.

She raised an eyebrow. "How does it make you feel?"

A naked woman in arm's reach of two clothed men? One of her feet was between the legs of the man in front of her, and she was very close to the man beside her. She looked at the viewer, daring them to take issue. She wasn't uncomfortable, but I was.

"Fine," I said. I was twelve.

"Do you wonder what a naked woman is doing with two men who are dressed? What do you think is the point of that?"

"Manet was just starting to discover photography so—"

"Dominance," she interrupted, turning from me to the painting. She'd had me late in life, and her tightly twisted bun was thirty-percent grey. "It's an expression of man's dominance over women. She's naked to them, and of course in his view, she's fine with it, because it's the proper order to Edouard Manet. The one with the stupid hat? Showing his friend what's between her legs. They'll dominate her, and she'll submit her naked body to both of them."

"Mom…" I tried to shut her up. I was afraid someone would hear her and see the thoughts in my head. The nude leaning back and spreading her legs while the two men stood over her, looking at her body and deciding how to use it.

"Yes?"

"Can you talk more quietly?"

"I'm not saying anything historians haven't. This is how men make women feel."

Like this? Like they have to pee but in a totally different place? I felt swollen and slick, in need of the attention of fully clothed men, and it was terrifying.

I'd been sexually aroused before, especially finding Daddy's porn magazines between the bottom of the bathroom drawer and the casing underneath. The skin and dicks and open mouths. The women in red stilettos and corsets. The stories that taught me the word *cock* and the proper use of the word *cunt*. They were very well-hidden, and I always put them back exactly as they were, until I wondered if he meant for me to find them. I put them back sideways. They disappeared the next day.

"Men," I said to myself on Funeral Day, eight years later.

Manet's painting still aroused me, but it made me angry too. The anger was easier to deal with. It had an object. I couldn't be mad at my mother because she was sick and she died, but I could join her in rage.

"Men will try to dominate you," she'd said on Bra Day. "They think it's their right. Their privilege. They will do everything they can to degrade you. They'll strip you down to body parts if you let them."

I looked at the wood floor of the Met as I remembered the scene at the Frick eight years earlier. I could hear her in my mind as if she was still alive.

"It's not their fault. They're raised that way. You need to find a strong man. Use him to make yourself stronger, and if he loves you, he'll want to be used for your betterment."

"Is that why you married Daddy?"

"Your father is another kettle of fish. I let him use me for his betterment because I love him."

He was my kettle of fish now. I had to be strong for him. I had to take care of him and make sure he had the life my mother would want for him. Everything else was a waste of my strength and my womanhood.

Chapter 65

PRESENT TENSE – DAY ELEVEN

I slept at some point. I'd rolled off the footboard like a clumsy one-night stand, used my feet to get the duvet back over me, and waited for the motion-sensor lights to go back on even as I denied caring.

The sun was reflecting the white of new snow. The brightness was crisp and unforgiving.

"Good morning," Adam said from the door that connected our rooms, fully dressed in slacks and a button-front shirt.

I turned away. I couldn't look at him. Of course he was relaxed.

He pulled the duvet off the floor and threw it on a chair. He opened my legs and inspected me as if checking under the hood. His manner was humiliating and degrading.

And...?

Arousing. Oddly. Goddammit.

"Good morning," I said. I didn't want him to know I was mad. I wasn't supposed to care, and I wasn't giving him the power of my jealousy.

He ran his fingers over the sheets, examining the corners at an angle. I'd admit I was curious about what he was doing, but I was too annoyed to ask.

He crossed to the other side of the bed and stopped at the footboard. Considered the surface with a fingertip. Watching me, he put his thumb in his mouth, releasing it with a pop, and drew his wet thumb over the place I'd ridden.

He put his thumb back in his mouth.

"You still have the sweetest cunt I've ever tasted."

I should have been ashamed of the way he treated me. Of the way he checked on me. Of what I'd allowed him to do to my body. But my shame came from one place only. I'd failed. I'd been weak, and I'd disappointed him. I'd said I'd do what he told me for thirty days. That was the deal and I'd gone into it as payment for a smooth ride out of the marriage. I'd failed to keep my promise. Again.

He sat on the edge of the bed, disappointment pouring off him.

Well, I'd had a reason to get my rocks off.

"What's Serena's taste like?"

He didn't answer right away. He unstrapped my left side. I bent my arm. Stretched. Bent.

"As I recall, her cunt tastes like regular Tuesday cunt."

"Tuesday cunt?"

"Yeah." He got up and went to the other side of the bed. He'd navigated the sides of my bed a dozen times in the past twenty-four hours, and each time, he wound me tighter. "A regular Tuesday cunt. Nothing special. Not funky risky Saturday night cunt." He undid my left side. "Not Sunday godly worship cunt. Tuesday cunt."

Once released, I sat up and rubbed my wrists. "What does mine taste like?"

"A footboard." He stepped back and stretched his arm toward the bathroom. "Get a bath ready. I'll be back in four minutes to clean you up."

He left. He didn't spin off in a huff or back out with a promise of something devilish. He just... left.

The shame of getting caught failing was greater than any other. Not the shame of my nudity, being checked over like livestock, or the humiliation of being turned on by both. Failing was straight shameful.

I turned the bath on as hot as it would go and sat on the little wooden stool, watching the column of water ripple in the center of the steam. I couldn't breathe. I didn't want to cry. I was stronger than that.

But apparently, I wasn't. I didn't know anything anymore. Not about my husband. Not about myself. Nothing.

By the time Adam came back in, the room was in a complete fog and my blubbering had gotten wet and loud. He crouched in front of me, putting his hands on my shaking shoulders.

"Oh, Diana," he said tenderly, pulling me to him.

I couldn't resist. Wanted to but didn't, because I did want to even though I didn't. I held both desires in my mind as he slid along the side of the tub until he was sitting with my naked body stretched across him. I cried harder because I was confused. He confused me. I confused me. My feelings and desires zigzagged all over the place.

I cried and cried. My husband held me, wrapping his arms and legs around me as the bath tap roared and steamed. He didn't say or ask anything, just held me and rocked me.

I let him. I didn't have the strength to explain myself. I let him comfort me. Let him command me. Let him envelop me completely. I cried, but I was dormant inside. My guts had been emptied into him through my tears. When he leaned into the tub to turn off the water, I missed the shelter of his arms but didn't need them anymore.

"I can give myself a bath." I wiped my eyes with the backs of my hands.

"I know." He rolled up his sleeves. "But it's my prerogative."

When his sleeves were rolled up to the elbow, he held out his hand. I took it, letting him help me get in the tub. My skin stung at the waterline as I sank in and stretched out. Adam dunked a washcloth, wrung it, and pressed it to my face.

"Talk about it," he commanded.

He didn't ask me if I wanted to or if I felt all right. He told me what to do, and in that was an odd relief. I didn't have to choose whether or not to be intimate. I didn't have to decide whether or not to burden him or pull back into a shell. He didn't say tell *me*. He took himself out of the equation by commanding me to speak about it, whether it was to him, myself, or the four walls.

"I can't put it in order," I replied.

"Tell it as it comes to you."

I took a deep breath and told it as he ran the washcloth over me. "What you're doing right now? You're washing me like I'm a puppy, or like, your car. You might love those things, but they're objects. Do you see that? How you're just efficient? I don't... I didn't know you were like that. And I'm mad at myself for not seeing it and I'm mad because... I'm mad at myself because it turns me on. All of this shit. I thought I'd just tolerate it, but instead I'm turned on all the time. And last night, I wanted you. I wanted you so bad. I didn't want to hump a piece of wood. I wanted you to fuck me, but you went to fuck Serena. And you had to. You had to fuck her because I left you and why should you give me anything when I took everything from you? I'd fuck her too."

I started to cry again. He worked the insides of my thighs with the washcloth.

"I'm better than this," I said through my tears. "I'm better than a possession. I run a multimillion dollar company with my husband, and I haven't worried about sales or the bottom line for days and days. Who am I now?"

I leaned back and let him scrub my feet.

"You're a submissive." He stated a fact.

"Women aren't naturally submissive."

"Most aren't."

"But I am? Fuck you."

"It's not an insult. It's not a feminist issue. It's a bedroom issue. I've denied this from the minute I met you because I didn't want you to be submissive. Submissives scared me. It was you who opened my eyes to it. Once I did that, I saw you for the first time. You're submissive, and the Dominant in me always knew it." He gently put my foot into the water. "It doesn't have to be shameful, and it doesn't mean we're not getting divorced."

The tap dripped. My skin tingled. His hand brushed the surface of the water, making a rippled V behind it.

"It's hard for me to…" I had to stop to clear a lump of gunk from my throat. It threatened to come up in a sob as soon as I spoke. "To be here while you fuck Serena. I'm not saying I blame you. But it's hard."

His expression didn't change. No surprise. No rush to comfort. "Why is it hard?"

"You're my husband." I covered my pussy with my hands. A reflex I didn't understand but was powerless to control.

"And?" He moved my hands away.

"There is no 'and.' There shouldn't have to be."

"Explain it to yourself. Out loud so I can hear it."

I knew what he wanted to hear. The truth. In words. The part of me I shoved aside because it was reactionary and immature.

I couldn't deny him.

"I'm jealous," I whispered.

"Ah." He ran his fingers over the surface of the water again, detouring up my knee, down my leg. "Tell me what makes you think I'm fucking Serena."

"The light went on last night and didn't go back on." I didn't tell him I'd gotten up to see him at the door. I wanted him to deny it. Tell me it was a cat or a bird. Make an excuse.

"I know I told you I'd be in the next room. I'm sorry I left. I did go over there to check on her. The furnace is old. If it breaks in the night and she doesn't feel comfortable coming over here, she could be in trouble."

"You were there for a long time."

The water cooling, he stroked my leg with real affection this time, lost in thought.

"We did talk for a bit. Maybe it was forty-five minutes. She's lonely." He looked at me. "Like you were when you were married to me."

"If you kissed her, would you tell me?"

"No."

"No?" Why did my voice crack? I didn't even love him. I was fighting through the thick dregs of our relationship.

"No. I'd leave you." His hand lay flat inside my thigh and stroked to my center. "I wouldn't touch you again."

But he was touching my legs tenderly, and that was his answer. I'd spent all night telling myself he could fuck her if he wanted, and he was telling me he hadn't.

"It's not fair for me to pull you in two directions," I said.

"It's not fair that Stefan and Serena are here at all. The cold weather isn't fair. Stefan being in the city isn't fair. I can make a longer list if I added everything I've done, but the water's getting cold."

He helped me out of the bath and wrapped me in a thick towel.

"Thank you," I said.

"I still have to punish you for disobeying me."

I looked at the floor, ashamed and annoyed at the same time.

"Talk," he commanded.

"It sounds awful. 'Disobeying' you."

"Did I ever even give you an order before we came here?"

"No."

"Bedroom games. That's all it is. But they're serious, and when played right, everyone wins." He took me by the chin and made me face him. "I haven't felt right in a long time. I need this corner of my world to be under control. You are the one great love of my life, but you don't need this. You might like it, but you don't need it. I do."

I nodded against the pressure of his hand.

"Now, you can safe out, or you can dry off, take care of your business, and be downstairs in your nightgown, where I'll punish you. Got it?"

"Yes."

He dropped his hand and started out. He stopped himself and turned when he was at the door. "You might like it."

"Yes," I repeated. I almost said *sir*, but I bit it back. I'd kept sharing in the contract so I could remove the *sirs* and *Masters*. I wasn't giving it up for a slip of the tongue.

Chapter 66

PRESENT TENSE - DAY ELEVEN

What if I pretended it was all right? What if I told myself to go all in? To not let a hundred years of the feminist fight get in the way? Just forgot it for the rest of the month? What if I chose to play this part with everything I had? For fun? Because it wasn't so bad. Because I enjoyed it. Because I had more to gain than to lose.

I'd have to choose it very deliberately and consciously. Could I? *Could I?*

I made a big question mark at the end of the sentence and went downstairs. A simple breakfast of toast and fruit had been left out with a handwritten note.

I'm in the office.

I ate in front of the wall of windows looking onto the sea. The backyard and beach were covered in flat white snow. I wanted to go and wreck it. Write my name in footsteps. My mother and I had built a snow woman in front of our building once, and the doorman had put a hat and epaulettes on her until he found out she was a woman. He laughed and took his hat back as if gender prevented one from opening doors.

And there I was, eating toast and wondering if I should get on my knees when I entered the office.

I put the plate in the sink, washed up, and went to the west side of the house. Adam was at the desk. A chair was set up next to it. A robe was draped over the back.

He looked up when I was almost at the door, and he stood, lifting the robe.

"I'm sorry," he said. "We have to break scene. Put this on."

"What does that mean?" He helped me push my arms through the sleeves. I belted the robe.

"It means we have two problems. Which one do you want first? The one we can do something about or the one we can't?"

"The one we can't. This way we can end with something to do."

"Good." He showed me his phone.

SEVERE STORM WARNING
High winds and precipitation.
Power and communication outages expected
east of Hither Hills State Park.
Take precautions.

"Should we leave? For safety?" I asked when I handed the phone back.

"We should. But Thierry and Willa took the car into Queens yesterday, and if I tell them to come back to get us, all four of us will be stuck."

"Five. Serena's five."

"Five. We've done this before. It'll be fine."

"Okay, what's the other problem?"

"It's a pricing problem on two retailers." He turned the laptop toward me, and I bent to look at it. One of our biggest retailers had discounted a title and the other one had matched it.

"Crap. How much have we lost?"

Adam handed me my phone. "A few thousand. Which one do you want to take?"

"I'll call Lake and you call Shonda."

"Good." He sat down and slid his chair over. I didn't know why until he pushed the laptop halfway over to me. He was making room for me to sit next to him.

"Adam?"

"Yeah?"

What did I want from him? I couldn't get an answer together. He answered me as if reading my mind, his face opening into a knowing smile.

"I'm still punishing... Shonda! Hey, we were just looking at this price and..."

He went on like a normal person. I shook away the submission I'd just accepted and got on the phone. I could accept it again later.

It was half an hour before I realized I'd used his name and he had no problem with it.

Chapter 67

PAST PERFECT

I was wearing my favorite blouse. The one with the flying birds. We'd gotten a table at Metropolis for the company's anniversary dinner, and I wanted to look extra special.

Adam wore a suit, as always: navy blue with a crisp white shirt. Tall and straight, with wide shoulders and a tight waist, he fastened platinum cufflinks shaped like smooth pyramids. He ignored me and spoke to me at the same time. Something about work. Blah blah blah. It was important, but I didn't care. All I saw was his hands, how muscular and wide they were. How each finger was active and articulated when he straightened his cuffs.

As he threaded his belt through the loops, my knees turned to jelly. We'd been together long enough to have bedroom routines, but at least not long enough for them to be tedious.

That day, I wanted something different. I couldn't communicate it, but I felt it in my marrow. I wanted to bend in ways I'd never bent before.

No, I wanted him to bend me. The thought of him pushing me down, moving me, using me turned my insides into a pool of warm liquid.

"Adam." My voice cracked. All I could see were his hands holding the belt.

"Yes?"

I was supposed to tell him what I wanted, but I couldn't. I wanted him to tell me what I wanted then demand it. I wanted to be free of want. Of decisions. I wanted those hands and the beautiful monster that belt locked away.

I still don't know what came over me, but I got on my knees in front of him.

He didn't move. I didn't look at him, because I didn't know what to do. I could have taken his cock out, but that would have broken the spell.

He touched my cheek. I turned toward it, just a little, lips parted, and took his fingers in my mouth.

With an authority that shocked me, he put them down my throat, and I took them. All the way. He shoved them in as if testing how deep he could go. I held back my gag reflex because if he wanted me to take his hand, I would. Just to please him. To prove how much of him I could swallow.

I looked up at him.

He was Adam. Same guy, but different. I didn't have the words to explain it, but I knew he'd heard what I wanted. He took out his fingers, and I breathed.

I wanted him to get his dick out. I wanted him to give it to me. I didn't want to show any aggression.

So I put my hands behind my back. I looked forward, waiting for his hands to come into my vision and undo his pants.

And waited.

"We have to go," he said. "We can pick this up later."

Fear pinched the corners of my heart. I was on my knees in front of him with my eyes cast down and my hands behind my back.

I looked up at him. He was too tall in my vision, rising up in perspective, his crotch huge and his face a tiny dot on the horizon.

I put my hands on my hips. "Fine."

I got up, and we went to dinner, driving to Union Square in

silence. He'd been right. We hadn't had time for a quick blow job. What stuck with me was the pressure on my knees, his fingers owning my mouth, the way my chest jutted forward when I locked my hands behind me. He'd rejected my posture. He didn't want that from me. I was glad we were equals in all things, and when I thought of it, I held his hand as it rested on the gearshift.

When we got to the restaurant, I was cranky. I assumed I was hungry or dehydrated. Even after the first course and a glass of water, I was still sour. I chalked it up to a bad day and didn't connect it to the aborted blow job. That was nothing. That was a tight schedule cutting off a good time and it wasn't new.

I'd bitterly changed my stockings because there were holes in the knees. It bothered me more than I admitted, and the bother had the rank stench of a disappointment you couldn't admit to. So it festered and curdled until I got to dinner, unable to tell myself the truth. I'd wanted to be dominated. I'd wanted to submit and he'd stopped it because, he said, time was tight.

But I knew he was saving me from my worst impulses, and the shame of even having them sealed my lips tight. By the time we got to Metropolis, (early, I'll note) my gratitude and disappointment mixed together to turn my mood muddy and dull.

If the pat on the back on my father's couch was the beginning of the end, that night was the middle of the end.

Chapter 68

PRESENT TENSE – DAY ELEVEN

The stockings were black and stretched to mid-thigh. The lace tops had clear silicone on top that kept them up. After I'd put on a pair of black stilettos, I looked at myself in the mirror. The stockings made a border around my triangle, and when I twisted to see my back, my ass looked rounder and more appealing.

"Turn around," he said from the doorway, catching me admiring my own body.

He didn't say please or ask. He didn't add an upswing to his voice at the end to suggest a question. He hadn't even said hello. I turned so he could see me from behind, then from the side, then front.

I could tell from the way he looked at me, leaning in the bedroom doorway with his arms crossed, that I was the sexiest thing in his universe. In five years with him, had he ever looked at me like *that*? He'd looked at me as if he wanted to eat me alive, looked at me as though he desired me, but there was an edge to him now, and that edge cut my own desire, opening it like a wound.

"Last night." He pushed off the doorframe. "You took what was mine. I trusted you, and you fucked the footboard."

He came in and put his hand under a lampshade, clicking one, two, three times until it was at its dimmest setting. Then he stood behind me. I felt him there, looking, planning. He moved around me, stood in front of me and over me. His silence was predatory. His posture was feral, yet completely in control.

I'd had no idea who I'd married. Had I been stupid and naïve, or shrewd?

"Your breathing's heavy." The back of his hand coursed from my collarbone, over my breast, the hard nipple, to my belly. Inside his manner was the threat of the threat, just enough to bring my awareness to the surface of my skin. "Hands at your side. Legs shoulder width. Don't look at me unless I tell you to. Don't make a move to touch me unless I say."

I dropped my eyes to his shoes. Not being able to look at him meant I couldn't see what he was doing or tell what he was feeling. It was disconcerting, and at the same time, the mystery was sensual. I listened. I felt the air stir. I paid more attention.

"I've been thinking of how to punish you, since I can't use paddles or crops. My hands would get tired giving you all the spanking you deserve."

I tried not to smile. I bit my lips. Pressed them together. Thought about kittens trying to cross Fifth Avenue at noon.

He leaned into me. I resisted the urge to turn around and face him.

"It wouldn't be funny if I really did it the way it was meant to be done." I couldn't swear it because I couldn't see him, but it sounded as if he was smiling too. "Not a stroke count. No. I'd stop when your ass was the right shade of pink and you'd surrendered so fully you stopped begging me to end it."

He grabbed the flesh of my bottom and squeezed. The surprise made me gasp and the flood between my legs came so fast it hurt.

"You want to come so bad, you're going to come. You're going to come until orgasms are agony. You're going to beg for pain."

He stopped. I didn't think he was done, but he cut himself off. I thought to agree. I considered "sign me up," discarded "when do we start?" and opened my mouth to give a simple, "yes," when we were interrupted.

I was working late at the office one night. It must have been eleven o'clock. Adam came in and asked me something. I jolted, surprised to find I'd been sleeping sitting up.

That was how it felt to hear footsteps in the hall. They yanked me from a fugue of sexual promise and churning hormones. I looked over at my husband. His head was turned toward the door, his clenched jaw a fierce line at his throat.

He leapt for the door, blocking it just as Serena showed up wearing a puffer coat, jeans, and boots. She looked at me and I looked back, frozen in place.

It took a second for us to regard each other. Her in boots and a puffer. Me, naked and still, my hands at my sides. When Stefan had pulled her into the driveway on a leash, I'd been disgusted and frightened. She was an animal. A slave. A piece of flesh to be used. And what was I, standing stock-still in the middle of the room in stockings and heels, held still not by ropes or chains, but by a man's will?

An understanding passed between us. She knew why I didn't cover myself in the dim light. She wasn't disgusted with me the way I'd been with her. My shame was my own. In the split second she saw me, I couldn't deny the shame was there and I couldn't blame her for it.

My body broke out into prickly pink heat.

I was ashamed and I was safe at the same time. I felt the shame physically as a weight on my hips. A liquefying warmth. A tightening of my nipples.

"What?" Adam barked, blocking the doorway.

She cast her eyes downward.

Look at him. You fucking bitch, look at him. Do not submit to him.

"I'm sorry," she said, hands at her sides. Their position filled me with unreasonable rage. I wasn't the jealous type, especially not over a man I was leaving, but I was boiling over her posture. Even her voice, which wasn't weak or warbly, just submissive, made me want to slap her. "There's cold air coming from the vent."

Adam's shoulders lowered a quarter of an inch. My body reacted by subtly leaning on one hip. I balled my hands into fists.

"Wait downstairs."

She spun and was gone.

Adam took his hands off the doorframe and turned. "It's going to be below zero tonight."

"She needs to fix her own fucking furnace," I said.

He let out a short laugh. "Her mother was the only female plumber in the tri-state area too. You'd think."

"Yeah. You'd think."

He put his hands on my biceps and drew them down, unclenching my fingers to weave his into them. "Give me a minute. It might need to be reset." He circled his arms around me and clasped my hands behind my back, pushing his body against mine.

"The furnace isn't the only thing that's going to need a reset," I groused.

"You're not usually so self-interested."

"I've never gotten this much attention before. It's making me selfish."

My comment was meant to be funny, but it wasn't. I was telling him he hadn't paid enough attention to me when we were married, and though I didn't mean exactly that, and though I would have denied it if he asked, that was the only one way to interpret my comment. I realized the sharpness of the remark as the last syllable came out.

"Lie on the bed," he said before I could rush to apologize. He let go of my hands and stepped back. "I'll be back in a few minutes. If your fingers or the footboard smells like Friday cunt, we're skipping agonizing orgasms and going straight to pain."

As I got my leg up on the bed and he had one foot out the door, I called him back. "Adam?"

He stopped and turned to me.

"What's on Friday?"

"Gratitude."

"What?"

"Thank God it's Friday."

I laughed so hard I didn't hear him leave, but I swore he was laughing too.

Chapter 69

PRESENT TENSE - DAY ELEVEN

Ten minutes had passed since I heard the back door whoosh open and slap shut. Ten agonizing minutes since the front light of the studio had flashed on and nine minutes since it went dark. Six minutes since I'd gotten under the covers. Three minutes since I slipped out of the bed and looked out the window. A minute since I put on pants and a sweater.

Thirty seconds since arriving at the front hall closet. A pocket of cold air surrounded the door, and my nipples tightened when I approached the front window.

I put my fingers on the glass. The sky had turned the orange of low clouds lit from below and the air was heavy with freezing rain and snow.

Wait for him? Do as he commanded? Or satiate the wild, predatory hunger of my curiosity?

The ocean seemed louder than ever, and the breaking waves looked more like toothy jaws ready to eat us alive.

This was more than curiosity. It was bitter cold. Deadly cold. The kind of cold inside the kind of storm that killed children and old people. My husband had been put in charge of a woman who played at incompetence for her own gain, and though I was sure he could handle her, there was nothing wrong with offering him support. I didn't know a damn thing about furnaces, but I could calm Serena down, hand him a wrench, boil water... whatever. Anything but lying in bed doing nothing.

My coat smelled of Manhattan and my scarf poked out of the pocket. It had embroidered hawks on the ends. He'd handed it to me at the door of the loft. I didn't put the coat on right away, just stood there with the lapels in my fists.

I'd given up being his wife, hadn't I? Surrendered my role as partner. Relinquished rights, privileges, and duties. What good would it do to go out there? I'd be taking advantage of my past intimacy with him. Breaking him down and leaving him anyway, and why? Pretending to be his life partner was wrong, unethical, and almost immoral. I was sure it wasn't simple curiosity. I cared deeply. But the curiosity sat in the room with its arms crossed and its foot tapping, saying, "Are you sure it's not about me? *Are you sure?*"

I was fucking sure. I might have given up on loving him, but I'd never promised to stop giving a shit about him.

And I admitted, as I laced up my boots... I wanted my orgasms.

Smirking, I slipped through the dark house and out the side door.

Chapter 70

PRESENT TENSE – DAY ELEVEN

It was colder and wetter than I thought possible. Wet snow fell on the ground layer of drier snow and immediately froze to a hard shell. My feet cracked it into ovals as I walked. I hadn't had a hat or gloves on the warm day of the drive from Manhattan, so I wrapped my scarf over my ears and tucked my hands under my arms.

Good thing the little house was just across the yard. Thirty steps at most. I curved my path to match Adam and Serena's steps, putting my feet into the cracked ice of Adam's footprints. The wind burned my exposed skin, and the sleet singed my cheeks.

Snow started filling the footprints. I rushed to step into them, but it was hard to see anything through the storm.

He did right to come back with her. He was a good man.

I got turned around in the wind and wound up on the side of the studio building. The light from the window was diffused by a layer of frost. Was there a door here? I would have sworn there was a side door, but I found no seam and no knob. I rubbed the frost, not feeling the cold glass or anything. Maybe I'd mistaken the warmth of the light for actual warmth. But the heat from inside the house had melted the inside of the frost just enough to let the fractal ice slip down.

Through the window. Quickly. Because I only saw for a moment.

Adam. Pointing firmly and talking.

A painting. Red. In human-not-human shapes.

Serena, hands on a low table. Feet on the floor.

A long cutting board in Adam's hand.

Serena was naked from the waist to the knees.

The cutting board was a paddle.

I wasn't cold, because my anger was so hot.

My feet were no more than weighted blocks, so when I went to lift one to go inside and choke someone, I didn't feel that it wasn't moving. The rest of my body spun around with the intent to move, shifting with inertia and falling on the handrail for the side steps.

The door had been three feet away and I couldn't see it in the snow.

All I had to do was walk up them, but I was falling. The foot that had tripped me—the one that had frozen in place—loosened and I went into free fall, smacking my hatless head on the stone steps.

As my vision erupted into sparks, I had a last question.

Do you love him?

Chapter 71

PERFECT

Hold your breath.

    You can hear the night birds call.

    His face blue in streetlamps.

    His feet warming yours.

    The breeze clicking the blinds.

    A car alarm a million blocks away.

    His hand on your cheek.

    What should we name her?

    You're not even pregnant yet.

    But I will be.

    You're getting ahead of yourself.

    Lenore.

    No.

    It's my grandmother's name.

    Did your great-grandmother read a lot of Poe?

    Probably.

    You want a bunch of ravens circling the building?

    You don't care.

    You want children before your insides turn into cancer.

He pinches your arm.
You like it.
You like him on top.
Your mouth yields in the dark.
The night birds fall away, and he begins again.
I like Olive.
It's a color.
And a boy can be Oliver.
You'll agree to anything.
He enters you again. You're sore.
You like it.
You whisper.
More please.

Chapter 72

PRESENT TENSE – DAY TWELVE

When is love? Is love when your heart swells at the sight of him? Is love when you fall asleep on his shoulder? Or when you fold him into sections so you can fit him in your odd-shaped envelope?

Did you love him when?

Is love when he saved your family's company, or is it when you twisted your bodies into knots in the middle of the night?

Did you love him when you told yourself it was time to love him or leave him? When you needed him? When you knew he'd give you children before you had to have your womanhood removed?

When he loved you?

When it was convenient?

Did you only love him when it suited you?

My head throbbed. I smelled the sheets. Felt damp human warmth all around me. Heard breathing.

Time folded in my unconsciousness.

It didn't fold in half, joining beginning to end in a neat jump. It folded in threes like a letter, past lapping tightly over present, tucking together to fit the shock of my senses.

Her voice.

His.

Warmth.

Blackness.

Nakedness.

Light.

His hard dick against me.

His arms.

Her sobs.

The smell of him slowly finding me, teasing me with half-consciousness. The smell of him in our life together. When I believed I loved him and when I feared I never had.

Folding like a letter left on the counter, signed in a shaking hand one day and kept in a drawer out of cowardice for a week. The edges spread and tucked back ten times until it was finally left for him. The man who smelled like the earth and the grass in it. His arms folded like a letter around me, but without the cowardice or malice of my letter folding.

My God, what have I done?

I said it in my sleep, but not out loud. I was only capable of input. The sound of breath and the hiss of the sleet on the windows. The glow of the lamp against my eyelids. The taste of blood in my mouth and the sting of the wound where I'd bitten my tongue.

Spread me like a sheet of paper. Write your life on mine. Fold past and present together like a letter. I am yours.

Chapter 73

PRESENT TENSE

My mind was awake, but my body slept heavily on its side. His form against my back was gone, and she whispered so close I could feel the mist of her spit.

"You don't respect me. You think I'm some kind of victim. You look at me with pity. At least you did. When you saw me leashed with Stefan, you had this look on your face. I see it all the time. It's disgust. Like I'm shit on your shoe. Like someone needed to save me but you weren't going to be the one to do it.

"You know I make fifteen thousand dollars a day to walk down a runway, right? I can stuff coke up my nose. I can drink absinthe with princes and kings. But I don't. If I did that stuff, I'd lose myself, and I wouldn't have that *thing* I get from being a slave. Go look at a magazine spread. When you see me, you'll see what I mean. I own that page because I'm owned."

My bottom lip tingled as if she stroked it. I smelled her breath on my face. Her voice was barely audible, but my half-dream wound around it.

"You're afraid. You're afraid I'm taking him away from you, or you're afraid you're the same as me. Or both."

She pulled my lip out and let it go, then she kissed it.

"Lady, you should be fucking shaking in your boots."

Sleep ate her words, digested them, and forgot their specifics, leaving only a vague discomfort behind.

Chapter 74

PRESENT TENSE – DAY TWELVE

I was going to tell him as soon as I got up. Explain everything, probably in one long sentence. As wakefulness came over me, my hands felt warm and dry and the bump on my head felt heavy. I touched where I'd hit it. The throb of it made a rapid smacking sound.

No.

The sound was coming from the next room.

I got up on my hands, shaking off sleep. The storm was fierce. Snow and sleet pelted the rain-rattled windows.

The sheet was warm on either side of me, as if I'd had company. The table night light didn't illuminate much in its dim yellow glow. The lamp shades were square with stained glass squares and rectangles in deep reds and browns. Adam's room.

The rapid-fire smacking, accompanied by squeals and cries, was coming from my room. And a man's voice through the wall. My man.

Fully awake, I sat up straight. My head spun around the hub of the bump on my forehead. The duvet slipped off. I was naked. Adam's bed was higher than mine, with a bench at the end and high posts with bars up near the top. The frame looked innocuous and

297

decorative enough, but there was a track along the vertical posts to adjust the height of the bar.

I wrapped the duvet around me and dragged it behind as I walked toward the adjoining door. The voices got clearer as I got closer.

"Say it," my husband commanded.

"I'm sorry," Serena sobbed right before the smacking sound.

The door to my room was ajar, and though I could only see a slice of what was going on, it was enough of a slice to build a scene.

Serena had her hands on my footboard, bent at the waist with her sock feet apart. Her jacket was hiked to her armpits, exposing the pockets of her designer jeans.

Adam stood over her. "You forgot something."

He hit her ass with the paddle. *Thwack.* Because her jeans were on, it lacked the same snap I'd heard at the Cellar, when the paddle hit the skin.

"Sir." Her tears and groans mixed together. "I'm sorry, sir."

Thwack.

"Who else?"

Thwack.

"Diana. I'll say I'm sorry to Diana."

Thwack.

"I thought you were better than this."

Thwack. Thwack. Thwack.

He hit her so hard and so fast I made a noise in my throat, and he turned, paddle in hand, sweat beading on his brow. Our eyes met through the slit of the open door, and when he took it by the edge, I didn't know if he was going to slam it in my face. He was devastating. This was the man he'd been holding back. The man he'd tried not to be all those years for my sake. He was pure power. Pure control. A fucking god.

Because he's beating a woman?

I answered my question.

Because she needs it, and he's a god who delivers it.

The truth of it went against everything I believed.

I took a step back, because I felt another truth.

I envied her. He was giving her a connection I'd refused. Her basest self was on show for him, begging him to put her right. She trusted him. I thought I trusted him, but not the way she was trusting him. Her vulnerability was raw and painful, and as he beat her bottom, so was his. I wanted that intimacy. I wanted to give him every inch of my skin, but I'd locked myself away.

Standing in the hallway, watching his chest rise and fall in that tight, sweaty T-shirt, I was still wrapped up against him in a thick feather blanket.

I dropped the duvet, letting the white cloud pile at my feet, naked in front of him.

"Stand in the corner and think about what you've done," he said to Serena while looking at me.

I shuffled back to his room.

When I got to the middle of the floor, I spun and faced the doorway. He was already there with his worn T-shirt stretched over his chest and sweatpants that made no secret of his arousal. His erection—the erection I'd lived with as a matter of course for five years—was now a powerful threat of dominance and beautiful pain.

Something in me purred. I had questions, but I could satisfy my curiosity later. He closed the door.

In two steps, he was across the room. He didn't reach for me in tenderness but took a fistful of hair and pulled my head back. He looked at the bump on my forehead.

"It's fine," I said in a breath that begged him to finish what he'd started. "Take me."

He threw me on the bed facedown.

"Show me," he growled.

I reached behind and spread my cheeks apart. He was going to fuck me. Finally. All I wanted was his cock. I felt his fingers in me. Three, pushing in. I shuddered.

"What were you doing looking in the window?" All his vocal control was gone.

"Fuck me."

He pulled my hair again. "I give the orders."

"Yes, sir."

I let go, and he guided himself to my opening.

"You could have died. If I didn't know you. If I didn't know where to look. You could have died."

He didn't wait for an answer before ramming into me all the way. I cried out in pleasure when he pushed against me, stretching me open. I took my hands off my ass and gripped the bedspread, and he redirected them, bending them so they were firmly and uncomfortably upward, pinned behind my back, circling my wrists with two fingers.

Immobilized, secure yet awkwardly positioned, with him using his other hand to yank my head back, I was thoroughly in the moment. I was his. My husband fucked me as he'd never fucked me before. In our relationship and our marriage, he'd never owned me like this. For the first time, I didn't feel loved, I felt possessed. And for the first time, I craved his ownership. He turned me on my back, spread my legs out and up, and entered me again. When I put my arms around him, he pulled them off and pressed my biceps into the bed, thrusting so hard and so deep it hurt. Yet I spread my legs wider to take him to the root.

I cried his name. I thanked him, and when I was so close I thought I'd burst, I grit my teeth and focused on the pain.

"Come," he said through his teeth. "You're so fucking beautiful. Come."

I thanked him again before I stiffened and let the orgasm ripple through my body. Maybe I screamed. Maybe I just opened my mouth. I was sure I was near unconscious all over again.

He let go of my arms and took my legs behind the knees, folding them and exposing me. His cock slid out, and he rubbed the slick length along my seam, where I was swollen and bare. The tide of another orgasm rose. I tried to reach for him, but my arms were behind my knees. He'd twisted me immobile.

"God. God, I'm—"

The sentence got lost in another climax. I strained against him and he held my body still as he ran his shaft along me.

"Stop," I gasped. "Please stop. Hurts. It…"

I came before I finished, surrendering completely to the pain, letting it twist around the pleasure. My screams and my tears echoed both.

Only then did he pull away, and only enough to grab me by the arms and put me on the floor, twisting my loose, pliable body until I was on my knees before him.

I worshipped him. I felt the supplication to a Master in my bones.

This was what it was to submit. To forget. To have my entire world revolve around a single thing. I felt sleepy yet alive. Boneless and ambitious. All the contradictions fused into a simple desire.

Please him.

I put my hands under me, grabbing my ass cheeks and pulling them apart. I bent at the waist, dropping my head between his legs. Without reservation or preference, I lifted my ass to show him his options.

"My fucking God," he said, almost in awe. His T-shirt landed on the floor, and with more authority, he said, "Straighten up. Hands off the floor."

I lurched up. He stood in front of me, cock at eye level. I opened my mouth.

"Take it," he said. "Like I taught you."

I opened my mouth as wide as I could, tongue out, throat open.

"Good girl." He fisted the hair in back of my head with one hand, put his dick at the tip of my tongue with the other.

I only tasted myself for a second. With no slow grind or test thrusts, he shoved it down my throat. I didn't wrap my lips around him. I just kept my mouth open, held back the gags, focused on him and his pleasure.

"Yes," he said. "Keep your mouth open. I'm going to fuck it."

He moved me to his rhythms. My jaw ached and my lungs gulped for air. He pushed my head into him and pulled it away when it suited him. I let him. I became his instrument. We moved together, and his tempo changed to something slower and harder. I knew he was close because I knew him.

He sucked in a breath, pulling out. "I'm going to come down your throat and you're going to swallow it."

I looked up at him and nodded, then he held my head still and fucked my mouth. Five thrusts. I took a gulp of air, and he buried his dick in my face. The base pulsed against my lower lip.

Even as a Dominant, he smiled when he came.

Chapter 75

PRESENT TENSE – DAY TWELVE

When I tried to stand, I nearly flopped over. He caught me and pulled me up to the bed, folding himself on top of me. Only in that silence could I hear Serena crying on the other side of the door.

I thought his first words after a monster fuck like that would be poems about love and satisfaction. But her voice reminded me of what had brought us to that moment, and he exhaled in deep resignation of everything that was wrong.

He'd been punishing Serena.

He was mine, and he'd given her something that was mine.

And I let him fuck me.

Jesus. What's wrong with you?

I took my arms away from him and let my legs fall away. He must have felt me draw away, because he rolled off me, rubbing his eyes. I felt naked without his body clothing me, but Serena's sobs were a third person in the room.

"What happened?" I asked. "Why were you punishing her?"

"She's topping from the bottom."

"What does that mean?"

"It means I fucked up."

He stood. I twisted to see him. I hadn't seen his naked body in two weeks and I wanted a moment to admire it, but he pulled on his sweatpants.

"Should I be hurt?" I asked.

"Are you?"

"I think so."

Was I? Hurt. Satisfaction. Betrayal. Joy. Warmth. My feelings were a box of puzzle pieces. They were meant to fit together, but it was going to take some work to see the whole picture.

"Are you admitting you care about me?"

"Are you kidding me right now, Adam Steinbeck?"

"Yes. No. Of course not." He took a deep breath and sat on the edge of the bed. "I lost my shit. Serena broke the furnace to get to me. And when I thought about what could have happened to you, I lost control."

"Get to you? Like, how?"

He moved hair from my forehead. "You knocked yourself pretty good. Does it hurt?"

"Only when you touch it." I slapped his hand away. "What does she want from you?"

"Attention. Excitement. Punishment. I think a way out of her relationship with Stefan. It doesn't matter." He paused for a second, and her crying came through the door. "She wants aftercare. She's not getting it."

I'd seen aftercare in the dark room with the window at the Cellar. I remembered the tenderness and intimacy between Dom and sub.

I wasn't the jealous type, but if he gave her aftercare, I would skin them both alive.

Maybe I was the jealous type after all.

"Thirty days," I said. "You're mine for thirty days."

We watched each other for a long time. Everything drifted away. Serena's sounds, the click of sleet on the roof, the rattle of the windows. I didn't shift my gaze from his blue eyes. This submissive shit was so ten-minutes-ago.

"Diana?" he said without shifting away.

"Maybe the contract says you can share me, but I don't share you."

"Do you know you do this thing where you drill into people by just looking at them?"

"And?"

His lips tightened in a smile so slight, I would have missed it if I wasn't watching every change in his face.

"And." He leapt forward and kissed me, surprising me with it even though he was right in front of me. "And I admire the same things about you that I did before you left me." He stood. "Let's take care of business."

He opened the door to my room. Serena was standing in the corner closest to the door, her face streaked with tears.

"Stand here." He pointed at the center of the doorframe.

She stood exactly there. Her legs were closed. She was slouched in a sexless submission.

"What do you have to say?" he asked Serena.

She looked at me through puffy, red, yet strangely satisfied eyes. "I'm sorry."

"Explain what you did."

"I broke the furnace."

"I can make this even less fun, Serena."

She took a deep breath that hitched. "I wanted to come between you and Master Adam."

"I'm not your Master."

"Yes, sir," she said. That bothered me more than Master, because those were my words to him. "My Master is gone and there's no one to punish me. Adam wouldn't do it, so I gave him a reason to."

"If Stefan knew this about you," I said, "why has he been gone so long? He could have come back."

They both looked at me as if they knew something I didn't and they were trying to figure out if I was close to putting together some puzzle. I was outside the circle. I'd always been outside the circle.

I wanted to be inside the circle. I wanted to understand what they understood. I wanted to participate fully in Adam's secret life. I wanted him to be mine inside that life, if that was possible, because we could never go back to who we were.

And I realized that I was inside the circle. I'd claimed a place there.

"Stefan knew," I said. "He knew and he was playing a game with us."

"With me," Adam said, and Serena stood there with her eyes glued to the floor, denying nothing. "Welcome to my world, Diana."

Chapter 76

PAST PERFECT

A little ad appeared on the side of my screen. A Manet exhibit at the Met. There hadn't been a Manet show at the Met since Mom died. I clicked to see which paintings were included, but found the one I wanted to see was still happily in Paris. Then I went looking for a picture of it. I had to see it.

I let it take up my entire screen. I wanted to crawl into it. Understand it. Live it.

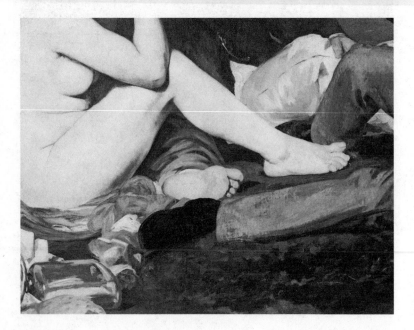

The blanket under her ass. She could probably feel the rocks beneath it digging into her skin. Was it cold enough to make her nipples hard? Her left leg, the way it dropped, the men had to see her pussy. Were they commenting on how wet she was? Who would take her first? Or would one take her mouth while the other—

"I got your dry cleaning." Kayti came in with a clear plastic trail behind her.

I hurried to shut the browser tab before she saw. "Okay." I cleared my throat and tried to remember what I had been doing before the ad showed up.

"You should wear this one to Metropolis tonight." She flipped the clear plastic up, revealing my red blouse with tonal birds. When I moved, they looked as though they were in flight.

"Good idea," I said, still squirming in my seat from the painting. "Bring your card. We might have to leave early."

Chapter 77

PRESENT TENSE – DAY TWELVE

He bathed me for the second time. In five years of marriage, he'd only bathed me when I bled from the D&C. Without the sadness of the lost baby or the tears of the previous bath, his hands were slow and erotic. He touched every inch of slick skin.

"She's been begging me to hurt her every time I go over there. Stefan gave me the green light to fuck her, not paddle her. I've caused a ton of trouble with him. Put your head back."

I faced the ceiling, and he poured water over my head. He was pensive and far away, but different from his distance in Manhattan. He wasn't closed off. He was both vulnerable and commanding in his own thoughts.

"But he wanted you to."

He leaned his forearms on the edge of the tub. His fingertips dripped until he turned his hands over and rubbed his right palm with his left. "He wants to open the door to… things. I want the door closed."

"What things?"

"Things I don't want."

"What? Tell me."

"No!" he barked. He never barked. His voice was most powerful when it was steady and strong.

I drew my knees up like a frightened child and hated myself for it.

He was hiding something. A man without secrets didn't have to yell.

"You didn't fuck her, did you?"

I hated that I had to ask. Before Montauk, I never would have.

No, not before Montauk. Before I left a note on the counter, I never would have asked such a question. But I'd set him loose.

"Of course not." He put the pitcher aside and sat straight on the stool. "She doesn't want to be fucked as much as she wants to be hurt. You can sit up."

I sat up, and Adam snapped a hand towel off the rack and dried his hands with his elbows resting on his knees.

"You know what this trip has taught me?" He waited for an answer with the front of his shirt bath-wet and the seam between his lips straight and serious.

I wrapped my arms around my bent legs and cupped my hands on my elbows. "I can't imagine it taught you anything you didn't already know."

"I have limits. Hard limits. But I don't know what they are until it's too late. And I just... I'm not ready for this again. The affectation with these people. The overdrawn courtesy. You see what it's covering up?" He flung his arm toward the wall behind him, pointing at an imaginary Serena. "He manipulated her, and she played me. I can't even get on his case for it, because it's so normal. And I should have seen it coming. Should have seen it a mile away and played the game instead of falling into it like a schmuck."

I put my hand on his, letting the water drip onto his pants. "You've been away from it for a long time."

I squeezed his hand. He looked angry and forlorn, holding on to a thousand words until he found the right handful. I slid to the center of the tub, getting up on my knees. I leaned over to him and moved my hands up his arms.

"You're going to be all right," I said with every ounce of conviction I could. "It'll all come back. You're amazing. I mean…" I needed more specific words. Accuracy counted or he'd think I was bullshitting him. "You make me feel safe. I've been walking around in this body my whole life and it's been like dragging around a liability. It's weak, and it wants, and it's built like a magnet for pain. Men look at me on the street… not just me, all of us…women… and it's scary. I'm scared all the time. I didn't know that. I thought it was just how a person felt. Not until you brought me here and I wasn't scared to give my body to you."

"That's you, Diana. You're finding yourself. Don't let the high cloud the reality."

"No." I squeezed his biceps. "I want the high. I want it so badly, and I want the reality."

He shook his head, gave one of my hands a short squeeze, and reached for the towel. "Up."

I stood, and he wrapped the towel around me, tucking one corner tightly under the other until I was snug. I leaned into him and he wrapped his arms around me, resting his chin on my head. I could see a quarter of his expression in the mirror, and even from that oblique angle, his trouble ran deep and turbulent.

Chapter 78

PRESENT TENSE – DAY THIRTEEN

Adam wasn't in bed when I woke. The storm had been relentless. Communication held. The power flicked to the generator. Snow drifted to the bottoms of the windows. I felt wrapped in a white cushion of icy batting, protected from the rest of the world. When it stopped, the world went quiet and bright.

By noon, the sun was bright, and a blue plumber's van parked in front of the studio.

Things weren't getting done in New York. Zack's departure had opened up a five-gallon drum of worms, and they were getting out. We couldn't have chosen a worse time to be away from the office.

"Dad's slipping," Adam said, holding his phone to me over breakfast. "He can't keep up."

I read Kayti's email outlining all the line editing, invoicing, and production decisions she still had on her desk. No mention of the divorce. But she wouldn't email Adam about my slip. She'd email me, and I didn't have my email.

"It's a different business than even four years ago," I said. "Do you think they need us to come back?"

"Do you?"

"No. Yes. I don't know. I want to finish. We have two freelancers we can pay rush fees. And I can do the Islands piece myself."

"I can run these invoices. Yeah, you take care of the editing." He nodded to himself, folding his bottom lip in thought. "You should take the office. It's quiet." He turned back to his work and spoke absently, "When the sun is down, you're mine again." I turned to leave, but he grabbed my hand, pulling me down. "And you need to stay away from Serena. You understand why now."

"Yes, sir."

He took me by the back of the neck and kissed me, and though only his lips touched me, he kissed me with his whole body. He hadn't kissed me like that in Manhattan, ever.

Chapter 79

PRESENT TENSE – DAY THIRTEEN

I tucked my laptop under my arm and headed for the office, passing the library. Serena sat in the winged chair there, bare feet tucked under her, flipping through a magazine. I was supposed to stay away from her, but I was so curious I changed direction and went into the library, settling into a thick wooden chair that reminded me I was sore.

"Good morning," I said.

"Hi."

I opened the laptop. A folded piece of paper fluttered out.

"How are you doing?" I asked, opening the note. "After last night?"

Remember how you got sore. – Adam.

"Fine. Why?"

I tucked the paper into my pocket, hiding my smile. As if I could forget where the pain came from.

I shrugged. "Just checking. Girl to girl."

She didn't respond right away. Just flipped through her magazine. I started my edit when she spoke up.

"You seemed into it."

"I was."

"I've had a few Masters since him," she said absently, as if mentioning the weather. "But none like Adam. He's got the right balance."

"Of what?"

"Cruelty and compassion." She closed the magazine. "I'm sorry about your head. It was supposed to be more fun."

I closed the laptop halfway. This conversation needed my attention. "It wasn't. We didn't come here to play. Not with you."

"Adam knows how it goes. He knew the minute I asked him to punish me straight out. Which he could have just done."

"I thought Stefan didn't want Adam punishing you."

She shrugged. "Things happen."

Her submission pushed the boundaries of pure aggression. I started to wonder if, five years before, she'd broken Adam on purpose.

"Whatever it is you're playing, I don't want it."

"Why not?" Her dark brown eyes had Venus flytrap lashes that caught my insecurities when they blinked. "You can handle it."

"You're not interested in me. You're interested in Adam. My husband. I'm sorry you couldn't have him, but he loves me."

She hung her head, and while her face was out of my view, I thought she was sad. I was wrong. When she looked up, I saw that she'd been hiding a smile.

The low rumble of an engine cut through the dead silence of the icy world outside. A car door slammed. Voices, muffled through the windows and walls.

Serena stood and pulled down her skirt. "No, he doesn't love you."

"You think you know him so well?"

"He can't love a submissive. Once he breaks them, he doesn't want them. I learned the hard way."

"Serena!" a voice called from across the house. Stefan. "Come!"

Serena's lips went slack and her eyelids fluttered. Just before she spun on her bare heel and ran toward the front door, she let out a gasp that I couldn't deny sounded a little orgasmic.

I needed to see what she did when she saw him, so I got up to follow.

Adam stood in the doorway. I nearly crashed into him.

"Stay in here," he said, pushing me gently back. "Please."

"Why?"

"Just stay and finish editing. I'll come get you."

Without another word, he slid the pocket door closed, shutting me away from the rest of the house.

Chapter 80

PRESENT TENSE – DAY THIRTEEN

Adam and Stefan stood in the exact center of the yard, in the middle distance between the houses, as if intuiting the point of no return to their safe spaces. They talked, but their footprints in the snow showed their bodies had circled around each other. The plumbers left, and still they were talking.

I watched from the glass door to the veranda. The same door I'd stood at when Stefan choked Serena to orgasm.

She'd left the paddle. I didn't realize I was running my hand over it, feeling its smooth curves, its weight in my hand, the caress of its warmth.

What are they talking about?

I'd waited in the library, behind the closed pocket door, until I couldn't take it any longer. I slipped into the kitchen and ate something. The house was empty, or so I thought. Serena was standing in the office, watching Adam talk to Stefan.

"What are they talking about?" I'd asked.

"Me. Us."

"Who's us?"

"Adam and me."

"There is no Adam and you."

She never answered. I went upstairs. That was when I found the paddle.

I'd watched through a crack in the door as Adam paddled Serena. I was intensely and deeply jealous. He hadn't touched her skin. He gave her no pleasure and took none for himself. Yet the act was intensely sexual. Intimate. The pain. The emotions. His rage. Her shame.

I swallowed, realizing how my hand had drifted over the paddle's surface as if it were a lover. I tapped the edge on the tip of my nose as I remembered the scene, then I pressed it to my lips. Paused.

I kissed it. A blessing. An understanding. Closing my eyes, I accepted the place of that tool in the world.

I put it on the window seat.

The paddle had terrified me and now...

I didn't have a chance to complete the thought. Adam and Stefan headed back to the house. Below me, the door opened, and Serena walked out, hair flowing behind her.

Adam continued into the house. I heard his footfall downstairs. The closet door. The stairs creaking under him.

Outside, Serena reached Stefan. He turned and walked into the studio. She followed. Adam came into my room as the couple disappeared into the side door.

"What's going on?" I asked without turning around.

I felt his breath on the back of my neck.

"Nothing."

I turned. "Nothing? You were talking for two hours."

"Nothing you need to worry about." He reached for the bump on my head.

I slapped his hand away. "I'll decide what I need to worry about. Is he going to punish her?"

Did I sound too eager? Did I sound as if I wanted to be a part of it?

I didn't sound concerned about her, that was for sure. It had taken two weeks for that to change.

Adam folded his lips between his teeth, tilting his head at me, as if considering carefully before he spoke. "You're not part of this world. You never will be. That's by design."

I crossed my arms. The wall between us got thicker and higher, and I didn't know why. I didn't know what had happened in the last two hours to close him off. "Was he mad at you?"

"Of course. But he was more concerned about her."

"Concerned?"

"Why are you challenging me? What's the problem?"

"Me? What's my problem? You and me, we were so close last night, and now you're shut down. You're hiding things. This is the problem, Adam, it was always the problem. You keep things from me."

"No, the problem was you leaving me notes on the kitchen counter."

God, I wanted to punch his face. I walked out. Or I tried to. He grabbed my arm.

"Let me go."

"You want to know what we talked about?"

I jerked my arm away.

"He wanted to punish me through you. Then he wanted to punish her. He wanted to share you to punish me, then paddle you while I watched. Then he wanted you to serve him while Serena watched."

"Serve him?"

"Jesus, you're so curious." He said it as if it were a moral failing.

"You brought me here." I was stiff as a board, a finger pointing up and a jaw set so rigidly I spoke through my teeth. "You held my life over my head. You endangered my family's company. You put me in a car I didn't know you owned and brought me here. All that's bad enough, but I chose to go along because I trust you and I had more to gain than lose. Up until now. As of now, it's all changed. You showed me things I never thought I'd see. You dangled a new way of thinking in front of me, and yeah, I was curious. But now I'm not curious about other people. I'm not curious about your secret life. I'm curious about me. I'm curious about what I'm feeling, and I can look it in the face for the first time. I don't have to be afraid, and I'm so free. I'm so…" I held my hands out to him and tried to grasp the feeling. My face stung with tears, but I held them back. I couldn't let this devolve into crying and comfort. "I didn't know I'd feel like this. I didn't know giving control would make me feel in control. I am fearless, but only because Adam Steinbeck is showing me who I am. Without you, this part of myself that's open now isn't an opportunity. It's an open wound. Every time you shut down, it bleeds. I get small and scared all over again."

I blinked, squeezing out tears. I didn't want to cry, so I grit my teeth together and breathed slowly through my nose. Cleared my throat. Held it together. I needed to finish this conversation. *We* needed to.

As if he understood what I couldn't say, he didn't wipe my cheeks or put his arms around me. He put his hands on his hips and looked down. It wasn't a submissive gesture. He was giving me space to get myself together without his scrutiny.

"You didn't cross off sharing," he said. "You were right when you said I wouldn't share you. But he knows you didn't redline it, so he's trying to hurt me by pressuring me to share. Even if it's not about him touching you, if you even kneel to him from ten feet away, it's sharing." He finally raised his face to me. "He can't force me to, and he can't force you to. But I crossed a line with Serena. I'll get a reputation. It's a small community. But I'm not doing it."

"If it's from ten feet away?"

"No. And the fact that you're even considering it? It's uncomfortable for me."

"I'm just trying to make your life a little easier."

"That's the sub talking, and that makes me uncomfortable too." He took my hand. That little touch cracked me open. I had to hold back another sob.

"Because subs aren't supposed to talk?" I bristled just enough for anger to temper the sobs.

"Because that the sub is you."

I had questions about what he'd expected of bringing me to Montauk if not to bring out my inner submissive, but he was missing the point.

"Well," I said, "that was your wife talking."

A door slammed across the yard. Adam and I froze, hearing indistinct voices, the faraway words of a man and the softer cries of a woman.

Adam stood between the window and me. He didn't move.

"Another show?" I asked.

"Probably. But not what you think. Punishing a woman who likes to be punished can get complicated."

I could have shown him I trusted him by showing no interest in what was outside, but my body reacted to the unknown in the way it always did. I stepped toward the window and looked over Adam's shoulder. He moved behind me, and we watched together.

Serena brushed the last of the snow from a picnic chair and spread a blanket over it. Stefan sat down and crossed his legs. She bowed to him and walked to the left side of the yard, where the snow was untouched.

"It's pure devotion," I said. "And she doesn't mean any of it."

"She does."

"She wants you."

"Serving him still satisfies her."

Serena walked into the fresh snow, making grey footprints in the flat white expanse. Adam put his hand on the small of my back. She walked a straight line, then followed it back and jumped to leave a blank space.

"Why is the paddle on the window seat?" he asked in my ear.

"Serena left it."

"Your lip marks are on it."

I looked down at it. In the angle of the winter light, a dull *O* broke the sheen of the wood finish. I could deny they were mine, but what would be the point? The instrument was meant to be used.

He took a deep breath against my neck. I couldn't see him, so I couldn't tell if the sigh was arousal or annoyance.

Serena jumped once, making a single divot, jumped again, and walked a line parallel to the first. She ran back to the start and made a diagonal.

"What you did to Serena last night," I said. "I want you to do that to me."

"Why?"

Serena finished the letter *M* in the snow.

I'M

I'd been brutally honest when I left him, but I'd been shallow. There was a more brutal, more honest truth to be told.

"I need it." My voice cracked.

Adam took half a step back. When I started to turn to face him, he held me in position, watching Serena in silence.

I'M SO

"You need it?" he asked.

"Yes. I can't explain why. Seeing you give that to her… I was jealous, but there was something else. I know you were angry, but I wished I was her. I wanted to be free."

I'M SOR

He ran his fingers down my back. "I want to break you right now. I've never wanted anything more in my life. At this point, I don't know whether to take you home and pretend this never happened or take you deeper with me."

"It's too late to pretend it didn't happen."

His hands caressed my ass, running under it and between my legs, getting his finger under my panties.

I'M SORR

"This works better if you're turned on already."

My clit was swollen and hungry for him. My eyes closed when he touched it. He was going to give it to me. My fear was the flame under my desire.

"Yes, sir."

He sucked in a breath. "Put your hands on the glass."

I bent at the waist. Adam leaned over me and picked up the paddle, putting it in front of my face.

"Kiss it again."

. I'M SORRY

I kissed the wood reverently, letting my lips linger on it. The plane that was going to hurt me, dominate me, challenge me to be less and more than I'd ever been.

Adam ran his hand over my ass, up to my lower back, which he pressed down while he tapped my bottom with the paddle.

"Up," he said.

I pushed my ass up for him. The very act of offering him my body for his domination relaxed my muscles and quieted my mind.

How had I ever lived without this?

I'M SORRY D

"We go until she finishes your name. Ready?"

I nodded. My body responded with ecstatic vibrations humming with the sound of sexual pleasure.

"Say words."

"Yes, sir."

I heard the whistle in the air before the pain, which was more intense than I dreamed possible. I screamed. Stefan looked up. Serena stopped and met my eyes through the window. Stefan barked at her, and she continued.

Adam hooked his fingers in the waist of my underwear and slid them down, tapping my ankles to let me know I had to step out.

"I don't like screaming, but I understand you might not be able to help it. Open your mouth."

I did. He stuffed my underwear in my mouth.

I'M SORRY DI

Stefan was still looking up at us. Serena glanced up when she could take her eyes off her feet. Could she see me? I hoped so. I wanted her to know Adam was claiming me.

"What's your name?" Adam asked, stroking and tapping my ass.

"Eye-ah-uh."

The next stroke hit like a blowtorch, and I screamed into the taste of my cunt, twisting my legs. He pushed me straight, tapped, struck again.

I'M SORRY DIA

He rained a series of blows on my bottom and the backs of my thighs, first one side, then the other, then both. Burn on burn. He stopped for a moment to touch me, grabbing raw skin. I groaned from deep in my lungs, and he paddled me again.

Yes, I cried. My face was slick with tears. Tears of relief. I accepted that I needed something in this. Some release that had built up my entire life. A reset button. A reboot. A place where I only had to bend.

I was submissive.

I'M SORRY DIAN

I saw Serena finish the N through a fugue. I was floating, and Adam was the rope that held me fast to the earth with his will and his pain.

I'M SORRY DIANA

"What's your name?" His voice cut through the soothing vapor of my surrender, transmitted through the clouds to kiss me with approval.

The high had nothing to do with the pain. The high was pleasing him. The high was from my choice to leave my own will behind, go further, endure more, give more.

I said my name.

My name was a rumble in my throat.

My name was a single, long sound.

My name was the shape of my body leaning on the window.

The light got dimmer as Adam leaned into my face, blocking the window. His hands framed my face.

"You are so deep in subspace," he said as he pulled my panties from my mouth.

I hoped that made him happy, because I wanted him to be happy, and I had no control over the dreamstate I'd entered.

He picked me up under my arms and knees and carried me to the bed before laying me out on my stomach. I couldn't do more than follow him with my eyes as he got things from the bathroom, arranged my body comfortably, put a blanket over me.

"Was I all right?" I asked, surprised by the huskiness of my voice.

He knelt by the side of the bed to be at my eye level. "Unreal. You're not broken, but I didn't expect you to take so much. Didn't expect subspace."

"Is that good?"

He wiped away tears I didn't know I'd shed. "Just stay still and let me take care of you."

The pain on my bottom was split by a line of cool balm. Adam spread it wherever I burned. Slowly, he worked it in, aggravating the bruises and raising another heat. He pulled my legs apart and massaged the insides of my thighs. I was coming out of subspace and into more familiar territory.

He put his hands on my hips. "Up on your knees."

He helped me move until my ass was up and I was exposed. He spread me apart. I was coming down from the high, and the pain of his touch made me cringe. When he ran his thumb over bruised muscles, I squeaked.

He slapped me lightly. "Shush. Trust me."

Before I could agree, he put his tongue around my opening, circling it. I was on fire, so close that when he sucked on my clit, I burst apart. But he didn't stop. He gave me orgasm after orgasm, until I was awake, aware, and screaming in ultimate pleasure.

I had only had the simplest words.

Good. Yes. Mine. Yes. More.

Chapter 81

PRESENT TENSE – DAY FOURTEEN

In the hours after he brought me back from subspace, I'd told him about the Manet. I'd never told anyone about it, and when he pulled up the painting on his phone, he said, "Wow. I wonder how many awakenings this thing is responsible for."

He'd fed me dinner in bed, and I fell asleep in his arms. He didn't pat my shoulder or look far away. He was completely, unequivocally present.

I woke at dawn with his hand on my cheek. His lashes flicked and his body rose and fell with his breath. I turned my head and kissed his palm, moving my lips to form words my throat wouldn't agree to make.

"*I love you.*"

I loved complying. I loved hushing for him. Pleasing him. Trusting him.

I got out of bed. My body ached, and my ass was black and blue. It hurt to get dressed and walk down the stairs, but in a way, that reminded me of the pleasure of the day before.

The sky was the same deep blue as the ocean, tinged lighter at the horizon. I'd been in the house two weeks and hadn't walked on the beach.

The ocean called me. I felt strong, sure, joyful as I got on my coat and hawk scarf.

Tell him you love him.

I was going to tell him, and I was going to stand straight and tall when I did. Then I was going to kneel and he was going to fuck me like he owned me.

It was a plan.

I opened the back door and walked outside, shutting it behind me with a squeak and a slap. The sea was louder than I expected, and the salty wind bit my cheeks. I crossed the wooden deck, its furniture cushioned in smooth snow piles.

Down the wood stairs to the snowy grass, I steeled myself to tell him I loved him. Then we'd go back to Manhattan and…

And what? What if we had the same problems? What if my infatuation with this new Adam was no more than that? An infatuation with excitement and adventure? What if all the same shit reappeared in a week or a year and he was as distant as he ever was? Could I leave him twice? Could I ever screw up the courage again? And how old would I be? How much closer to the day I had to face what my mother had faced?

The backyard grass ended abruptly with a fence. Beyond it, the rocky beach took over. The sea undulated back and forth. The line between wet and dry made a sine wave thirty feet from the fence.

"It's high tide," a voice said in the blustering wind.

I snapped my head in the direction of the sound. Stefan in a pea coat and wooly ribbed cap. His eyes were riveting blue and his hands were in his pockets.

"It doesn't usually get this close. It concerns me."

My decision to go outside the gate was overruled by good sense. "I'm sure you have flood insurance." I put my hands on the top of the gate but didn't open it.

"Of course. But it won't stop the water if the water wants

to come. We hold it back and it pushes forward. One for one. *Quid pro quo.*"

He was intimidating even when he smiled. Even when his hands were stuffed in his pockets and he was saying something general and philosophical about the tides.

"I'm sorry about what happened," I blurted. "I can explain."

He shook his head. "Don't. You did nothing wrong. I'm the one who's sorry. I love Serena, but she has a way of creating trouble." He leaned on the fence and looked over the ocean. "Have you seen the rocks on the beach? Schist mostly." He dug into his pocket and pulled out a fistful of small stones. He held them out to me.

I couldn't see the stones well. The sun just peeked over the horizon. It was still not quite daylight, but one stone stood out to me. It looked like a heart. Not a paper heart folded and cut, but a muscle. A living thing.

"This is interesting." I pointed at it, and he rolled it to his fingertips, holding it up. His hands were deft as a magician's.

"Yes," he agreed enthusiastically. "It's quartz. Not special, but this?" He pointed at what looked like a valve in the dark, but it was actually a rough fractal twisting around the smooth shape. "Coral from the Gulf Stream. It can attach to rocks and get carried away to foreign waters."

"It's beautiful."

He handed it to me. "It only lives one summer season up here. Then it dies and leaves this. Take it."

I took it and put it in my pocket.

"I thought he had no business bringing you here," Stefan said.

"And you changed your mind?"

He laughed to himself. "No, actually. But I understand his desperation." He put the rest of the stones in his pocket. "I'm losing Serena." He brushed a line of snow off the top of the gate. "When I leave her alone to respect her space, I lose her. When I pin her down, I feel her leaving me. If I thought a trip to the suburbs for thirty days of vanilla sex would bind her to me, I'd try it."

"Vanilla's a state of mind."

"Touché." He smiled ruefully. "Nothing lasts forever, I guess."

"I'm sorry." I kneaded the rock in my cold fingers. I felt for him in a way I hadn't felt for Adam when I hurt him. I hadn't steeled my heart against Stefan.

"I saw you here and I thought, 'Ah, talk to her. She's in Serena's shoes. She'll tell you what to do.'" He waved off his own stupid ideas. "The desperate strategies of a desperate man."

I put my hand on his shoulder. "It's going to be fine."

"The owner of all your pain and pleasure has arrived," Stefan said, indicating behind me with a jerk of his chin.

Adam was taking big steps across the back deck. He wore a fresh shirt and trousers, but his shoes were untied and he wasn't wearing a jacket.

"I didn't tell you to get out of bed," he said when he was close.

"You never needed to tell me before."

His look crumpled me like a piece of paper with the wrong words on it. The many ways to tell a man to go fuck himself shot up my throat, only to be trapped behind my teeth when I locked my mouth shut.

"I see how much you want to be punished," he said, holding up one finger. He slowly lowered it. "Knees."

Knees? He wanted me to kneel in front of Stefan? Over what? I was touching Stefan's shoulder but there was a fence between us, and more importantly, fuck him.

"Huntress. Do not disobey me."

His tone didn't speak to the Diana who told him to fuck himself. It spoke directly to the part of me that needed his ownership. I couldn't pretend that his voice wasn't a physical force to that need.

I put my knees in the snowy grass.

"So pretty from this angle," Stefan said. The same guy who had just spoken to me in desperation was now the voice of humiliation.

"She is," Adam replied. Then, by a change of tone, he spoke to me. "Crawl back to the house and wait for me in your room. Go."

I'd said I wouldn't crawl for him. I'd stated it explicitly in black and red and white. But I'd also said he couldn't hit me with a paddle and he couldn't gag me. I also said I wouldn't call him sir.

I'd leapt over my own boundaries, and let him leap over the rest.

I put my hands on the cold deck. I had to stop. My heart was beating too hard and my pussy went code red with need. Hands and knees in front of these men, I fell back into where I'd been the day before.

I must have taken too long to think about it. Even as I knew I was going to do exactly what Adam asked, I hesitated.

He unbuckled his belt and yanked it out of the loops in one move. He stood right in front of me, crotch to face, and folded the belt in two. "Open your mouth."

I did, and before the obscenities I had ready came marching out, he put the belt in it.

"Bite."

Stefan laughed derisively, as if he was partnering with Adam in this particular leap over a sub's limits.

My knees were getting cold. I had to decide to obey him or not.

I bit down into the leather of my husband's belt.

"Now. Crawl inside. And keep your ass in the air. I'll see you upstairs." His tone wasn't unkind, but it did reveal an expectation of compliance. He wasn't asking. He was neither impatient nor shrill.

I'd been living with a god all these years and never knew.

He snapped his fingers and I dropped to my hands. "Go."

My body jerked to obey as if his will was a natural force. I moved one hand, then one knee. The shallow layer of ice and snow crunched under me.

My mind fell into a swoon. I was permitted to do this, first by myself, then by Adam. His protection made it possible. I felt them behind me, watching my disgrace as my tongue tasted the leather of the belt. My ass still hurt from the paddle. The thought of the sting of that belt on top of it didn't cause fear, but a hopeful anticipation.

When I got to the door, I had to stand to open it. In the reflection of the glass, I saw Adam standing silently, facing the ocean, in the middle distance between Stefan and me. His back was as strong and solid as a brick wall. I slid the door open and got on my feet.

I took the belt out of my mouth. I probably wasn't supposed to even be standing, much less removing it without permission.

Adam still stood, feet spread apart, hands balled into fists at his side. Stefan hadn't moved either. Only the tide had shifted.

What did he want me to do?

What did he need me to do?

His room faced the back. I ran upstairs. I could be obedient and satiate my curiosity at the same time. But by the time I got to his room and pressed my nose to the back window, they were gone.

Chapter 82

PRESENT TENSE – DAY FIFTEEN

He came behind me, swooping into the room with the force of the sun's gravity. He took me by the back of the neck and pushed me down to my knees.

I wouldn't have tolerated that a month ago.

Not the violence or the attitude.

But this was Montauk.

I stayed on my knees, head down, hands on my thighs. He stood over me, snow crusted on his boots and melting sludge onto the hardwood.

"Don't talk to him. Not without me in the room."

Still in my submissive posture, I answered the only way I could. "Are you kidding me?"

"I don't trust him."

"Maybe you should try trusting *me*."

I kept my eyes on my hands. My position contradicted my words, but I had a deep feeling I knew was correct, that Adam would hear me better if we were still in the game.

"I do," he said.

"Really?"

He laid his hands on my shoulders and slid them down my back, hooking his fingers under my arms. He picked me up, and we faced each other. Those lips, those eyes, the stubble on a jaw that defied geometry. I couldn't look at it. I unbuttoned my coat.

"No," he said. "I guess not."

"Now you're talking." I threw my coat on the bed and sat in the upholstered chair. He was making my knees weak. "Stefan and I were just talking. It wasn't anything. He wasn't trying to come between us."

"What were you talking about?"

"Rocks. And Serena. You'd think, with what he does and how he acts, that he doesn't love her. But he does."

Adam sat on the bed. "He does. Of course. What you see is what they need. But that doesn't mean he's not a predator."

"I've handled predators."

"Yeah. Maybe. As the old Diana, you did. But you're changing. I can see it. It's like watching a flower bloom. You're so beautiful when you let go. But you're leaving and you're taking the change with you, and there's not a goddamn thing I can do about it. All I get is the time here. Two more weeks. Then you're on your own, and there are going to be dozens of men like that. Trust me. They're in the fucking woodwork, and when you're single—"

"Wait—"

"—I have to tolerate it, but I can't watch it. Not here."

"—let's—"

Stay together.

Be married.

Start over.

I couldn't choose between them, and the words got caught in my throat.

"I need time," he said, and I cut myself off. "I need to decide if we should finish this."

"Do I get a say?"

He stood. "Technically, yes. But if we go home now because I stopped it, you get everything. Done."

"This stopped being about McNeill-Barnes a week ago."

"It was never about McNeill-Barnes for me."

Right. I knew that. It was about me. Him. It was about our marriage.

"I want to stay," I said.

"I know."

He walked out and closed the door.

Chapter 83

PRESENT TENSE – DAY FIFTEEN

He'd left me with a feeling of unease. He wasn't telling me everything. I was ready to explode, and he was holding back. When he held back, I held back, and I couldn't do that anymore. He might turn back into Manhattan Adam and a million crappy things could happen, but the idea of signing divorce papers when we got back was absurd.

What do you want?

I knew what I wanted. I got dressed, showered, and ran downstairs to tell him.

He'd left me a note on the counter.

Went into the city to see Charlie. Back by dinner.

Fine. Actually, this would do nicely. I put bread in the toaster and composed the note in my head.

Stefan came in from the gym. "Hello. How are you?"

"Good. Great, actually."

He leaned on the counter, arms crossed. "I wanted to ask you something about yesterday."

"All right." I hoped he wasn't going to ask me to talk about

Adam. I couldn't speak for him. I was about to say something polite in that vein when Stefan's phone rang.

He plucked it out of his pocket and looked at the screen. "My mother. I'll come back later?"

"Knock first."

He took the call and rattled off a good-humored conversation in what must have been a Scandinavian language. He waved and went out the back door, crossing over to the studio.

I rummaged through the drawers in the library until I found a notebook and a pencil. I slid the wingback chair to the dresser, and I began the relationship the way I'd ended it.

> *Dear Adam,*
>
> *After everything we've been through, there's no easy way to tell you this. So I'm just going to spit it out.*
>
> *I love you.*

Out the window, the morning sky was a clear glass blue and our way together was in front of us. I rewrote the note a hundred times and finished in the late afternoon, over lunch. He'd gone out to decide whether to stay and finish, but I knew what I wanted and I needed to tell him before he opened his mouth. He needed to know I was committed to staying before he told me his decision.

I left my note on the kitchen counter. Seconds after I turned my back on it, the long black car crunched down the drive.

He was back.

Chapter 84

PRESENT TENSE – DAY FIFTEEN

Dear Adam,

After everything we've been through, there's no easy way to tell you this. So I'm just going to spit it out.

I love you.

I never thought I'd ever say it again. Believe me, if I thought we had a chance, I wouldn't have written you that other note. But you made the chance. You did it. You showed me the you inside you and the me inside me.

I ran upstairs when I saw the car. Threw on one of the short nightgowns he liked and went into his room. He'd go to the kitchen to look for me. Get a glass of water. See the note. Come upstairs.

It was going to be great. I didn't have an ounce of remorse for a damn thing. Yes, I'd left him. Yes, it took a lot of balls. Yes, I was going to reverse it, and yes, I felt very good about that.

Thup. The car door.

Scrape. The bags.

Click. The front door.

Murmur. Adam and Thierry talking.

Click. The front door again.

Squeak-snap. The closet door opening and closing.

Creak. Footsteps on the stairs.

He didn't go to the kitchen. Wonderful, handsome, caring, dominant man. He came right to me. I got on my knees and elbows, spread my legs, and raised my ass. He was going to have to fuck me without the note. He'd find it after, but I wanted him to find it without warning, the way he'd found the first note. The symmetry made my self-discovery feel complete.

He was in the hall. I could hear him. He opened the door to my room first. Would he come through the hall or the door between our rooms? I adjusted to face the door between the rooms, showing him his options. Serving him.

Those seconds of waiting were the purest satisfaction. Nothing had ever felt so good to me.

He came through the adjoining door. Stopped. I knew from the sound.

My heart was pounding.

I wanted to look at him so I'd know what he thought, how to adjust, how to do everything he needed, the way he needed.

"Perfect," he said.

Yes!

He threw his coat on the bed and kneeled behind me. When he stroked my bottom, the bruises ached, and when he ran his fingers along my seam, he touched every ache that had been building since he'd left.

"Everything about this is perfect." He slid his hands up my body and curled his body over mine.

I went flat under the weight of him. "You're staying?"

"If you want."

I fell into the happiness. He'd find the note and know I wanted more than a two-week finish. One bite of joy at a time.

"Thank you," I said. "And thank Charlie."

He spoke softly into my ear. "We have a lot to talk about, but not tonight. You're going to break tonight. You're going to beg me to stop."

"I won't."

He got off me and stood. "Get on the bed. Legs up."

I crawled up the high bed and got on my back, opening my legs for him. The nude woman in the Manet looked right at the viewer and dared them to have a problem with her. She was going to let those two men do whatever they wanted whether anyone approved or not. I was her.

"What's your safe word?" he asked.

"Pinochle."

He took one of my feet and put his lips to the inside of my ankle. Had any kiss ever been so sexy?

"Why?"

"When my mom died, my father and I stayed up late playing pinochle because we couldn't sleep. I felt safe."

He dropped my ankle and pulled down the horizontal bar, sliding it along the track. He rested my feet on it. "You're safe here too."

Adam opened a wooden box, and I heard the clink of metal. He came into my vision with a silver object. It looked like interconnected and fused rings, shined to a flawless polish.

"Give me your hands."

I held up my hands. Adam guided them into the rings, where they crossed together, wrist to wrist, and held them over my head.

He stepped out of my view. I heard him get undressed, buttons, belt buckle, pants sliding down. He took his time, until he stood over me in only his unbuttoned shirt.

"You look terrified," he said. "And aroused."

"Listen to the arousal."

He pulled a long silver chain from the wooden box, slowly so that each little ball in the chain flicked the edge and I could get a long look at the rubber-tipped clamps at the end.

"Charlie convinced me all the shit I was worrying about wasn't worth worrying about."

"Like what?"

"I've never loved a woman I've broken. I can't do it to you. Can't turn you into something you aren't. Something I don't love."

He extended his finger and, with a swift motion, spun the chain, making it helicopter and wrap around, sheathing his finger in ball chain. With the clamps tucked into his palm, he got his shirt off.

"What I feel for you," he said, tossing the shirt away. "It's worth protecting. I hated how I felt when you left, but now I don't want to lose it."

"You won't."

Kneeling between my open legs, he put his hands on my breasts and slid them down, the texture of the chain making a line of sensation on my skin.

"I've never loved a sub. I've never wanted to love a woman who's part of that world. I could never get past the negotiations, the scenes. It felt disposable, and that kept me from loving anyone." He dragged his hands over my thighs and back again, resting them on my tits. "If I can love you, even if you don't love me—"

"But I—"

"Hush. Let me finish. I need to see if it's possible. Only answer yes or no. Will you do this with me?"

"Yes."

"I'm signing everything over even if you say no. Easiest divorce in the world. Will you still stay here? Yes or no?"

"Yes."

He pinched my nipples and pulled. His chained finger hurt my left side in a way that went right to my core. Then he brought his hands down again, and the finger with the chain wrapped around it found my clit.

"Yes," I said as he dragged the tiny silver balls along me, back and forth until he slowly put that finger inside. Every ridge started a new wave of sensation. I pushed against the paired roughness and smoothness, and slowly he pulled out.

"The fantasies I've had these past years," he said, unwrapping the chain. "I couldn't even let myself put you in them." He let the wet chain dangle from his fingertips. There were three clamps. "Destroying you is a dream I was afraid to have."

He took two of the clamps in one hand. Silver. Black rubber tips. About the size of bobby pins. He yanked on my right nipple with the other hand, rough, assured, as if doing a job efficiently.

He clamped it. I must have made a face or something, because when he took the other nipple, holding it out, he said, "It doesn't hurt now. Just wait," and clamped it. The chain ran down my belly and ended in another clamp.

"Oh," I said. "Oh, no."

"Don't make me gag you."

He bent his head between my thighs and kissed my clit, ending with a suck. It was so good. Adam knew how to work a clit with a flick and a suck. Always. I was nearly lost in it when he pinched the nub and clamped it at the base.

I squeaked and closed my legs.

"Spread those legs. Show me."

I did, and he pressed them back, looking closely at how he'd done. He glanced up at me.

"I'm taking your ass. Not tonight. But before we go back."

He waited for my answer. Or, more accurately, he waited for me to say no. I was so deep in submission I couldn't say no, and still so deeply myself I couldn't say yes either. He smiled as if reading my mind and ran his tongue along the tight skin stretched over my clit. It felt as if he'd licked some deeper pleasure. A pleasure that had always been there, behind layers of skin and membrane.

I groaned deeply.

"You ready, huntress?" He moved the bar back up, letting my feet dangle in midair.

"Yes."

He positioned his cock at my opening and slammed deep into me. Stopped. His eyes closed and he bent his head.

"I'm sorry. I have to say this." He clamped his hand over my mouth and spoke into my ear. "I always knew. I didn't want to admit it, but I always knew this was you. It scared the hell out of me, and I denied it. I needed to love you more than I wanted to dominate you. Don't doubt for a second that I chose to love you."

He took his hand away and jerked his hips. With the hood of my clit peeled back by the clamp, every thrust felt like an explosion, like a kid setting off a mat of firecrackers on July 4th. The popping and cracking went on and on, and when he straightened himself and pulled on the chain that held my nipples and clit, an M80 went off. I strained against the wrist restraints.

"Don't come," he said, thrusting.

"I want to."

"Don't." He pounded me, fisting the chain, letting go, tugging one way and not the other until I thought I'd lose control.

"I need—" The sentence died. I was going to come whether he liked it or not.

"No, you don't."

He pinched one nipple clip then the other, taking them off.

They went on fire in a flush of explosive pain. I thought my breasts were going to burst, but Adam smiled, bit his lower lip, and fucked me harder.

The pain removed the need to come for a minute, but it returned stronger than before, as if the pleasure was too ambitious to let the hurt win. It had to come in a harder, heavier rush.

I barely had a chance to tell him how close I was. He knew. He straightened and pulled my labia open with two fingers.

That pain.

Between my legs.

"No!" I shouted.

"No screaming."

"Please!"

"Breathe through your nose. Look at me when I come inside you."

He took off the clamp. I held my mouth shut like a vise and sucked air in and out of my nose. The blood rushed back, expanding me in fire and pain. I was almost blind as my husband buried his cock in me and came in slower thrusts, groaning deep.

The pain flowed out, leaving a bigger space for the pleasure rushing to take its place.

"Come, Diana. Come."

I stiffened under him, arched, pushing him deeper. I cried and came so hard I didn't feel the cuffs cut into my skin, and it went on so long, I thought I was losing my mind.

● ● ●

Hours. He fucked me for hours. He tied me up and took pleasure and pain. He took control. He left me on the edge of orgasm for twenty minutes while he held my head down and put his fingers in my ass. It felt so good I begged him to put his cock in it.

He wouldn't, and I cried because I had no will or want after that.

He'd broken me, and I was so out of myself I didn't realize it until he went downstairs to get water.

He'd broken me and I still loved him.

Chapter 85

PRESENT TENSE – DAY FIFTEEN

Dear Adam,

After everything we've been through, there's no easy way to tell you this. So I'm just going to spit it out.

I love you.

I never thought I'd ever say it again. Believe me, if I thought we had a chance, I wouldn't have written you that other note. But you made the chance. You did it. You showed me the you inside you and the me inside me.

My god. We wasted so much time.

Let's make it all up. Let's go back home and do this all over again. I'll be everything you need and you'll be everything I didn't know I needed. We'll get the company going again. We'll be partners in the boardroom, and in the bedroom, you'll bring me to my knees whenever you want. You'll be my Master.

You win. I lose, but I win. I'm yours again.

I love you more than ever,

Your Little Huntress.

I must have fallen asleep, because it was four in the morning and

Adam still wasn't in bed. I was still floppy-limbed, sore, aching, made of dough that had been kneaded but not baked.

Had he found the note?

I didn't know how long he'd been downstairs, but if he went to the kitchen for water, he would have seen it.

What did he think?

Was he writing me a note back?

I got into my nightgown and tiptoed downstairs. He wasn't in the library or the kitchen. I found him in the dark office, framed by a window, facing the darkness between the big house and the studio. He was in pajama pants that hung low on his waist, just below the divots on each side of his lower back. His shoulders were rippled with muscles in tension.

I went in. The floor creaked. He looked around. When I put my hands on his back, he moved away, turning to face me.

"Hey, I was wondering what happened to you," I said. "I left you a note."

He held up his hand. The note was in it, folded into three parts, past over future.

If he'd read it, he didn't look incredibly pleased by what it said. Maybe he didn't believe it, or maybe he'd misunderstood it. Maybe I'd misunderstood. But suddenly I was off balance. I needed him. I was flailing and I didn't even know why. Quicksand or water. Falling fast or drifting slow. Everything in the world had turned upside-down, and I needed him to show me which way our shared gravity pulled.

"Talk to me," I said.

"I know you thought I brought you here to make you love me again."

"I do love you."

He took a breath so deep, his shoulders rose and his chest expanded. "I did something truly evil. I came here with you to break you so I could stop loving you. Then I could cut you loose easily. That's why I waited. I didn't know who I was if I wasn't loving you. I had to let that idea go. Took two weeks."

I didn't get this. He loved me but didn't want to? Was that it? I was confused.

"Did you read the note?"

"Yeah." He tossed it on the desk as if it was a contract with missing redlines. "I did. And it didn't surprise me. I knew it. You loved me, and I loved you."

"Why do you keep using the past tense?"

He flicked my note aside and picked up a piece of paper under it. He wedged it between his index and middle finger and handed it to me. "This was on the counter."

It was a card. I opened it.

> *D—*
>
> *We need to talk.*
>
> *—S*

"Okay? So?"

"I decided today that I could do this. You are submissive. You proved that yesterday and I still loved you. I failed to stop loving you, and I hate failing. But I could get something better. You. I could live without lies, and you could be mine. You could make the impossible possible."

"You're freaking me out. What does that have to do with the note?"

"If you'd stop interrupting, you'd know."

I went cold. His tone wasn't dominant with expectation of obedience, but commanding in its disappointment. I'd been on my knees. I'd crawled. I'd offered my body to him as an object to use, but he'd never made me feel worthless.

At home, he couldn't have gotten to me. But in that office in the early morning dark, I was cut open, broken, vulnerable. He'd taken my armor, carefully unlocked it, slipped it off, and hidden it. When he spoke that pointless phrase in that tone of voice, I was in no position to hear it without hurt.

"Go on," I said with no tools to stop the tears from coming.

"This note. I know you're not fucking Stefan. But it presupposes that you're accessible for a chat. That's on him. You didn't do anything wrong. Nothing about it is a big deal, except it told me

you've crossed over into the world I left, and then, I just changed."
He snapped his fingers. "Like that." He tapped the note on the heel
of his hand, pausing to think. "If I wanted you in this world, I
would have brought you along. I would have started a little kinky
and broken you by our first anniversary. But it's not what I want.
Not then, not now."

"You stopped loving me? Over a note?"

"It's not the note. I have love for you, it's not what it was and
it never will be again, but what little there is? It's mine, and I'm not
giving it up. I'm not going to destroy the only woman I've ever
loved. That's why I'm letting you go."

What was my expression? Open-mouthed, head shaking, eyes
squinting, brows knotted, I must have been a sight.

"You can't do this," I said.

"I have to."

"You made me love you and now—"

"You never told me you didn't want to split up. I didn't know
until it was too late."

"You just… hours… we were doing it for hours. Did you not
love me that whole time?"

A tiny crack played across his hard expression. "You were
perfect."

"Stop it!" I shouted. "Stop it now. Tell me I'm yours!" I pushed
him as hard as I could, but he didn't fall. "You love me! You're
mine. Do you understand? You fucking bossy asshole. You prick.
You motherfucker, you're mine and you love me!"

He took my face in his hands and leaned down so I could see
him clearly. I looked away, but he shifted so the only thing in my
vision was him, slowly shaking his head.

"I'm sorry," was all he said.

"Fuck you," I sputtered.

No. We'd entered this room as husband and wife. Dom and sub.
Business partners and friends. If we left this room as something else,
we'd always be that something else. We'd be ex-things. Ex-partners.
Ex-husband and wife. Ex ex ex.

Once we were out of the room, there was no going back.

I took one step closer to him and lowered myself to my knees. I was at war. He hadn't told me to drop, and I did.

"Diana. Don't."

I bent at the waist and pressed my palms and nose to the floor.

"This is what you wanted." I spoke into the floor. "Take me this way."

"Do you think I went to all this trouble to make you kneel? If I needed to get a sub for a month, I would have just gotten one and given you your divorce."

He stepped over me, and I scrambled to get in front of him. I dropped to my knees and put my face and hands to the floor again.

"Last night," I said into the fringed edge of the rug, "what was last night?"

"Get up."

I didn't move.

"It felt like love," I said.

"Diana, you don't have to submit."

"I trusted you. I trusted it was real."

"Get up!"

"Fuck you! Tell me! Was it real?"

He took me by the arms and pulled me up. I was jelly in his arms, but he fought gravity and good sense.

"It was very real, but I realized how toxic it was. To have someone I love in that world. Don't you get it? I'd stop loving you completely."

"You won't," I said. "You love me. I don't know why you're doing this. I don't know what the game is... but you love me."

He let me go, and I stood on wobbly knees.

"Thierry will drive you home tomorrow. I'll fill out the papers. We're done. It's for the best."

"Fuck you," I said. "You love me."

I dropped to my knees again. I was out of breath, heart pounding, tense, and shitty-feeling, inside and out.

He patted my head, leaving me on the floor as he went upstairs.

Chapter 86

PRESENT TENSE

He'd disappeared behind a door. Willa had packed for me. Outside my window, Stefan and Serena loaded up his shitty pickup and left.

I got in the back of the limo alone. Thierry didn't ask where we were going.

I was going home.

Chapter 87

The day my life changed was different than any other. I kneeled and was stepped over. I begged and was refused. I submitted, but no one claimed dominion over me.

The limo was quiet. The tires made no sound over the Southern State. The windows were closed against the wind. My sobs were silent, the way they were before he taught me how to cry.

The day everything changed, I felt different. I had work to do. A life. Bills. A mortgage. But all my routines seemed foreign and futile. Did I ever perform them? Did they ever matter?

The morning my life changed, I sat in the back of a limousine, staring at a small swatch of fabric that lay in the corner like a wound. It took me fifteen minutes to decide to pick it up.

It was a piece of the stocking he'd ripped off me to rub my feet, a million years ago, when he loved me.

I had a sense of impending doom. A gut feeling that I was ruined. I couldn't believe in healing. Not for me. Because I wasn't a victim here. This was my fault.

All of it. I'd been lazy and fearful. I'd left him and told myself I'd been courageous, but I'd been a coward.

And if my pain was my fault, I had to take responsibility for it. I had to fix it. I had to fix myself, of course, but this man I loved needed help too. I scrunched the stocking up in my fist.

He didn't have a choice.

Why?

He said to trust him.

Why?

He told me he's preserving his love.

Why why why?

Something wasn't adding up.

He can love a submissive. He can and he does.

I was right with myself for the first time, even in pain, because to submit is to understand your sun and your shadow. To submit is to know your place is not always a *where* but sometimes a *when*. To submit is to accept your power and to embrace that your place is both *now* and *forever*.

To submit is to choose. To hunt. To chase. To decide.

To submit is to dominate.

Adam was mine.

I chose him.

I'd thrown him away, and I could choose him again. I could finish this. I could stand by what I wanted, who I was.

There were two weeks left in our arrangement.

They were mine, and so was he.

TO BE CONTINUED...

Acknowledgments

I've been thinking about this book for a long time. Over a year ago I sat in the front seat of my car in a Starbucks parking lot, breaking the story with Lauren Blakely. So many moons later, and it's completely different, but without that first breakout with her I never would have been able to start it.

So first, thank you Lauren for taking that time with me.

I pitched *Marriage Games* to Mary Cummings at a poolside bar in Hawai'i (it wasn't that glamorous, truth. But doesn't it sound so delicious? "I pitched the story to her at a poolside bar in Hawai'i." Glitter just pours off that sentence) I also pitched her a release concept.

Turns out, she was about to pitch me a release concept, and it was the exact same one. It was like we were puzzle pieces. Mary and Ever After have been what a publisher should be. Supportive, unintrusive, constructive, and collaborative. Kudos to her, Taylor, Sarah, and the entire Diversion team.

My husband has done me the service of just being himself, and supporting me in his quiet way while I work. My kids think all I do is work. In fact, they get hours of my time a day. They're greedy, and I love them for it.

Laurelin Paige stayed up until 4 a.m. reading the first draft.

She had a million other things going on, but she beta'd it and then, unbelievably, she did it again after I chopped off the ending and replaced it with the one that wound up here. If you want to know what the original ending was, you'll have to wait until I'm dead. Amy Vox, Bethany, Jenn – more wonderful betas than I deserve.

Cassie Cox, my tireless editor, rushed the hell out of this so I could get it to print. I bow low, because she caught more than a few clunkers. As always, I sound like me, but with better grammar.

My Camorra, ladies and one gentleman, thank you for your support. You guys went into the breach when I had to check out of social media for awhile. Thank you.

Jean Siska checks this and all my books to make sure I at least sound as if I know the law.

Janice and Candace – (blows kiss) thank you for the fast turnaround on the proofs.

Jenn. Speechless. Wind beneath my wings and all that corny shit that makes me gag.

You.

Yes you.

Blogger. Fan. Supporter. Service provider. Advice-giver.

I'm forgetting you.

I'm sorry.

Other Books by CD Reiss

THE GAMES DUET

Marriage Games
Separation Games (January 2017)

THE SUBMISSION SERIES

Beg
Tease
Submit
Control
Burn
Resist
Sing
Coda

THE CORRUPTION SERIES

Spin
Ruin
Rule

STANDALONES

Forbidden
Hardball
Shuttergirl

CD REISS is a *USA Today* bestseller. She still has to chop wood and carry water, which was buried in the fine print. Her lawyer is working it out with God but in the meantime, if you call and she doesn't pick up she's at the well hauling buckets.

Born in New York City, she moved to Hollywood, California to get her master's degree in screenwriting from USC. In case you want to know, that went nowhere but it did give her a big enough ego to write novels.

She's frequently referred to as the Shakespeare of Smut which is flattering but hasn't ever gotten her out of chopping a cord of wood.

If you meet her in person, you should call her Christine.